HARD LIGHT

ALSO BY J. B. TURNER

Jon Reznick Series

Hard Road

Hard Kill

Hard Wired

Hard Way

Hard Fall

Hard Hit

Hard Shot

Hard Target

Hard Vengeance

Hard Fire

Hard Exit

Hard Power

Hard Duty

American Ghost Series

Rogue

Reckoning

Requiem

Jack McNeal Series

No Way Back

Long Way Home

J. B. TURNER

HARD LIGHTS

A **JON REZNICK** THRILLER

THOMAS & MERCER

Published by Thomas & Mercer, Seattle

www.apub.com

Amazon, the Amazon logo, and Thomas & Mercer are trademarks of Amazon.com, Inc., or its affiliates.

EU Product Safety contact:
Amazon Publishing, Amazon Media EU S.à r.l.
38, avenue John F. Kennedy, L-1855 Luxembourg
amazonpublishing-gpsr@amazon.com

ISBN-13: 9781662527371
eISBN: 9781662527364

Cover design by @blacksheep-uk.com
Cover image: © Chris Wynn Photograp © VideoFlow / Shutterstock;
© Itani / Alamy Stock Photo

Printed in the United States of America

To my mother, with love and gratitude

Prologue

Summer 2024

When she left the house high up in the Hollywood Hills on that sultry summer night, she had no idea what fate awaited her. She was still loaded from the night before: pills, powders, and booze lingering in her bloodstream. She checked her watch. It was just after midnight. The smells of jasmine and trail dust hung heavy in the air. But in the distance, the alluring, seductive lights of the city beckoned.

Mirlande Jean-Baptiste slid into the back of the waiting Rolls-Royce, her mind racing. This was going to be the night it all began. Growing up in Haiti, she had dreamed of being famous. She had fantasized about making it in America. Making it in the big city. Her destiny, or so it seemed, was already written in the stars.

The car pulled away and turned onto Mulholland Drive, heading along the winding, twisting road. Past multimillion-dollar houses concealed behind high walls, high hedges, and shielded by towering palm trees.

When she passed her favorite view of the city—the vista from the Hollywood Bowl overlook—she smiled, momentarily spellbound, surveying the downtown lights of Los Angeles. Her eyes followed the snaking trail of headlights and taillights on the freeway. It all looked so unreal.

She sniffed hard. The lines of cocaine still coursed through her system. She fidgeted with her fake fingernails, picking at her cuticles.

Mirlande looked at the eyes of the driver in the rearview mirror. "You mind if I smoke?"

"Go right ahead, miss," the driver said.

Mirlande pressed a button and the rear window slid down. She casually lit up a joint, inhaling the marijuana deep into her lungs. She stared out over a sea of lights as far as she could see, expelling smoke through her nose. She had never seen so many lights. Her own village, outside Port-au-Prince, had no lights. No electricity. No anything. Dead dogs on the street, open sewers, bodies of police and gang members drenched in blood. Men and women scavenging for scraps. She was glad to have escaped.

The City of Dreams had entranced her from the second she'd gotten off the bus at Union Station. She had fallen under its spell. The city had beckoned her with promises of riches and fame. Three months ago, she'd been doing two-dollar meth hits and lines of angel dust in an alley in Skid Row. Now she was being driven in a Rolls-Royce.

Mirlande's hands tremored around the joint. She willed them still. She'd been kept awake by pills and coke supplied by her new, super-wealthy boyfriend, a hotshot film director. Her mother didn't believe Mirlande knew such people. The previous day, Mirlande had sent her photos of her with her big shot boyfriend. Her mother, a religious woman, had been aghast. Mirlande dragged on the joint as she contemplated her existence—a streetwise escort. It was hard to believe. She was only sixteen.

Mirlande didn't care what her mother thought. She felt at home in Southern California. She liked the warmth on her skin.

The high heat in summer, even the wild Santa Ana winds that whipped up wildfires. She loved it all. But more than anything, she loved looking down on the city, nestled high up in the Hollywood Hills. Life was good.

Mirlande had been set up in a cool apartment. She was hanging with important, powerful people. She sensed she was going to make it big. She felt it in her bones. She took acting classes that her boyfriend paid for. She dreamed of her future, morning, noon, and night. She talked with her boyfriend about getting a film agent. A manager. She went to industry parties. She wanted to meet creators and creatives.

Mirlande's foggy mind snapped back to the present. The SUV headed onto the freeway. Within minutes, the car was driving down North Gower and then hanging a right onto the Boulevard in West Hollywood.

She caught sight of the red neon lights of the club. Her heart began to beat a little faster, dazzled by the nightlife. Revelers were lined up around the block to get in. She threw her joint out of the open window. A smattering of paparazzi were jostling to photograph celebrities. It was just another Saturday night in LA. She would love to be photographed and have her picture splashed over all the papers.

The car pulled up and the chauffeur opened the rear door.

Mirlande stepped out, escorted into the club by tattooed security guards. The place was pulsating. Buzzing. Deafening house music thudded mercilessly. Strobe lights hypnotized. Trip-hop beats interspersed with an R&B classic. She loved it. She loved the smell of sweat and expensive cologne.

Her boyfriend, not surprisingly, was sitting in the best VIP booth.

Mirlande wrapped herself around him, kissing him hard on the cheek.

"Here she is!" he said.

Brett Miller was a young-looking seventy-four-year-old. He was sitting by himself, bottles of champagne on ice. He was grinning like a jackal. His skin was dark mahogany. He flashed his eighty-thousand-dollar smile as she snuggled up to him. "You okay, honey? People treating you nice?"

"Couldn't be nicer. You're so kind to me."

"Hey, lot more where that came from, believe me. Big plans for you."

Mirlande felt herself tremble with excitement. "Seriously?"

Brett poured them both a glass of vintage champagne. "You know what I'm going to do?"

"What's that?"

"I'm going to make you such a fucking star, bigger than all of them. Better than all of them. A year from now, you won't believe the life you'll be leading, trust me. That's all you have to do: trust me."

"Have you got a part for me?"

"A part? Are you kidding me? It's all lining up for you, honey."

Mirlande Jean-Baptiste's head was swimming as she picked up her glass of champagne and took a small sip. The taste was divine. She had dreamed of this since she had first arrived in Florida from Haiti, penniless and shivering. Charities had helped clothe and feed her. But apart from that, she had been on her own.

Brett was fantastic fun for his age. He was crazily indiscreet. She had told him that, and he'd laughed. He snorted whatever and fucked whoever, wherever he wanted. He just didn't seem to care. He enjoyed risky behavior. He said his therapist wanted him to undergo regression therapy to see if there was something in his childhood that made him act out such outlandish fantasies. But Brett had told the therapist he was too busy getting loaded!

Brett reached into his jacket and took out a small vial of cocaine.

Mirlande smiled and undid her top. "You want a special?"

"Yes please," he said. He liberally sprinkled some of the powder onto her chest, quickly inhaling the contents with a fifty-dollar bill. He sniffed hard, his eyes red as he began to talk incessantly. "I can see it now. Your face on billboards across the city. Maybe across the States. The world. You're perfect. Have I ever said that?" Sniff. "I've got so many . . . plans." Sniff. "People. It's all about people. This is a people business. I want to introduce you to some great people."

Mirlande pecked him again on the cheek. He was adorable. He was old enough to be her grandfather, but she was past caring. And he took Viagra.

He sprinkled some more cocaine onto the table. He chopped it into neat lines with an Amex Black Card. He was ultra-high income, along with his high-risk actions.

"Powder your nose, honey," he growled. "You're going to love it."

Mirlande took a fresh fifty-dollar bill he rolled up, and snorted three lines, one after another. She felt like her head was going to explode. Waves of euphoria ran through her veins. She heard herself laughing, heart racing like a runaway horse. "Pure. The stuff on the streets is nothing like this, let me tell you."

She kissed him, not caring about his age. She tasted the residue of the coke on his tongue. She thought of how her life was going to be.

Thirty minutes later, they left and rocked up at another club. They were escorted in by security, who showed great deference to Brett.

He was in his element. "You're all absolutely fucking gorgeous!" He was again shown to the best VIP booth in the club. The champagne flowed. Coke was snorted. And snorted. More and more.

Brett beckoned over the owner of the club. "Bring me some of your psychedelic tea," he purred, winking at the menacing-looking guy.

The man returned a few minutes later with two cups of pungent-smelling, reddish-brown tea.

Brett drank his and began to laugh.

"What is this?" she said.

Brett leaned in close. "Ayahuasca. You like to trip like last night?"

Mirlande shrugged. "Why not?"

"Drink up. You're gonna love this, honey. This is out of sight."

Mirlande gulped it down quickly, the bitter aftertaste leaving a nasty flavor in her mouth. She sipped her glass of champagne.

"You okay?" he asked.

Mirlande felt as if the world was speeding up. She felt more uninhibited. She got to her feet and began to dance to the music.

Brett watched her, laughing harder. He was enjoying her display, digging the music. Digging her spirit. She danced with abandon, eyes closed. She was being pulled in by the music. By the incessant beat. Quicker and quicker.

She felt herself being kissed. And groped. She opened her eyes and Brett was in front of her, demonic eyes boring into her as flames consumed him. Insects began to crawl across the floor, blood dripped from the lights.

The nightclub ceiling began to tip over, turning her world upside down.

Mirlande felt hands on her. She was spinning out of control. She closed her eyes. She felt agitated. She opened her eyes. The apparitions were all around. Spectral figures. Ghosts from the past. Visions. She was gripped by terror.

She turned to look at Brett. His face was melting slowly. The sound of the beat was getting louder. She tried to move but felt herself falling down steps. She felt herself being chased.

Chased through the streets, ghosts all around. Coyotes howling.

Mirlande ran toward the lights, screaming for help, demons and spirits suffocating her as it all turned black.

One

The call came just before dawn.

Jon Reznick was on his second black coffee of the day, staring out over the dark waters of Penobscot Bay. The lights of a few lobster boats returning to the port of Rockland dotted the landscape. He reached over for his cell phone, wondering who could be calling at this ungodly hour. He hoped it might be his daughter, Lauren, still based in Jakarta for the CIA. He hadn't heard from her in weeks. He picked up the phone, not recognizing the caller ID. "Yeah, who's this?" he said.

"I'm looking to speak to a Jon Reznick?" a man's voice said cautiously.

Reznick was reluctant to identify himself because of his line of work. He was invariably called on a secure line by the Feds or the CIA. "Who's calling?"

"My name is Captain Frank Garcia. LAPD, Venice Beach. Is this Jon Reznick I'm speaking to?"

"How can I help?"

"Do you know a man by the name of Angel Ramos?"

He had served alongside Angel for years. Iraq, Afghanistan, Somalia—during his Delta Force days. Angel had been the toughest man he had ever known. "Yes, I do. Why?"

"A man we believe to be Angel Ramos has been found dead. I'm sorry to be the bearer of bad news."

He'd known that Angel was a chronic alcoholic. Reznick wondered if his friend had drunk himself to death. "How did he die?"

"We're still investigating that."

"Where was he found?"

The cop sighed down the line. "It's not very pleasant."

"It's a simple question. Where was he found?"

"A dumpster in a back alley in Venice Beach. I'm sorry."

Reznick closed his eyes for a beat. "Has he been formally identified?"

"That's one of the reasons I'm calling. We need your help."

"I have to be honest, I haven't seen him in years."

"The medical examiner hopes you can help him. Ramos doesn't have any family we know of."

"How did you get my number?"

"During the autopsy, the medical examiner found a piece of paper with your name and number scribbled on it in Ramos's sneaker."

"You kidding me?"

"No, sir."

Reznick looked out at the dark waters. The peace and calm all around him, all that he loved about Maine, was a world away from the craziness of Los Angeles. He knew Angel could be highly volatile. Had he drunk himself to death?

"Are you still there, sir?" said the cop.

"Yeah, I'm still here. Do you want me to head out there?"

"No need. The medical examiner would like you to jump on a Zoom."

Reznick felt waves of sadness wash over him, thinking of Angel meeting his end in such a way. He wondered if Angel had been homeless and crawled into that dumpster. The last time he'd seen Angel, he could tell his old friend was in a bad way. Drinking crazy amounts, depressed. That had been fifteen years ago when they met up in Miami.

"Sir? I'm sorry . . . So, are you able to help the medical examiner?"

"Anytime he wants. Set it up."

A short while later, with the sun peeking over the horizon, bathing Penobscot Bay in a cotton candy pink, Reznick sat in front of his iMac in his office upstairs.

It was still the dead of night in Los Angeles. On the Zoom call, wearing a white medical coat, smiling back at him, eyes tired, dark shadows underneath, was medical examiner Dr. Robert Gleisner.

"Mr. Reznick?" Gleisner asked.

"Yes—speaking."

"Appreciate you helping out like this. Sorry about the loss of your friend."

"Appreciate that."

"Did the LAPD outline what happened?"

"Not in detail. Just enough to know that my friend was found in a dumpster."

The doctor scribbled some notes. "Never an easy thing to do an identification, especially with you thousands of miles away. So, without further ado, have you got any questions before I start?"

"I guess so. The first question is, are you sure this is Angel Ramos?"

"That's the working assumption, Mr. Reznick."

"So you're not sure of that."

"Not one hundred percent. But we're pretty sure it's him. So we need someone who knew Mr. Ramos to identify any markings on him. We would take that as an identification."

"I might be able to help you with that."

"We have spoken to people who knew him down in Venice Beach. But they couldn't tell the LAPD anything. We have no dental records to speak of, which is rather strange. So that's problematic. And that's why I'm so pleased you've agreed to speak to me."

"Not a problem."

"Let's get to it. Did you know or were you ever aware of any distinctive identifying features on Angel? Birthmarks? Inkings?"

Reznick racked his brain, thinking back. "There are several I know of. The main one being a distinctive tattoo on his chest."

"A distinctive tattoo . . . I'll need more detail. What kind of tattoo?"

"A heart with a dagger through it."

The doctor jotted down the details. "Anything else?"

"Angel Ramos also had the words *LOVE* and *HATE* tattooed on his knuckles. Left and right."

The doctor noted what he was saying. "That's very helpful. When did he get all that?"

"I'm pretty sure he was tattooed in South Beach, Miami. I think fifteen years ago or so was the last time I saw him, that's when he got those tattoos. Yeah, that's about right."

The medical examiner smiled. "That's all I need, thank you. You've been very helpful."

"Can you confirm the body you have has those same tattoos?"

Gleisner hemmed and hawed. "Correct. You've identified our body as Angel Ramos. I'm very sorry. Can you tell me any more about him? Just so we can get a better picture of this man."

"Angel was in Delta Force. You might want to reach out to the Army. Try the Pentagon. They should have medical records relating to Angel."

"Thank you for that."

Reznick leaned back in his seat and shook his head. "What more can you tell me?"

"What do you want to know?"

"Was he homeless? I know Angel drank a lot."

"That wasn't how he died, I can assure you."

Reznick took a few moments to contemplate that. He was surprised. He'd always thought Angel would drink himself to death. "You mean alcohol didn't kill him?"

"That's what I'm saying."

"I served with Angel in Delta."

The doctor took more notes.

"Just out of curiosity . . . I'd like to know exactly how he died. Just for my peace of mind, if nothing else."

Gleisner averted his eyes, pinching the bridge of his nose, exhausted. "Some things are best left unsaid."

"Maybe so. But tell me what happened to him. I identified him. I would appreciate you being a little more forthcoming."

"We have certain protocols . . ."

"I operate under protocols too . . . I deal with classified information in my line of work."

"I understand. But I must warn you, the details are upsetting, to say the least."

"Dr. Gleisner, I don't get upset too easily."

"I'm sure that's true."

"So I'm asking you to tell me how he died."

The doctor stared long and hard through the screen. "I'm very sorry to say that Angel Ramos was tortured to death."

Reznick felt his stomach tighten. He had seen the victims of torture up close. "Tortured? What kind of torture?"

"I have done my job for the best part of thirty years. I've never seen injuries like that. Angel Ramos would have suffered terribly. It would have been an excruciating death. Terrible."

"Angel was a tough, tough guy. He could be difficult. He was an angry man. But I never imagined someone would be able to overcome him. He had been trained to kill."

"Well, I'll tell you, Jon, your friend died a bad death. And someone inflicted great harm on him. Of that there is no doubt."

"How exactly was he tortured?"

"I've already told you too much, Mr. Reznick."

Reznick leaned forward in his seat, his face nearly touching the screen. "He doesn't have a family, as far as I know. I want to know."

Gleisner shook his head. "His body was discovered in a dumpster. When it was brought to the morgue, I saw classic signs of torture. Electric drills through his eyes and neck. Whoever did this was a psychopath. A raving psychopath."

Two

The shocking revelation about the vile nature of Angel Ramos's homicide was like a series of bombs going off at intervals inside Reznick's head.

Reznick sat in shock for a few minutes, digesting the grotesque manner of Angel's murder. He felt an emptiness, thinking of his friend being tortured to death. He could only imagine the horror Angel must have endured. He reflected on how they had drifted apart. It was sad that he had lost touch with Angel, but most of the men in Delta had.

Angel's personality had darkened over the years. He'd become violent when drunk, prone to bouts of uncontrolled rage, even among friends. His mood swings unsettled most people he didn't know. When Angel left Delta Force he had gotten a great job, working VIP security in and around Hollywood. Protecting the stars, he'd said. But Reznick wondered if the work had dried up. Had Angel's mood swings pissed off one too many clients?

The last time he'd seen Angel, his friend had seemed paranoid. Angel had talked about people out to get him. Reznick had wondered if he was displaying symptoms of post-traumatic stress. The deaths he'd caused and witnessed had affected Angel worse than most who'd fought in such hellish close quarters in

Afghanistan and Iraq. He'd once had a full breakdown and been hospitalized—raving, screaming. But then, after a month away, he'd returned, seemingly as good as new. Except he wasn't.

Reznick got up from his seat and went over to a cupboard, pulling out a treasured scrapbook. Photos of Reznick with his Delta colleagues in Baghdad and Fallujah. He took out a photo of him and Angel together, and carefully placed it in his wallet.

Then he turned and stared out of the window as a new day began.

Reznick felt strangely nostalgic now for Delta Force. Memories returned of tracer fire in the night sky. The call to prayer from ruined minarets. The explosions. The traps. The constant gunfire. Being cornered in Fallujah, stuck in filthy alleyways, the sewers overrunning, bodies in the streets; covering each other as they fought house to house. They had taken the fight to the unseen enemy. The Sunni militias had been like ghosts, disappearing and reappearing at will. Insurgents with nothing to lose. Baathists beheading Shia elders. Iranian-backed Shia militias exerting their authority. It had spiraled before the operation crashed and burned in the ashes of Iraq. Just like Angel Ramos.

Reznick brooded as the recollections flooded back of the American warrior whose parents were from rural Mexico. He remembered Angel showing him photos of his mother and father on their wedding day. Angel had been strangely moved, tears in his eyes.

Reznick went outside and headed down the wooden steps that led to the beach, adjacent to the cove. He wondered what more he could do. He had already done his bit for the medical examiner by identifying the distinguishing marks on Angel Ramos's body. But as the hours passed outside his beloved home in Rockland, he couldn't just let his friend's violent death pass by.

Reznick had so many questions. He was a couple of years younger than Angel, and when he'd joined Delta Force he had looked up to Ramos as a fierce, uncompromising special forces soldier. A man who was always first into battle. Angel had never shown any fear ahead of missions. Many people, Reznick included, had grown quiet as they contemplated what lay ahead on a high-risk mission. But Angel Ramos never had. He'd always been itching to make first contact with the enemy. It was hard for Reznick to accept that such a man could be snuffed out like Angel had.

But there had been another side to Angel Ramos.

Reznick remembered the last time he saw him, fifteen years ago. He'd spent a memorable weeklong vacation in Angel's hometown of Miami. There, he had seen his friend in a completely different light. As a soft-spoken, complex, sociable man, not a fearsome Delta warrior. His friend had seemed chill, being back in the city. Angel had taken Reznick out fishing for marlin, and Jon had watched the way he'd expertly baited the line and noted the patience he'd shown in order to catch the biggest fish of the day. Angel's dark eyes were impenetrable, or so it had seemed. But when he'd talked excitedly of playing Little League as a kid, his eyes had shone.

Day after day, they'd hung out. At a tiny Cuban café in Little Havana, where they'd drunk cortaditos, Cuban coffees. Angel had talked in rapid-fire Spanish as Reznick soaked up the warmth of the sun and the people. He had shown Reznick his old school, in Hialeah. He'd begun to reminisce about old friends. He'd taken Reznick to the graveside of a girl murdered in a drive-by shooting a block from Angel's childhood home. It was a side of the hard-living Angel Ramos that most people never saw. The quiet man.

They'd spent that week shooting the breeze, trying not to talk of Delta or Iraq. On the last day, Angel had shown Reznick his favorite bar in the city, a dive bar in Little Havana where he played pool with the locals. A band had played Afro-Cuban jazz.

His friend had been full of life, chatting to old pals. Then they'd headed to South Beach, where Angel was inked before they went to Mac's Club Deuce bar on 14th Street.

It was then, at that instant, on the banks of Penobscot Bay, that he realized he owed his Delta brother. He needed answers.

◆ ◆ ◆

When Reznick's plane touched down at LAX the following morning, he caught a cab straight to a luxury hotel in the heart of Venice Beach. He had booked an oceanfront room with views of the skatepark and boardwalk. He checked in, showered, and while he put on a change of clothes, he turned on the TV in his room. Governor Gary Clarkson was talking about decriminalizing loitering to stop prostitutes from being arrested. He talked about wanting to end the "stigmatization" of sex workers. He called for "understanding" in the community. Reznick turned it off and headed out. He walked a few blocks to the LAPD Venice Beach substation, located on the boardwalk. He thought it was the best place to start. He walked up to the counter, a tall desk sergeant eyeing him with suspicion the whole way.

"Can I help you?" the cop said.

"Looking for Captain Frank Garcia."

"Who are you?"

"Name's Jon Reznick. It's in connection with the death of Angel Ramos."

The cop pointed to a chair opposite. "Wait there, I'll see if he's available." He picked up the phone and relayed what Reznick had told him, then raised his voice. "He's here now, Frank. I'm looking at him."

Reznick sat in silence, studying the mug shots of felons on the wall.

The cop put down the phone and looked across at Reznick. "He'll be out in a minute."

"Appreciate that."

A few minutes later, a heavyset man wearing a crumpled navy suit, white shirt, pale blue tie and shiny black shoes walked up to Reznick and shook his hand. "Frank Garcia, nice to meet you. Follow me."

Reznick followed the captain down a series of corridors and into a secure area of the station, where he was shown into Garcia's tiny office.

"Shut the door."

Reznick did as he was told.

"You don't mind me calling you Jon?"

Reznick sat down on the other side of the desk. "Not at all."

Garcia leaned back in his seat and shrugged. "Jon, I've got to be honest. I'm surprised that you travelled all the way to LA."

"Why are you surprised?"

"I just don't understand why you would come all this way."

"Angel Ramos was a friend of mine."

"I get that. I respect that. Really I do. But the death of your friend is under investigation. This is a police matter. There's no reason to get involved."

Reznick stared at Garcia. "I'm just looking for answers."

"What can I say? This is a big city, and we have multiple investigations going on, as usual. I'd like to give you an update. But there's nothing. I'm afraid you've wasted your time and money. I don't have anything else I can tell you."

"I'm just looking for more details."

"What kind of details?"

"Well, I believe my friend died in an alleyway in Venice Beach, right?"

"Correct."

"It was an unusual death. He was murdered."

Garcia shifted in his seat.

"My friend was brutally tortured and then killed."

"Hang on . . . Let's not get ahead of ourselves. I don't speculate."

"That's a fact, isn't it?"

"How do you know that?"

"The medical examiner gave me that information."

Garcia winced. "That's not protocol. He wasn't at liberty to do that."

"I helped him identify Angel from his tattoos. He was just reciprocating with some information to help me understand what exactly happened."

"I'm sorry for your loss. Really, I am," Garcia sympathized.

"I'm not family. But I appreciate your sentiments."

"What I mean is . . . the loss of your friend. He was a veteran, right?"

"Yes, he was."

"It's tough. I get it. Adjusting to life after the military. That was the family he had."

"He wasn't the sort of person who got pushed around. So for him to end up the way he did tells me some seriously dangerous people are responsible. Angel might have crossed the wrong guys. I want to know more."

Garcia leaned back. "Bad shit happens in big cities. LA is no exception. We deal with all kinds of stuff. We have countless, simultaneous investigations of serious crimes. We usually get the bad guys. But it takes time. Investigations take time. There aren't enough hours in the day. We're stretched. So I'd appreciate it if you just accepted the fact that we're dealing with this."

"I'm not going to get in your way."

"Investigations are time-consuming. Interviewing suspects takes time. Forensics."

It was clear that Garcia was trying to brush him off. "Let me ask you something. Have you got any leads? Suspects? Was he killed in Venice Beach? Or was his body just dumped here?"

Garcia took a deep breath, exasperated by the questions. "Jon, I can tell you want to find out who did this. But that's our job. You're hurting, I get it. But I'm not going to give you or anyone else a report on an ongoing investigation. That's not how we work."

"I'm not looking for a running commentary. Just a few details. You must know something."

Garcia undid his top button and loosened his tie. "I'm genuinely sorry you've come all this way . . . What I can say is that there is a team of detectives investigating this. Smart people. And we will find whoever is responsible."

Reznick felt exasperated too. "Can you at least tell me about Angel's lifestyle out here? Was that a contributing factor?"

"What do you mean?"

"I mean, what was his lifestyle like in the last few years?"

"Don't you know what your friend was doing?"

"We went our separate ways . . . Drifted apart, I guess. Frank, just give me something."

Garcia winced again, as if reluctant to divulge anything. "Why are you so intent on knowing the details?"

"For peace of mind. Where was he working? Last I heard he was doing VIP close protection in Hollywood. But his life took a downward turn."

Garcia noted that down on a pad. "That's correct, Jon. By all accounts your friend was very skilled, knew what he was doing in security, martial arts, countersurveillance . . . He was smart and well respected. He was a personal trainer for a few years. He also worked the doors of some nightclubs. Tough parts of town. He worked all over."

Reznick pondered that. "You think he had a run-in with someone in his line of work?"

"I'm not going there, Jon."

"Where was he working when he died?"

"There's no easy way to explain this."

"Try me."

"Angel Ramos was a junkie. Heroin. Fentanyl. He was broke and homeless, living on the streets, Jon. Had been for a while."

"He was an addict?"

"I know, it's not an easy thing to accept. This city will chew people up no matter who they are. LA's a tough town when things aren't going well. People see success, bright lights, money. But believe me, it's easy to fall on hard times. Angel most certainly fell on hard times."

Reznick shook his head.

"Drugs are everywhere. Illegal and legal. Take your pick."

"Do you know what started his addiction?"

Garcia nodded. "From what we know, after speaking with homeless shelters, local clinics and doctors, he became addicted to painkillers after an injury. That might have been the trigger. From there he lost all his jobs. The money dried up. That's how he became homeless."

Reznick sat in quiet contemplation. It was tough to hear the stark truth of how life had turned out for Angel in LA.

"That's about all I can tell you. He was in a bad, bad place."

"The question then is who would want to kill a drunk homeless guy—a junkie—in such a way? I've heard of homeless people being beaten up. I've heard of homeless people being beaten to death. But I can't say I've heard of a homeless person having their eyes drilled out before they were brutally killed."

"Like I said, I'm not going to give a running commentary on the state of our investigation."

"The injuries he suffered . . . The only time I ever saw such things, firsthand, was in Iraq. Tortured victims of Shia and Sunni death squads."

Garcia held up his hand. "All right, Jon, I've given you what I can. I do have other things to deal with today."

"One more thing. When's Angel's funeral?"

"I don't know. Whenever it is, it'll be a pauper's funeral. He didn't have a dime, apparently. His bank account had three bucks in it. Three bucks and twenty-four cents. It's a sad way to go out from this world."

"I'll pay for the funeral. A proper Christian burial."

"You sure?"

"Positive." Reznick picked up a pen from the desk and a yellow Post-it. He scribbled down his cell phone number and handed it to Garcia. "Get whoever's in charge of the body to call me and I'll deal with that side of things."

"I'll pass on your number."

"Off the record, Frank . . ."

"Jon, I've been as up-front as I can be."

"I appreciate that. But I'm asking, man to man, have you got any idea who would want to kill Angel? Any leads at all?"

"Venice Beach Homicide is working this alongside six other outstanding cases. That's a lot."

"I get it. But the level of violence that was used to kill Angel Ramos is something you don't see every day. Am I right?"

"We see bad shit all the time, trust me."

"The circumstances of Angel's death, you have to admit, are the exception rather than the rule in homicides."

Garcia got to his feet and put his hands on his hips, as if eager to end the conversation. "I agree. But keep in mind, we deal with a big area. Culver City, Venice, Marina del Rey, quite a bit of the Westside. We're stretched pretty thin. Sorry I can't be of more help."

Reznick stood up. "One final thing, Frank. The last photo I have of Angel was taken fifteen years ago, when we met up in Miami. Have the police got an up-to-date photo I can have? For old times' sake, just as a memento."

Garcia opened a file and pulled out a color photo. "We had dozens printed up. Take one."

Reznick took the print in his hand and scrutinized his former Delta buddy. A wave of sadness washed over him. The photo showed Angel wearing a ripped and faded gray T-shirt, track marks visible on his arms. He looked emaciated, with long, straggly, unkempt hair and haunted eyes. "When was this taken?"

"Taken by a homeless pal of his on his phone, just a couple months before he died."

Three

Reznick headed along the graffitied backstreets of Venice, the smell of weed heavy in the air. It was hard to reconcile his friend as Reznick had known him with the image of the unkempt man who had died here in LA. As he walked on, past a cannabis shop, tattoo parlors, a liquor store, and a secondhand bookstore, he saw a group of junkies, some injecting in full view. Kids on skateboards whizzed past, weaving their way up and down the boardwalk.

A black guy sporting dreadlocks and Nike shorts, Bible in hand, was talking about God. "We all need to be saved, brothers and sisters. Only God can redeem us. He is our salvation. He is the one! Jesus Christ is our Lord and savior."

Reznick continued along the boardwalk. He wondered if Angel's mental and physical disintegration had gone hand in hand. Had Angel's addiction fueled his sense of hopelessness? It made sense.

The drinking might have plunged him into a deep depression from which he'd been unable to escape. Then the opioids, to kill the pain of an injury. And from there, onto heroin and a rapid downward spiral into a personal hell. But what exactly had propelled Angel's murderer to kill him in such a savage way? What had Angel done to deserve that? Perhaps it was a drug deal gone wrong. Or maybe he hadn't paid his debts.

A blond man on roller skates, smoking a joint and wearing green Speedos and mirrored sunglasses, sped past him. "You want some action, dude?"

Reznick ignored him and walked on, past a legless veteran, medals on his chest, crutches at his side, begging for money. He dropped a twenty-dollar bill into a dirty Lakers hat.

The man looked up, tapping the side of his head. "I'll remember you," he said. "I don't forget. I can look into your face and know everything there is to know about you. Thank you."

Reznick stared down at him.

"I got no one, brother. Not a fucking soul. So, thank you. Again. Thank you for seeing me. I'm not invisible. I'm here. Most people walk on by. But you fucking saw me."

Reznick crouched down beside the guy. "Things tough, my friend?"

The veteran had tears in his eyes. "You have no idea, brother. I served my country. I served it well. Now look at me. A bum. A washed-up bum. I can't piss straight. And when I do, I piss blood. Swear to God, I piss blood. I've got fucking AIDS. Dirty fucking needles."

"You need to get yourself to a hospital, man. Right now. You want me to help you?"

"Fuck hospitals, man. They'll detain me. Tried to kill a guy who tried to steal my stuff. They said I was paranoid. Crazy. I ain't going back. You hear me! I ain't goin' back!"

Reznick nodded. "I hear you."

"Who are you? You a veteran?"

"That obvious?"

The man dabbed the tears in his eyes. "Difficult thing to shake off. Army?"

"Marines. A few years in Delta."

The man whistled, shaking his head. "I met a few of you fuckers. Tough bastards."

"We have our moments."

The guy laughed. "I fucking knew it." Then he leaned forward and hugged Reznick. "You got that look about you."

"What kind of look is that?"

"I don't know. Intense."

Reznick felt sick at the state of the veteran in front of him. "I'm real sorry about your situation. Please, let me get you to a hospital."

"That's not going to happen. Besides, it is what it is, man. I've got to live like this. If you can even call this living."

Reznick nodded and sat down beside him. "I'm Jon, by the way."

The guy shook his hand. "Danny Duggins."

"Where you from, Danny?"

"A little town in Vermont. I went back and no one wanted to look at me. Talk to me. That's why I headed out west. At least it's sunny here."

Reznick smiled. "Danny, a friend of mine—a veteran—used to hang around here too."

"What was his name?"

"Angel Ramos?"

"Name don't mean a thing to me. I can't remember what happened a fucking hour ago, man."

Reznick pulled out the photo of Angel the cop had given him. "Wondering if this is someone you've ever met or known. This guy was a friend of mine. He hung out around Venice. But now he's dead."

The man stared long and hard at the photo. "I knew him. I saw him around."

"You did know him?"

"I didn't know his name. But I knew that guy. I just called him Chico; he liked that. I don't know why."

"Tell me about him."

"Chico. Nice guy. You say his name was Angel Ramos?"

"That's right."

"Never knew that. Here's the thing about your friend. Without a drink in him, when he wasn't loaded, he was very nice. But he was a scary motherfucker if you caught him on a bad day, know what I mean?"

"What else can you tell me?"

"He was an addict. Shared needles. Dumb fucking shit. We've all done it."

Reznick wondered if this guy was telling the truth, or just weaving a tale for a stranger.

"Terrible way for him to die." Danny shuddered.

"I'm sorry, what?"

"I said it was a terrible way for him to die."

"You know how he died?"

Danny nodded. "Crazy stuff, man."

Reznick wanted Danny to tell him what he knew. "So how did he die?"

"I'll tell you exactly how he died. Drilled his eyes out. Torture, man. That's what they did to him. May he rest in peace."

Reznick was stunned. The cops hadn't released any details about how Angel had died. "How do you know that?"

Danny shrugged. "I was the fucker that found him. Swear on my mother's life, God rest her soul, I discovered Chico."

"You found him? You found his body? Where?"

"In a goddamn dumpster, under some old clothes and food. I found him."

"Do you mind me asking . . . Where exactly did you find him?"

"Breeze . . . just off Speedway."

"What's Breeze?"

"It's like an alley. Breeze Court. I was raking about in a few dumpsters, looking for stuff. I'm kind of a dumpster-diving veteran. I've found all sorts of shit in dumpsters, let me tell you. TVs, baseball hats, guns. But I've had nightmares since I found Chico's body."

"Danny, this is important . . . Where in that alley was the dumpster?"

"Well, let me think. Memory's not too good. So . . . Oh yeah, I headed down Speedway, and then I turned right along Breeze. It was a black dumpster, graffitied. Next to a telephone pole and a garage door, painted orange."

Reznick made a mental note. "What exactly were you looking for in the dumpster, if you don't mind me asking?"

"I don't know . . . stuff I could sell. Old clothes. Furniture. The sort of shit people throw out. You can sometimes make a buck or two, maybe more, selling shit on the beach. Tourists will buy any crap."

"And that's where you found Angel?"

"Yeah, man. I was the one. I freaked out. I was shaking. Crying. Blood all over the inside of the dumpster, eyes drilled out. I'll never forget it 'til the day I die."

"And you called the cops."

"I called them. I have a shitty old phone." He pulled a discolored Nokia out of his back pocket. "I used this."

"You don't know who did this?"

"Me? How the fuck am I supposed to know who did this? I can barely crawl ten yards without my sticks. I just happened upon your friend's body. I was sick, right beside the dumpster. Sick as a dog."

"So it was in an alley . . . Breeze, right?"

"Right. Ten yards in, just off Speedway, black dumpster, graffiti all over it. It was in there. The body."

"That must've been tough to see. A guy you knew. Hung around with."

"It was tough alright. No man deserves to die like that. Like a dog. I have flashbacks about it. His face. Nightmares, man. About his face. God rest his soul."

Reznick stared at the poor guy on the ground.

"One final thing, my friend," said Danny. "Chico, the guy you said was called Angel . . . he was cleaning up his act."

"What?"

"I mean, before he died, the last couple months, he was clean. Going to AA meetings. No booze. No drugs. Chico had gone straight. That's what's so fucking sad."

"Are you sure?"

"Course I'm fucking sure. He came over and talked to me. I saw him running too. Sweating the shit out of his system. The junk. I swear, Chico wanted to start again. He was lifting weights. And he looked fresher. His eyes were alive."

Reznick was floored, thinking Angel had been turning his life around just before he was killed. "Let me ask you something. Did he tell you what exactly had motivated him to change?"

"One reason. He wanted to get clean for his daughter. He wanted to find her and have her back in his life."

Reznick felt as if he'd been hit by an oncoming freight train. "He had a daughter?"

"Chico? Sure, that's what he said. He said he saw his daughter in his dreams. When he closed his eyes he saw her. And he prayed he would one day see her again in real life."

Reznick felt his throat tighten. It was heartbreaking to think that Angel had been murdered just when things had been getting better. "What else did he say?"

"Said he wanted to make things right. He wanted to be a father to her. A real father. He was ashamed she became an addict as well. And that's why I think he'd vowed to change. Which he did. She'd gone off the rails too. He felt responsible. He'd heard she was working as a prostitute for wealthy clients. It sent him crazy. He knew his daughter needed his help. He wanted to find her. God is my witness, man, Chico told me that. She was his flesh and blood. He had to save her."

Four

Robert Kassan might have been known to most A-list stars and the movers and shakers in Hollywood, but his name was not known outside of the elite, wealthy circles of Los Angeles. Art dealer to the stars, his company bought and sold rare artwork and ancient artifacts on behalf of his favored clients, but he preferred to keep a low profile. He lived alone in a modern house, nestled on a cul-de-sac in the upscale neighborhood of Brentwood, on the Westside of LA.

His property was hidden behind giant hedges and fifteen-foot walls, with electronic surveillance scanning for any intrusion. The seclusion was important. Unlike many of his wealthy clients, he had never been featured in major newspapers or magazines. This urbane, well-dressed, and fiercely discreet man moved in rarefied circles, but even when attending glitzy LA and Malibu parties, he still managed to studiously avoid his photograph being taken.

Kassan had moved to the city twenty years earlier. Back then he'd had no contacts and no money, or so it had seemed. But he'd had an innate ability to seek out virtually priceless works of art from around the world. Since then, Kassan had cultivated deep and enduring business relationships. His clients were fiercely loyal. His personal friendships were invariably business-related. His exclusive art gallery on North Rodeo Drive in Beverly Hills catered to only ultra-high-end individuals, who invariably bought the art through offshore companies their lawyers had set up.

Kassan drank in moderation, and did not smoke or take any drugs—almost unheard of in Los Angeles. He liked nothing better than driving over to the Hollywood Reservoir to hike, and also swam and jogged to keep in shape. He boxed, once a week, at a gym down on San Vicente Boulevard. A fastidious dresser, he bought his suits in Milan and London. Despite being one of the city's most eligible bachelors, he remained unmarried by choice. He was a workaholic.

Networking was his thing. When he wasn't sourcing upscale art for stars, he was schmoozing with multimillionaires and billionaires. He attended parties and film premieres, and was invited to the beachfront homes of seemingly every film star, producer, and entertainment lawyer in Hollywood. His biggest clients were the A-list actors who wanted to invest their money in fabulous modern artworks—Picassos, Pollocks, Hockneys—or rare ancient artifacts—from the Middle East, Greece, Egypt, and Africa—to adorn their homes. Art was a smart investment.

His contacts across the globe—especially in Lebanon, his father's birthplace, and Crete, where he was born and raised—allowed him to access the rarest of sculptures, some Roman, some ancient Egyptian, some classical Greek. He had middlemen who had become close friends, who lived in Geneva and Zurich and worked in high-security storage spaces. They helped to source new art for his gallery. They were also discreet.

Occasionally he traveled to meet dealers and brokers across North Africa, the eastern Mediterranean, Turkey, and even Saudi Arabia. He was on first-name terms with billionaire Saudi princes who wanted the finest artworks to adorn their glass mansions around the world. But the film industry was far and away the backbone of his business.

Hollywood had always had its share of high-net-worth individuals who splurged on art. The more exclusive the better. Kassan's reputation was such that brokers who wanted to sell the rarest pieces came to him first, knowing his clients would pay the highest price. He was generous with commissions and kickbacks. Everyone got a piece of the action when he bought or sold a piece.

Kassan also ran a separate private art market out of Switzerland which offered first-look access to exclusive rarities. Those unique pieces that came onto the private market once every decade—if you were lucky. Hundreds of millions had poured in to purchase paintings and artifacts, from reclusive investors, film companies, Saudi princes, hedge-fund executives, and actors who wanted a great return on their investments. Tax-efficient, top-of-the-line returns.

That particular morning, Kassan was in his gallery with the head of a premier talent agency. The agency wanted to source the finest modern art to bedeck the granite walls of their new offices in Beverly Hills.

Kassan's cell phone vibrated in his pocket and he excused himself. "I'll be back in a minute," he said to his client. "Look around, see what catches your eye."

He headed up the spiral staircase to his office on the second floor, shutting the door behind him. Then he sat down behind his desk and took a deep breath. "Robert Kassan speaking."

"Robert, it's Jerry."

"Jerry, how the hell are you?" Kassan loved Jerry Levinson. Jerry was a partner at a top entertainment law firm in Beverly Hills. "What can I do for you, man? We still on for that squash game later?"

"That's why I'm calling. I'm sorry, but I have to cancel."

"You're killing me, Jerry. That's not like you. Is everything okay?"

"It's fine. The usual. Brett Miller wants to meet me urgently. So I've got to drop everything."

Kassan knew how valued a client the A-list film director was to Jerry. "I get it—not a problem, man."

"You know how it is, right?"

"Jerry, I get it. If Brett called me, I'd take the meeting, too."

"Which reminds me, you said you'd secure a two-thousand-year-old Roman bronze plaque for Brett."

"I most certainly did."

"You got any update on that before I see him?"

"I've been advised that the plaque is now in Geneva. In high-security storage."

"What price are we looking at?"

"Our guide price is five million dollars, but I expect if I made it available, private dealers would be knocking over each other to get it for six or seven."

"Is that the price?"

Kassan had already reserved the artifact for 1.8 million Swiss francs—equivalent to around two million dollars, depending on currency fluctuations. "Jerry, I love you. You're a good friend. So . . . let me see, I suppose I could be persuaded to part with it for five million dollars. How does that sound?"

"Time frame?"

"One week."

"Perfect. Robert, I've got to go. That's Brett on the other line. But I'll let him know about the plaque. He'll love it."

"Incidentally, how is he?"

"Are you kidding me? I love the guy, but he'll be the death of me."

Kassan laughed. "I'll liaise with Geneva and be in touch."

He ended the call and opened up his computer. He sent an encrypted message to his brother, who was also his accountant, instructing him to transfer one million dollars in commission to the art dealer friend in Beirut who had found the artifact in a private collection in Naples. But he also instructed his brother to send ten percent of the sale price—five hundred thousand dollars—to Jerry Levinson for brokering the whole thing.

Then he headed back downstairs and attended to the needs of the talent agent, who was eager to buy rare art in order to project exquisite taste and a sense of power.

It was the name of the game in Hollywood: the intersection of power, art, and money.

Five

Following the meeting with Danny, Reznick had walked the Venice boardwalk, lost in thought. He made his way from the ocean along the winding paths beside the canals. He craved vengeance for his friend.

A burnt-orange sunset bathed the side streets and sidewalks, casting shadows of the palm trees that lined the beach town. Beautiful homes overlooked the waterways. He walked on, occasionally passing a jogger or a cyclist going the other way.

As he took in the vibes and ambience of Venice, he felt restless. Mile after mile, he thought of his late friend and Delta comrade—a brother in arms. He listened to a voicemail from Captain Garcia, giving him the details of a local undertaker. Reznick called him and agreed to pay the full amount up front—fifteen thousand dollars—to ensure a dignified burial for his ex-Delta buddy.

As he ended the call, he watched the tattooed skaters smoking weed speeding past, headphones on. A group of girls smoked on a corner, next to an arcade. A long-haired white kid in his late teens, wearing cargo shorts and a ripped T-shirt, injected himself in full view. Reznick wondered what had happened to America. Was this it? Was this happening across the country?

Reznick stared at the kid as his eyes rolled back in his head from the hit. It was the sickening reality for hundreds, maybe thousands, of people across Venice Beach and the rest of Los Angeles. The same pitiful existence that Angel had been reduced to. Addicted to drugs, thinking there was nothing else to live for. Lying around in the sun, wasting away. Stealing, or selling drugs, to afford another fix. A vicious cycle.

Reznick walked on. He felt pangs of hunger, and realized he hadn't eaten for twelve hours. He headed over to a food truck and bought a couple of fish tacos. He sat down on a bench.

The sound of hip-hop from a nearby bar spilled into the evening air.

Reznick ate his tacos, watching some kids playing hoops. Then he got up and walked past a crowd of pumped-up bodybuilders lifting some serious weights. He wondered if Angel had hung out here. He imagined he would have. Back in the day, Angel had been a phenomenal weightlifter. Insane upper-body strength. Super-fit. But not because of steroids. He had built his body and muscles through hard work in the gym. Weight training. Running. Swimming. He had done it all.

The music was getting louder.

Reznick thought about Danny, and wondered if others in the transient community in Venice Beach had known Angel.

The more he thought about Angel's horrible death, the more he contemplated what sort of people Angel had crossed. Was it heroin dealers who had tortured and killed him for not repaying a debt? But the torture element, even for a small-time dealer, seemed way out of proportion. Maybe Angel had pissed off people higher up the food chain. Had he been more heavily involved in the underworld of vice and drugs? It had been so devasting to hear from Danny that Angel had gotten clean just before he died.

Reznick walked down a side street directly opposite the Venice Fishing Pier. He went into the Hinano Cafe, a cash-only dive bar. Inside it appeared to be made up of old boat parts; there was sawdust on the floor, five big screens on the wall showing a variety of sports, and a jukebox playing an old country song by Merle Haggard. The kind of music his father had loved back in the day.

Reznick walked up to the bar and sat down on a stool. He ordered a Scotch on the rocks.

"Beer or wine only, pal. Take your pick."

"Gimme a beer."

His eyes danced around the bar. A couple of surfer dudes playing pool with their girlfriends, a fisherman dancing along to the music, and a homeless guy outside, looking in through the window. A couple of bikers were sitting near the back, nursing beers. It was that kind of place.

Reznick liked the vibe. He drank his beer as the music played. He could definitely imagine Angel hanging out here. Angel had been a heavy, heavy drinker. He could drink from sunup to sundown. He wasn't a big talker, and he'd liked to drink alone. But this place was the sort of grungy hangout he'd have enjoyed—wallowing in self-pity, with the faded memories of his military exploits.

Reznick showed the recent photo of Angel to the bartender. "This guy ever drink in here? Face look familiar?"

The guy shrugged. "I just started a few days ago, man. Sorry."

Reznick stayed and drank a few more beers, until the place closed. Then he tipped the bartender twenty dollars and started to head back to his hotel. But as he turned off the boardwalk and down a side street, he saw red lights flashing at the other end as paramedics crowded around someone on the ground. He walked toward the scene, wanting to get up close.

"Get back, sir," a young cop said. "Nothing to see here."

Except there was.

The legless veteran he had spoken to only a few hours earlier—Danny Duggins from Vermont—was lying there, not moving, face white as a ghost. Blood spattered on the ground; a needle in his arm.

Danny was dead.

Six

The following morning, after a fitful sleep, Reznick felt drained and exhausted. His thoughts were preoccupied by the sudden death of Danny Duggins—whether from an overdose or murder—so soon after the brutal torture and killing of Angel Ramos. The pair had known each other. But drug deaths in a city like Los Angeles, or any big city, were not so unusual.

Reznick got up and went to the bathroom, splashing cold water on his face to wake himself up. He put on a gray tracksuit and Nike sneakers, and headed out for a run. The sun tried to peek through the early-morning fog that had settled overnight. He ran along the boardwalk all the way to Santa Monica Pier, sweating heavily. He checked his Fitbit. He had run just over two miles.

Reznick bought a bottle of water and swigged it, quenching his thirst, then walked to the end of the pier until he got to the fishing platform. A lone fisherman was casting his line, cigarette in hand.

The middle-aged fisherman looked around. "Nothing so far, but I'll get something. Don't worry about that. Always do."

Reznick smiled back at him. "Nice spot you've got."

"Fantastic. Once the fog lifts, it's heaven. Can't think of a better place on God's earth."

Reznick peered out over the ocean. "Yeah, pretty spot."

"Where you from?"

"Me? Out of town. Maine."

"Long way from home, bro."

Reznick swigged some more water.

"You here on business?"

"Just looking around."

"Let me tell you. That's how it started with me. I'm originally from Seattle—weather there is a complete bummer. Came down here in the mid-eighties . . . and thought wow! This'll do for me. Not crazy hot like inland or out in the desert. Just the perfect temperature. Love it."

"I can see the attraction."

The fisherman reeled in his line, bait still hanging from the hook. He cast out again, watching his line hit the choppy water. "Patience, that's the secret."

Reznick nodded. "Nice talking to you, my friend."

"Take it easy, pal. And be careful. We've got plenty of crazies hanging around the beach."

Reznick walked off the pier and did some stretching. Then he set off back to Venice Beach. When he got there, he headed off the boardwalk and meandered around the canals, getting a feel for the bohemian area.

An old woman reading a book was sitting on her patio overlooking the water. She smiled at him. "Good morning."

"Good morning to you."

"I'd love to join you. But my knees aren't up to jogging anymore."

"Enjoy your book, ma'am."

Reznick returned to the boardwalk, jogging past lifeguard towers, kids playing volleyball, and a middle-aged Lycra-clad woman doing yoga, her headphones on.

He breathed in the salty sea air. The endorphins were kicking in.

Reznick felt the sweat on his back, his heart racing. He felt a whole lot better, his head clearer, than he had when he'd woken up. He walked over to Muscle Beach, where he pumped iron with a crowd of super-fit bodybuilders.

Reznick headed back to the hotel to shower, then went to get breakfast at the nearby Sidewalk Cafe. He had finished his eggs and toast and was on his third coffee of the morning, while checking his phone for messages and emails, when he heard a familiar voice.

"You still hanging around, Jon?"

Reznick looked up and saw Captain Frank Garcia approaching. Garcia was wearing jeans and an LAPD T-shirt, clearly off-duty.

"Hey, Frank, how're things?"

"You mind if I join you?"

Reznick pointed to the seat opposite.

Garcia sat down. "I'm surprised you're still here."

"The funeral is in three days. Didn't see the point of flying all the way home just to fly all the way back."

"I see." Garcia ordered an omelet and toast with coffee.

"This your regular haunt?" Reznick asked.

"It is."

"I was over in Santa Monica earlier, on a run. Real nice place."

"I live in the Ocean Park neighborhood there."

"Can't beat living by the sea."

"You're from Maine, right?"

"You got it. So you live near your work, Frank. Ocean Park to Venice . . . that's an easy commute."

"True."

"You got a family?"

"Yes I do."

"Your family like it in Santa Monica?"

Garcia shook his head. "Everyone thinks it's paradise here. That's what they think they're moving to. A beach paradise. Don't get me wrong, a lot of Venice has been gentrified since the 1990s. That's when the tech companies moved in. Software developers brought in a lot of wealth."

"Still got a gritty feel to it."

"No doubt about it. A lot of the older cops, retired now, who were around in the seventies, said there were serious problems back then. Lot of them gang-related. Now, it's a different place. But still, it's not all it's cracked up to be."

Reznick drank some more of his coffee. "I was surprised at the scale of the homelessness."

"You have no idea how bad it is. Housing is unaffordable in Venice. Unless you're an actor, director, or a tech guy with bags of money. You know the types—go around on their fucking hoverboards."

Reznick laughed. "I ran around the canals. Nice area there too."

"Nice? I don't know about that."

"Looked pretty nice to me."

"Last month there were two violent rapes in that area."

"Seriously?"

"Three months ago, there were a couple murders on the same night. Woman raped and thrown in the canal, where she drowned. Homeless guy beaten to death by a group of kids."

"Sounds like a nightmare."

"It's all over California. But Venice Beach, I don't know . . . The area attracts some real lowlifes. No disrespect to your late friend."

"I understand."

"A lot of the homeless . . . they're sad people. Batshit crazy, some of them. But a few of them are dangerous and should be locked up."

"So why aren't they?"

"They are, and then they get released. Some are good people. Just down on their luck. Some are hearing voices in their heads, paranoid, screaming and shouting into the night, roaming all around the beach, the canals, night and day. It's scary. A few commit petty crimes, or they fight, deal drugs, stab strangers for cash. We catch them, they get locked up. And then they're released. The cycle goes on."

Reznick shook his head. "That's a recipe for disaster."

"You said it. Some of the homeless move away from Venice. Most just hang around, year after year, scratching out a living, panhandling, breaking into homes. Summer is when it all goes crazy."

"You must worry about your family."

"Damn right I do. I've got a wife and two teenage girls. They love the beach. But my daughters don't appreciate the risks. Santa Monica is nice. But it has its sketchy parts too. I worry. But I'm a cop."

Reznick smiled. "That's what parents do, right? Worry."

A waitress served Garcia his breakfast. He waited until she was out of earshot as he sipped some coffee. "I'm sorry about your friend."

"Angel? Yeah . . . he fitted the Venice Beach profile for sure. He was homeless, he was an alcoholic. He was down on his luck. But I was speaking to a guy on the beach who said he'd gotten clean before he died."

Garcia shrugged. "Maybe. Maybe not."

"Any further developments in the investigation?"

"Jon, like I said before, these things take time. Don't bust my balls on this, I'm eating my breakfast."

Reznick finished his coffee. "You must have an inkling."

Garcia ate his omelet and toast in silence, shaking his head, not wanting to continue the discussion.

"I want to know if you have any leads. Come on, Frank, give me something. What do you know?"

"We have leads. Satisfied?"

"What kind of leads?"

"It's complicated. Leads take time to chase down." Garcia leaned forward and whispered, "Don't get involved, man. That's all I can say."

Reznick was surprised at the response. "I'm just asking questions. Besides, I'm already involved."

"I know you are. I'm just trying to let you know without letting you know, if you get my drift."

"You know who might be involved?"

"Maybe."

"Just maybe?"

"We're following up on some leads, like I said. But no one's talking. I can't say any more."

Reznick ordered another coffee and the waitress refilled his mug. "Okay . . . I understand."

"Think about it, Jon. Where you have drifters, homeless, junkies, all trying to carve out some kind of life, and then you see the unbelievable wealth that exists—people lose their minds. They'll do anything for fame. For money. I've seen it all."

Reznick sipped his coffee, trying not to scald his mouth. He stayed quiet, sensing that Garcia was opening up as much as he could.

"The people that did that to your friend . . . they're bad people. Evil."

Reznick nodded. "Agreed."

"So if you're hanging around for a few more days, all I'll say is be careful."

"You think I might be at risk?"

"I'm saying be careful. The people who killed your friend have money, and they kill for fun."

"Are we talking organized crime here?"

Garcia finished his omelet, wiping his mouth with his napkin. "I've said too much already. My advice? Go home. Try and forget this. No good will come of any of it."

Seven

The clouds were low, swollen with rain, the smell of cut grass in the air. The weather was fitting for a funeral.

Reznick stood graveside at Woodlawn Cemetery in Santa Monica, alongside a female mourner and the priest. He felt numb as he watched the coffin being lowered into the California soil.

The priest lowered his head as Angel was laid to rest.

Reznick looked at the only other mourner. A middle-aged woman dressed in black, sunglasses on, looked down into the grave.

The priest closed his eyes. "The Lord bless you and watch over you. The Lord make His face shine upon you, and be gracious to you. The Lord look kindly on you and give you peace. In the name of the Father, and of the Son, and of the Holy Spirit."

Reznick bowed his head. "Amen."

The priest turned and spoke to the woman for a short while. He then walked over to Reznick and shook his hand.

"Father, thank you for that," Reznick said.

"God bless you for allowing Angel to have a Christian burial."

Reznick nodded.

"How did you know Mr. Ramos?"

"We served together. He was in Delta Force. We served for years overseas."

"That must've taken its toll on Angel's soul."

"It didn't at first. But these things linger I guess, over the years."

"Thank you for this," the priest said. He turned, facing the grave, and whispered a few prayers in Latin.

Reznick waited until the priest had walked away. Then he approached the woman, who had taken off her sunglasses and was dabbing her eyes with a white handkerchief. He extended his hand and introduced himself. "Thanks for coming. Do you mind me asking how you knew Angel?"

The woman squeezed her eyes shut as she fought back the tears. "Are you family? I didn't know he had any family."

Reznick shook his head. "Just a friend. My name's Jon Reznick."

The woman's face was streaked with tears. "My name's Christine."

"Nice to meet you, Christine. So, you knew Angel?"

"Me and Angel go way back. When I first moved to LA, he looked out for me. We worked out at the same downtown gym. He worked security, clubs, VIP protection—pretty cool stuff."

"So that must've been a few years back, right?"

"A long time ago. Ten years, maybe more. We lost touch."

"He fell on hard times, I think."

Christine nodded.

"Do you mind me asking . . . were you Angel's partner? Wife?"

"I was his girlfriend at one time. Had hoped to get married. But you know how it is."

"I'm sorry, not sure I understand."

"I had to leave Angel for my sanity if nothing else. I couldn't help him. No one could help him. He was spiraling out of control. Drink, drugs. I was scared. Mood swings. He began to self-harm. So, I had to turn my back on him. Broke my heart."

"That's tough." Reznick turned and acknowledged the priest, who was getting into a waiting car. "Do you want to get a cup of coffee?"

The woman shrugged.

"I know this must be a difficult time. But I'm looking for answers about Angel's death."

"I heard he was murdered."

Reznick nodded. "I believe so."

"What do you want to know, Jon? Are you a cop?"

"No, I'm not."

"You look like a cop."

"Trust me, I'm not. You want to grab that coffee?"

The coffee shop was on the corner of Lincoln and Pico.

Reznick picked a table in a quiet corner, overlooking the parking lot.

A waitress approached.

He smiled at Christine. "What would you like?"

"Coffee and a slice of apple pie with cream."

Reznick ordered the same.

"Did I say my name is Christine?" she asked.

"You did."

"I'm sorry, mind's a bit slow. I'm on medication."

"It's nice to meet you, Christine. Sorry it's under such circumstances."

"Me too. What a waste."

Reznick sat in silence as the waitress returned with their order.

"Enjoy!" she said cheerily.

He waited until she was out of earshot. Then he leaned closer to Christine. "I'm so sorry, again. I appreciate you coming."

"I thought he was the one." Christine shrugged. "Story of my life." She picked up her mug of steaming coffee, wincing slightly. "That's hot."

"How did you hear about the funeral?"

"Purely by chance. I occasionally attend church, down in Venice. And someone in the church mentioned that they heard Angel had been found dead. I was horrified. It had been a few years . . . but still, I was fond of him."

"I'm glad you found the time to attend."

Christine cut off a bit of pie with her fork. "What can I say? I sit around most of the day. Xanax keeps me from blowing my brains out."

"You mind me asking what you do?"

Christine ate some pie, shaking her head. "I'd rather not say."

Reznick drank some of the scalding coffee. Maybe she wasn't too proud of her occupation. Or maybe she was just a private person. He changed the subject. "So, you both moved to LA and hung out?"

"Pretty much. Angel was a bit wild. And I mean wild. When he got a drink in him, he got kind of crazy, unpredictable. But everything seemed to be going well in the first year I knew him. He had a good job, working in film. He was making good money. That was a decade ago. A lifetime. I could see a future."

"What happened?"

"Life happened."

"What do you mean?"

"His personality seemed to change. I don't know if he was doing drugs. The film industry . . . there's a lot of drugs there. And he was working long hours. Then his drinking went from heavy to blackout drunk every night. He wouldn't come home some nights. I thought he was seeing some other woman. So I left."

Reznick shifted in his seat.

"What can you tell me about his daughter?" he asked.

Christine seemed to be searching in her coffee for what to say next. "Next to nothing. I had no idea she even existed. But neither did he, I think. From what I heard, the girl moved to LA to try and find her dad. She found him in a bar in Venice."

"Help me out here. Angel didn't know he had a daughter until she got in touch?"

Christine nodded.

"How did he take it?"

"Apparently, Angel was happy to see her. He was loaded most of the time. But he had talked to his pals around Venice about making money to provide for her. When he was with me, he had got tight with some druggies. He seemed to spiral not long after that. Angel went through a series of jobs. Eventually, he didn't work anymore. Actually, he couldn't work. He was on oxycodone for pain relief. He was a serious addict. Sometimes he disappeared for days at a time. But he could never shake his cravings for the drug."

"That must've been tough for you."

"It was devastating. He tried desperately to get another job. But all the interviews came to nothing. People could see he was strung-out, not sharp. He was also out of shape. I think he lost his confidence, and then he began talking about seeing people—people following him."

"He was paranoid?"

"Very. I don't know if it was the drugs. The medication he was on to stop him having epileptic fits."

Reznick gulped his coffee. "He had epileptic fits?"

"More and more. He was working at some club. A guy shot him. The bullet went into his forehead. He survived, thank God. But he started having fits."

Reznick felt like he knew nothing about the hell that Angel had endured these past few years.

"His personality seemed to change after that. There was no going back."

"Tell me about his daughter."

"What can I say? A friend in the church said she was very pretty. Apparently her mother was a young woman from Mexico Angel had run into in Miami. But it was a one-night stand. Or so I heard."

"That's brutal, to learn about all that. For his daughter too."

"Can you imagine how she must have felt? She didn't know who her father was for all those years. When she finally tracked him down, he was in a bad way."

"What did his daughter do when she got here?"

"Apparently she tried to look after him. She moved in with him. He had a horrible little apartment on 4th Street. She cooked for him. Cleaned up. But he went downhill fast. Then he lost his apartment. And he became homeless. But his daughter was desperate to help him. The girl tried."

"What's his daughter's name?"

"Her name is Camila, with one *l*. But from what I heard, she used a different last name to Angel. Her mother's name. Cortez, I think."

Reznick made a mental note. "What exactly happened to her?"

"I don't know for sure. I know she left. But I heard that Angel had miraculously managed to clean himself up just before he died. He was desperate to find his daughter. He felt responsible for what happened. But she was a bit wild herself, to be honest."

"How?"

"She needed to earn money. She wanted to get him somewhere to live. To help him get back on his feet. And she wanted quick money. She began escorting."

"Not a good move."

"Don't judge, honey. Sometimes there are no good options. I've been there myself."

"Sorry, I didn't mean to insinuate anything."

"It's fine . . . but Camila. She got drawn into that fucking world. Creeps, losers, drug-taking abusers, I've hung out with them all. She began working, so I heard, up in the Hills. Wealthy clients. Home visits. Bar girl for a while. Someone said she worked as a yacht girl, out in the Caribbean. It's all just prostitution by another name. But her disappearing out of his life was, I think, the final straw. Angel got clean for a little while. And then he wound up dead. Go figure."

"Do you know if Camila knew her dad had cleaned up his act?"

"Probably not."

Reznick nodded.

"It's just another hard-luck story in this city. She moved here to find him. Then she tried to help him. But she couldn't. I'd had to get out when I did for my own sanity. Still, sad to think what happened to him."

Reznick stared at the tough thirty-something woman opposite him. "You did the right thing, walking away. You've got to protect yourself."

"But I didn't do anything to reach out to him. It would have been easy for me to track him down. I heard he was hanging around the beach. He was boozing with some nutcases he called friends, and his daughter, from what I heard, was fucking men twice her age or more in Hollywood. I can't deal with that. It's too fucking sad."

Reznick sipped his drink as he looked around the upscale coffee shop.

"Your first time in LA?" Christine asked.

"No, been a few times. You live around here?"

"If only . . . Santa Monica is lovely."

"Where do you live?"

"West Adams, in South LA. Not the best."

Reznick didn't want to share the details of the shocking nature of Angel's death. "I'm sorry again about Angel's passing."

"Glad you traveled here."

"He was a good guy when I knew him. Tough. But that was many years ago."

"We all end up the same way. Six feet under. I'm worried that's how his daughter will end up too. Forgotten, and left to die like her father."

Reznick chewed on that thought. "You don't know where she might be living?"

"No idea."

"Is there anyone that might be able to help me find her?"

"I don't know where she is."

"You got a number in case I track her down?"

"I don't give out my number to anyone." Christine checked her watch. "It was nice meeting you. But don't stay too long in this town. It'll chew you up and spit you out like all the rest of us."

Eight

The day after the funeral, the conversation with Angel's ex-girlfriend fresh in his memory, Reznick was still hanging around Venice Beach. He had made sure Angel had been given a proper burial. He had contemplated heading back home to Maine. But he had decided to stick around in LA, at least until he found out what had happened to his friend.

He had a couple of beers in the Whaler beach bar on Washington. Afterward, he strolled around the less touristy areas of Venice. He headed west on Lincoln Boulevard, past fancy duplexes and ritzy apartment complexes. Along Flower Avenue. Past a young woman, headphones on, carrying her coffee. Down Abbot Kinney Boulevard, past a juice bar and an upscale boutique, before heading along Cabrillo Avenue. He observed the modernist houses, with their floor-to-ceiling windows, visible above high hedges, and then walked along Altair Place, where palm trees shrouded cool bungalows and fancy two-story townhouses.

Reznick headed back to the beach and along the boardwalk. A barefoot white kid wearing a faded pink T-shirt was playing the guitar and singing a Beatles song as his girlfriend, wearing faded jeans, sat at his feet, chewing gum. Down on the beach it looked like a yoga group was practicing their poses. Out on the water, a surfer was paddling out on his board. Reznick walked on. It became grittier. He talked with vagrants, panhandlers, junkies—anyone really, trying to see if they knew anything about Angel Ramos. It was the same old story. A few shrugs. His instincts were telling him to head home to Rockland.

What had Angel been doing in his final days? And had that played a part in his horrific murder?

The more he thought about it, the angrier he got. There was a burning rage, deep within him. He wanted to hunt down the people who had killed Angel. But it was more than that. Angel had a daughter. Where was she now? She had been drawn into the seedy underbelly of the city too—into a world of sex, drugs, and bad choices.

She might be dead for all he knew. And as for who had killed Angel, the cops had a better chance of finding the bastards who had tortured and killed him than Reznick. It was easy to be cynical, thinking about the LAPD and their procedures. But he had believed Captain Frank Garcia when he said that his homicide detectives were on it.

But something deep down in Reznick's gut told him that he shouldn't walk away now.

He wanted answers. He *needed* answers. When it came down to it, he owed it to Angel. A debt of gratitude for being a comrade and a friend. Angel had never walked away from any firefight in Iraq or Afghanistan. Only Angel's fragile mental health and breakdown in Iraq had forced the military doctors to get him out of the firing line.

Reznick looked over toward a bench. A nun wearing a full habit was handing out some sandwiches and coffee to a disheveled older woman. He waited until she had finished tending to the woman before he approached. "I'm sorry to bother you, Sister. I was wondering if you could help."

"If I can," the nun answered.

"I'm looking to speak to people who knew my friend who died recently, Angel Ramos. Just trying to piece together his last days."

The nun smiled. "Angel Ramos? Yes, I knew him. Poor thing. But he was a lost soul. I hadn't seen him for a few weeks. He drifted in and out of Venice."

Reznick introduced himself, then told her, "I'm from Maine. I don't know Venice very well."

"It's a lovely place to live. But only if you have money and a nice house. Otherwise, life can be harsh."

"Is there anything you can tell me about Angel or his friends that could connect me to his old life? I may be grasping at straws."

"I'm probably not the person to speak to."

"Who is?"

"The person Angel spoke to, when he did open up, was the priest at our church here in Venice Beach. Father O'Donnell. Lovely man. Speak to him."

"He knew Angel?"

"Father O'Donnell is a confidant to many of the homeless in the area. Angel was quite close to him."

Reznick thanked the nun and headed to the church where Father Patrick O'Donnell was welcoming the homeless to the soup kitchen. He watched and waited until everyone had gotten their soup and bread before he approached the ruddy-faced priest.

Father O'Donnell looked up and smiled. "How can I help you, son?"

"Father, I was wondering if we could have a word. It's about a friend of mine who recently passed away. Angel Ramos. Does that name mean anything to you?"

The priest nodded as he took Reznick to the far side of the church, near the vestry. "A wee bit of privacy," he said. He sat down on a pew. "What a day. Take a load off, son."

Reznick sat down beside the priest and introduced himself. "I'm just trying to piece together the final days of my friend's life."

"I see. Where are you from?"

"Maine."

The priest cleared his throat. "That's a long way away."

Reznick smiled. "It is."

Father O'Donnell closed his eyes and crossed himself. "I only heard this morning about Angel. From one of the sisters. I believe something unspeakable happened to him. Ungodly. That's all I heard."

"He was murdered. Very brutally."

"In the name of God . . ."

"How well did you know him, Father?"

"How well does anyone truly know anyone else, Jon?"

"I mean, how long did you know him? Was he friendly?"

"He was down on his luck when I first met him a few years back. He was fighting people in the street. Getting locked up. And once he got out again, he'd be staggering around, drinking. He was a lost soul. Epileptic after getting shot, I heard. We tried. I tried. I could sense his sadness. Like he was never going to be the same man he once was. Like he had no hope. No future. Just a faraway look in his eyes. God rest his soul."

"Angel was a warrior when I knew him. That's how I still think of him. The man I knew, the man I served with, was strong, tough, resilient, and level-headed."

"He was lost to alcohol and drugs."

Reznick nodded.

"Why he ended up with that life and you ended up with your life, only the Lord above knows. I tried to help him the best I could. We all did. But sadly, Angel was headed down a very dark path, from which few ever return."

Reznick sighed.

"Tell me, Angel was a veteran, yes?" said the priest.

"One of the best. Angel served overseas with me. He won numerous military honors. Toughest man I knew. And that's what makes his death so hard to deal with. But he did suffer post-traumatic stress in Iraq. Almost certainly when he came back home."

The priest clasped his hands together. "You know what he told me about his medals?"

"What?"

"He told me he sold them all. He was broke."

"That's very sad."

"He told me he owed tens of thousands of dollars to drug dealers and loan sharks. And also to his daughter."

Reznick wondered if this was what had gotten him killed. "That's not good."

"They sometimes came here looking for him. Even to the church."

"The drug dealers?"

The priest nodded, his eyes hooded. "Covered in tattoos. Gang tattoos, I think."

"Did they rough you up?"

"They didn't touch me. But they were shouting at me and some of the sisters. Terrible atmosphere when they arrived. But he was never here, or not for long anyway."

Reznick felt frustrated, and he shook his head.

"The only two things Angel had were his faith and the love of his daughter. He lost faith when his daughter abandoned him. I saw her once or twice. But she moved away when Angel really hit rock bottom."

Reznick watched the nuns and volunteers mingling with the homeless. He leaned in close to the priest, his voice barely a whisper.

"I heard his daughter might be working up in the Hollywood Hills . . ."

"West Hollywood. That's what I heard. I've prayed for her life like I prayed for her father's. He used to weep for her. Angel knew that his daughter was working on the streets. And that is a terrible cross to bear for any father."

Reznick nodded.

"A call girl, or whatever it is they call it these days. He got sober on a couple occasions, and tried, unsuccessfully, to find her again. But she was in the throes of addiction by then, just like her father. I sat down with him on many occasions, listening to him weep for his lost daughter. Crying like the child he was. God rest his soul."

"Are you sure she was involved in prostitution, Father?"

"I am quite sure. She wanted to get into film, he said. She wanted to be an actress. But every young person dreams of that, don't they?"

"Did he confide in you who she was with, or if there were men who were controlling her?"

The priest gave a beatific smile. "Jon, you know that the seal of the confessional must never be broken. Even after death. All I can say is that people come to this town with big dreams. But those dreams are only illusions. It's a spell they fall under. That spell is soon broken when they come face-to-face with the reality of Hollywood. It's an unforgiving city."

"How do you mean?"

"I mean, when you're down on your luck, and you hit rock bottom, this city can be a wilderness of lost people. I remember a girl whose family lived in a nice part of Los Angeles. She was maybe seventeen, strung-out on crack and heroin, and our street outreach team found her in an alleyway one night. They got her clean, then back to her parents. She knew Angel's daughter. She told me about her. She was friends with her at one time. They were close."

"And you got that girl back to her parents."

"We did. We were lucky that the girl had tremendous support at home. Her parents were good people, but not Christian. They were artists. Creative people."

"Do you have a name for this girl?"

"Catherine."

"I'd like to speak to her. I'd like to try and help Angel's daughter if I can."

"A word to the wise, Jon. Be prepared for heartache. I fear the worst for Angel's daughter. She lost her way pretty bad. I don't know where she lives now."

"Do you have an address for the parents of the girl you helped?"

"I have an address." The priest reached into a pocket and pulled out his cell phone. He scrolled through a list of contacts. "And here it is!" He turned his phone toward Reznick. "They live in a place called Topanga Canyon, up in the Santa Monica Mountains. Very peaceful town. The parents are, how would I describe them . . . New Age types. They wouldn't mind me calling them that. They have kind hearts. Tell them I sent you."

Nine

Jerry Levinson might have felt the sun on his face and the wind in his hair as he drove along Mulholland Drive in his BMW convertible, but he was preoccupied with a sense of foreboding. He was on his way to see his hellraiser film director client, Brett Miller. Sunglasses on, blue skies above, it should have been a beautiful day in the middle of summer. But he knew the calm of his drive up into the Santa Monica Mountains was about to be broken. It would end with another volatile meeting. It always did with Brett.

Jerry had been summoned an hour earlier by a text message from Brett. It had said, simply, *We need to talk. Now.* It was very Brett. Short. Sharp. His first thought had been: *What now?*

It seemed like every day was another drama. Six months earlier, he had received a call from Brett talking about a prostitute, Charlotte Orton. He'd told Jerry that she lived down in the Valley, and he had paid her for sex. Weeping uncontrollably, Brett had said that she was going to go to the cops, claiming she had been raped by Brett and some of his friends.

Levinson was still in the middle of dealing with that incident, liaising with a private detective, Jay Johnson, who helped out his firm. Johnson was a feared, old-school, retired Los Angeles homicide detective who had countless contacts in the criminal world. When Jerry needed a problem to disappear for a client, he contacted Jay. Only Jay. And his answer would invariably be the same: *Leave it to me, Jerry. I know someone who can help.*

Jerry didn't ask questions. He was only interested in results.

Despite being a top client of Levinson's firm, Brett Miller was fast becoming a liability, with his predilection for young girls and his insatiable appetite for drugs.

Jerry had earned tens of millions of dollars working with Brett. A lot of the time it was just dealing with contracts. Other times it was acting as Brett's psychologist or confidant. Sometimes he was Brett's fixer, making sure his client's foibles didn't make the newspapers or TV. He used all his contacts in law enforcement, politics, and the media to protect the reputations of his clients.

Jerry drove on past the huge estates cocooned behind enormous hedges and fences; the gates staffed by multiple guards. He represented a number of the inhabitants of Bel-Air and Beverly Hills. He was the go-to entertainment lawyer for film stars, producers, and directors. A-listers who didn't mind paying his two-thousand-dollars-an-hour rate. But in return it felt like he had to be at their beck and call, twenty-four-seven, whether in LA or while on vacation. When they wanted Jerry on the other end of the line, they got him, no matter what.

He loved his work. He would kill for his clients. Perhaps not literally, but he knew plenty of people in the city who would, if the price was right.

Jerry pulled up to the electronic gate outside Brett Miller's compound, leaned out the window, and buzzed. "It's Jerry Levinson," he said. Video surveillance cameras scanned his vehicle. A few seconds later, the gates opened. He drove slowly up the driveway toward the sprawling, eighteen-thousand-square-foot modernist masterpiece of a home on Perugia Way in lower Bel Air. Miller had paid a cool thirty-five million dollars for it three years earlier. His films had raked in billions and billions over the last decade.

Jerry picked up his briefcase from the passenger seat. He was shown into the house by a butler, and escorted out to the back, which had stunning views over the city. The golf fairways of the Bel-Air Country Club were spread out before him.

He saw Brett sat slumped beside the poolside. "Hey, man!"

Brett stared ahead, his face flushed, an empty champagne flute and bottle on the table in front of him. He looked terrible, with dark shadows under his eyes, as if he hadn't slept in days. The film director turned around, his eyes bloodshot. "Where the fuck have you been, Jerry? I'm worried sick. You know I worry."

"I know you do. And I'm sorry, but it couldn't be helped. Traffic."

"Fuck traffic, Jerry. I'm fucking dying up here, man. I wanted you here hours ago."

"I came as fast as I could."

Brett closed his eyes and shook his head. "I'm sorry, man, I'm a bit strung-out. My life's a mess. And that's being charitable."

Jerry was used to his client's mood swings. Brett was notoriously hot-tempered—prone to crazy tantrums, on and off set. And he was also not averse to violence. His first wife had left him because of his abusive behavior and his cocaine addiction. He'd beaten her to a pulp when things weren't going well. He'd had to pay her fifty million to keep her quiet.

Brett motioned for his butler to leave them alone.

"Do you need anything, sir?" he asked.

"We're fine. Thanks, Charles."

"Very good, sir," the butler said, before making himself scarce.

Brett stared out over the golf course and shook his head. "I'm in the shit again, Jerry. It's bad. I need someone to figure out what I should do. I'm freaking out, man."

Jerry sat down and pulled his chair closer, until he was inches away from Brett. He placed his briefcase at his feet and took out a legal pad and pen. "Slow down, Brett. I'm here for you. What seems to be the problem now?"

"I'll tell you what the latest fucking problem is. I'm the fucking problem, Jerry."

"So, let's talk about this. Nice and calm. It's just me and you."

"A week ago, I was out. You know I like to party."

"It's not illegal. At least not yet."

Brett stared at him. "This is not a joking matter, man."

"I'm sorry. Go on."

"I was out, clubbing. I need to cut loose now and again. The girl I was with, cute thing, she got fucked-up, super-high, and storms out of the club. She was out of her fucking mind."

Jerry noted down the salient points. "And this was a week ago?"

"Correct."

"That must have happened to you before. A girl storms out of a club, right?"

"That's not the issue. The issue is the girl who ran out of the club got killed on the freeway."

Jerry felt his stomach tighten with tension.

"And if that's not enough, my friend says there might have been pap photos taken inside the club of us together, talking and getting high."

Jerry felt a pulse of aggravation behind his eyes. "And you only found out about it now?"

Brett nodded.

"Okay, let's get this straight. So, the girl ran out, but now you're hearing there are photographs? Compromising photos?"

"I believe so."

"Should there have been professional photographers inside the club?"

"Abso-fucking-lutely not. No-photograph rule. Paparazzi are sometimes spotted outside. But no way should they be inside. That's the rules. That why I go there."

"Name of the club?"

"Heaven."

Jerry wrote down the name. "What else?"

"There's online chatter that some blogger, Raymond Prince or something, is going to run a story about the girl and me."

Jerry wondered if this could get any worse.

"And I heard from my friend that a major newspaper—a tabloid newspaper, in London—is offering high six figures to get this story. Photographs, all of it. Man, this is fucked-up."

"Let's focus, Brett. Who's the photographer?"

"Her name is Heidi Stratton, some chick from England. She's based in LA apparently. Has a studio here in the city."

Jerry scanned his notes as he absorbed the information. He sat quietly, wanting Brett to tell him as much as possible. But his presence was also a way to reassure Brett that this was nothing to panic about, even if it was. "A lot of unfortunate events there."

"The understatement of the fucking year, Jerry. I can't deal with this. I can't fucking deal with this."

"Let's get back to the nightclub. It was over a week ago, right? And you only learned about the photos now?"

"And the girl being killed on the freeway! I didn't know shit about that until a few hours ago."

"Think back to that night. When you say you were partying . . . that means different things to different people."

"What do you think I mean?"

"You tell me."

"I was doing coke throughout the day. I must've had cocaine psychosis or something. I was out of my mind by the time I went to the club. We both were. She arrived separately. My manager had organized a car for her."

"Separate?"

"I sent a car to pick her up."

"Okay."

"Jerry, it was a fucked-up few days. We were doing huge amounts of blow. I think she drank some crazy drink that's like peyote, mushrooms, I don't know. All I know is that the girl started freaking out. She was out of her fucking mind. Then she disappeared. I mean she split, screaming."

"Did you go after her?"

"Fuck no."

Jerry nodded. "That's good."

"Why is it good?"

"If you had run after her, as if she was your date or girlfriend, and you had been photographed outside the club, that would have put a different spin on the story. It would be a real connection to the girl."

Brett rubbed the stubble on his chin.

"We'll get through this. I know this must all have come as quite a shock. Especially being told that the girl you were with had died."

"Fuck that. That's not my business. My business is me. I'm worried about me. About this story growing wings, putting me in a bad light. Linking me to this fucking girl. I can't have that. Photos . . . That's the worst part of it. I can't have that shit in my life."

"Who gave you the heads-up?"

"About the photographs?"

"Yes."

"Jimmy Gatz."

Jerry wrote down the name. "Who's he?"

67

"He works as a stringer for the *New York Times*. He's a photojournalist."

"And the girl that died? Her name?"

"I don't know."

"You don't know?"

Brett shrugged. "What can I tell you? I talk to a lot of people. I talk to a lot of girls. We drink. We hang out."

"A name would be useful."

"Mirlande, I think. Haitian chick. Sweet girl."

Jerry looked up from his note-taking. "I need you to be honest when I ask you the next question. I'm not looking for lies. I need to know the truth."

"You got it."

"How old was the girl?"

"She said she was twenty-one."

"And was she?"

"Probably not. No."

"Under eighteen?"

"Perhaps."

Jerry felt himself grimace. "Can you tell me more about the club?"

"All I know is that it's run by a guy called Curtis Strange. But it's owned by a Mexican dude. Carlos."

"Carlos Lopez?"

"You've heard of him?"

Jerry nodded.

Brett closed his eyes and shook his head. "What a mess."

"It'll be fine. You'll see."

"It needs to be, Jerry. If the story gets out that I was photographed with the chick that died that night, I'm fucked. It's the cops I'm worried about most. I want that element silenced. Investigations and shit. I want this locked down tight."

Jerry leaned over and patted Brett on the arm. "I will deal with this. This is what I do. I'm your fixer."

"Fix this for me, Jerry. Lock it down hard. I know you've got connections. Let's make sure this stays under wraps."

"Where's your wife?"

"She's out of town. Fucking Maldives or some shit. Environmental charity bullshit. If she finds out about this, about being photographed with a girl before she was found dead, she will divorce me. It would be the final straw. And she will fuck me over. I'll lose hundreds of millions. She will destroy me, man."

"You have a prenup, Brett. It's watertight."

Brett nodded and smiled. "That's right, I do. Thank God for lawyers!"

Jerry smiled. "But it won't come to that. I won't allow that to happen. I won't allow it. You've done the right thing, coming to me."

"What should I do, Jerry? Tell me, what should I do?"

"Leave it to me. Don't leave this property. Don't answer any questions if the cops turn up. Do not go clubbing, drinking, fucking, or whatever you usually get up to in your spare time. Just leave everything to me. I will fix this."

Ten

The house was located high up in the Santa Monica Mountains, in an isolated area on the outskirts of Topanga, about an hour away from the sprawl of the city. Shrouded in buckwheat flowers, it was nestled at the end of a dusty, winding road, with incredible views all around.

Reznick pulled up outside and surveyed the home. It appeared to be a traditional timber-frame house. A quiet, beautiful refuge from the craziness of Los Angeles. He switched off his engine and walked up the path.

A man with disheveled shoulder-length hair opened the front door. He wore an oversize Grateful Dead T-shirt and paint-spattered black jeans. "Father O'Donnell said you'd be coming up here. Nice to meet you. I'm Will, Catherine's father. Come on in, man."

Reznick followed him into a sun-bathed living room. Vibrant modernist paintings were hung on the walls, and Native American pottery and statues adorned every shelf. "I appreciate you seeing me."

Will shrugged. "Not a problem."

Reznick was introduced to Will's wife. She had a headscarf on and wore faded jeans with a pale pink shirt hanging loose, bangles on her wrists and beads around her neck.

"I'm Cindy." She shook his hand.

"I'm Jon. Lovely place you've got here."

Cindy smiled. "It's a place of peace. We like it. But occasionally we have wildfires, coyotes, even mountain lions to contend with."

Will led them out onto a deck with startling views of the mountains, wildfire smoke off in the distance. There sat a young woman on a paisley-patterned sofa, her arms folded. Reznick was introduced to the couple's daughter, Catherine, who smiled nervously.

Will pointed to a chair. "Please, have a seat."

Reznick sat down as the daughter shifted uncomfortably.

"Can I get you a drink?" Cindy asked. "Freshly squeezed orange juice? Water?"

"Black coffee?"

She nodded. "Great. I'm a coffee lover, too. I'll make us all some coffee."

Reznick made small talk with Will about the calmness up in the mountains. He noticed Catherine sat in a sullen silence. A short while later, Cindy returned with a tray. She handed him a mug.

Will cleared his throat. "So . . . How can we help you, Jon?"

"First, thanks for seeing me and letting me into your beautiful home. I won't take up too much of your time."

Will wrapped his arm around his daughter as if for comfort, before looking at Reznick again.

"The priest in Venice Beach thought you might be able to help me. I arrived in Los Angeles about a week ago. I'd been told my friend had died here." Reznick refrained from giving any of the gory details.

Cindy steepled her fingers as if in a contemplative mood. "I'm so sorry to hear that."

"Thank you. Anyway, I've been told that my late friend had a daughter. I didn't know anything about that. But I want to try and find her, to make sure she's okay, before I head back home."

Will nodded as Catherine sipped her coffee.

"That's why I'm here. Father O'Donnell said that this girl, my late friend's daughter, Camila, may be known to your daughter. I believe the church helped Catherine a few months back. I'm looking to get any information about where this girl might be."

Cindy smiled. "Father O'Donnell is a good soul. I like to help out with church activities a couple times a month. Soup kitchens, food parcels, that kind of thing. And yes, they helped Catherine, for which we are eternally grateful."

Reznick looked at the girl sandwiched between her mom and dad. "I'm pleased things are working out for you now, Catherine."

The girl blushed. "I got the help I needed."

"Father O'Donnell said you used to hang about in West Hollywood a while back. I'm not judging, trust me."

"That was then," Cindy interjected. "Catherine has moved on. She's settled now. She's going to college." It seemed as though she didn't want her daughter to have to relive a painful time in her life.

"That's terrific. Where?"

"NYU. I'm going to major in English Literature. I hope to be a writer someday."

"Good for you. Who's your favorite writer?"

"Arthur C. Clarke. I love science fiction."

"Nice. My own daughter went to college in Vermont. Bennington. She loved it."

The girl smiled. "That's a cool place."

"She thought so."

"So how exactly can I help you?" Catherine asked. "I will if I can."

"How well did you know Camila?"

"Well enough. We hung around for a while. She was kinda wild."

72

"I'm looking to find her. Like I said, I knew her father. He was a veteran, same as me."

The girl stared at Reznick. "How did he die?"

He winced. "I don't want to go into detail, but he was murdered just over a week ago."

"That's so sad."

"I'm just hoping to speak to anyone who knows his daughter. I want to make sure she's doing okay."

Catherine stared at him blankly, as if slightly medicated.

"Sadly, from what I've heard, she's in a bad place. I'd like to get her back on her feet again."

"Well, I'll tell you what I know."

"That'd be great," Reznick said.

"She was a friend of a friend. A bit scary. Don't get me wrong, Camila was very likeable. But she didn't seem to know when to stop. Partying, taking drugs, hanging out with creeps, that kind of thing. I was in a bad place too. I took the wrong path. But she was on a whole other level."

"So you partied with her now and again, but you weren't close friends?"

"Close enough. We'd go to a club or two on Sunset together—sleazy places." The girl looked at her parents. "Do you mind if I speak to Mr. Reznick alone? It's a bit embarrassing, talking about this stuff."

Cindy kissed her daughter. "Sure, honey. Your privacy is important to us. We'll leave you to it."

The parents disappeared into the house. Reznick looked out over the verdant views of the mountains nearby. "This home must seem a million miles away from the Sunset Strip."

"It does." The girl rolled her eyes. "It's a bit boring, to tell you the truth. But my parents love it. They're painters."

"It's a beautiful part of the world. Safe. Clean."

"True."

Reznick leaned forward, lowering his voice. "Catherine, I know this isn't easy, and I appreciate you seeing me. And your parents allowing it. But I'm just trying to get a handle on the places you hung out, where Camila might be now, that kind of thing. Or mutual friends or acquaintances, if there were any. If you feel uncomfortable with any of my questions, just let me know and we can move on."

Catherine shifted in her seat. "What do you want to know?"

"Did you and Camila hang out much?"

"Just at night, at the clubs. My parents already know this. And before you ask, we were with men. We were sex workers."

Reznick nodded. "I understand."

"They were sleazy. Some of the men were in the industry, some said they had connections. But it was bullshit. I realize that now."

"Do you mind me asking why you were hanging out with those guys? I'm assuming to get a start in the film industry?"

"Correct."

"And you were using drugs?"

"You kidding me? Everyone was. Weed, psychedelics, speed, coke, LSD . . ."

"Heroin?"

"Absolutely."

Reznick's heart sank. He thought of his own daughter, Lauren, getting embroiled in such a scene. It didn't even bear thinking about. "What about you?"

The girl shrugged. "I was chasing the dragon. Night and day."

"You were smoking it?"

"More or less. It left me broke, sick, unable to function. Pretty soon I was having sex with men in motel rooms on Sunset for money. So was Camila."

Reznick bowed his head. "I'm so sorry."

"Don't be. It was my doing. I was responsible for my actions."

"You were just a kid. You're still a kid."

"I was selling my body. I didn't view myself as a prostitute, but that's what I was. It's referred to as escorting, or being a party girl . . . but that's bullshit. I know that now."

"How did you get help from Father O'Donnell?"

"One morning, one of his outreach street teams found me in an alleyway off Sunset. I was unconscious. I'd been raped. They got me to a hospital. And they looked after me until I felt ready to contact my parents."

Reznick stared at the girl, noticing the slight tremor in her hands. "You're very brave. It takes a strong person to survive such trauma."

"That's all I'm doing. Surviving. It's going to take a long, long time to get my life back on track."

"I'm glad your parents are here for you. Are you getting any other support?"

"I'm seeing a clinical psychologist. Three times a week. They're helping me get through this. Sometimes I wake up in the middle of the night—sweating, anxious, not knowing where I am. But when I realize I'm back home, I calm down."

"It must've been tough for your parents, too. I've got a daughter in her twenties. I don't know what I'd do if she got caught up in the world you're describing."

The girl tucked some of her long hair behind her ear. "I'm alive. And I'm glad."

Reznick showed her the photo of Angel that Frank Garcia had given him. "Did you ever see this guy around? Venice Beach in particular?"

"Don't know him. But one face blurs into the next. Who is he?"

"This is Camila's dad."

"Really?"

Reznick nodded. "Did Camila ever mention him?"

"Just that she tried to get him help, but from what she said, he was an alcoholic, crazy when drunk. But I never knew what he looked like. I never met him, that's for sure."

"Was there a club you hung out at a lot?"

"Club Alpha."

"Where's that?"

"Just off the Strip. Fast crowd, money, plenty of drugs. Heavy-duty security. Horrible, actually. Nasty. Saw them kick and stab one guy in the alley out back. I can't remember the number of times I was carried out of there after collapsing in the bathroom."

Reznick shook his head. "Where was the last place you saw Camila?"

"Heaven, on West Sunset Boulevard. There's a big film studio three blocks away. A lot of the hotshot executives would roll in after midnight, loaded."

"And Camila was there?"

"All the time. I think that was the last time I saw her. Off her face in Heaven."

"Who runs the club?"

"A guy called Curtis Strange. Real sleazeball. He used to have sex with any of the escort girls who were working in the club."

Reznick sat in shocked silence.

"It was a bad scene. But I got lucky. I got out of there. I have parents who love me. I have parents who could pay for treatment to get me clean. Camila didn't have that . . . She was on her own."

Eleven

The underbelly of the city's glamorous, celebrity-fueled culture was not hard to find after midnight.

Reznick was back in the city, driving along Sunset, looking at the hookers and cops jostling outside the neon-lit clubs. A couple were making out in a doorway of a restaurant. A loner hid in the shadows, smoking. It was a world away from the peace and beauty of Topanga.

He parked a few blocks from Heaven, the last place Catherine said she had seen Camila.

Reznick headed into the club through a phalanx of tattooed, oiled-up, muscle-bound heavies, bronzed and clean-shaven. Hip-hop pounded out of huge speakers as he walked up to the bar, past scantily clad bottle girls. He found an unoccupied stool and sat down.

"What you having?" The barman had to shout to be heard above the music.

"Double Scotch on the rocks."

"Coming right up."

Reznick turned and stared at the girls, some looking way younger than twenty-one, who were pouting and flirting with a crowd of guys in suits. He had no idea if this was a nightclub, strip club, a sex club, or just a lap dance kind of place. He wondered what sort of man made up the clientele.

The bartender put his drink down on a monogrammed white coaster. Reznick paid the exorbitant price, leaving a ten-dollar tip.

"You part of the bachelor party tonight?"

Reznick shook his head. "Just hanging out."

"My name's Frank. If you need anything, just let me know."

Reznick was tempted to ask about Camila. He decided against it, wanting to speak to one of the girls first, if the opportunity arose.

Camila herself could be here, though that was a long shot. But he figured if she wasn't here, someone at the club might know her.

A twenty-something girl approached, and leaned in close. "You want a special private dance in one of our VIP booths, stranger?"

"No, thank you. Just having a drink tonight. Though I am looking for a girl. She's around your age."

"Well, you've come to the right place. You got a name for her?"

"Her name's Camila."

"I don't know any Camila, honey. But my name's Betsy. Will I do?"

Reznick felt uncomfortable with the whole vibe and setup. It was sleazy, boring, and wretched. He felt dirty. "Thanks anyway."

"I'll be here tomorrow night too, stranger."

"I'm just passing through. Take care of yourself." Reznick handed her a fifty-dollar bill.

"What's this for?"

"Just look after yourself."

Reznick got up from his stool and left the club. He headed back to his car and drove around to the side entrance. Then he switched off his engine and lights, watching the comings and goings. He hoped he might catch sight of Camila. He wondered if she was working in one of the so-called VIP rooms.

He swigged a bottle of water as he took a couple of Dexedrine, to keep him going into the night. A chemical crutch of his for as long as he could remember. He used the drug so much he didn't think much about it anymore. It kept him wired. He enjoyed the rush it provided. The edge. But he also knew that ingesting amphetamines, day in and day out, year after year, would fuck him up eventually.

He looked over at the entrance to Heaven. He wondered if the club owner was inside, tucked away in a back office. The more he thought about it, the more he realized his chances of finding her here were slim. Camila might be dead. She might be living in Wyoming. She might have cleaned up and moved to the suburbs.

The reality was, for a girl like Camila, if she was still in Hollywood, she was vulnerable. Being all alone in a big city meant there was a greater chance of her being exploited and abused by predators. Men who could supply drugs and money in exchange for sex. If they controlled her, they owned her.

A handful of scantily clad dancers emerged for a smoke break. He decided to take a chance. He got out of his car and approached them.

"Good evening. I'm sorry to bother you girls," he said. "I'm looking for a girl called Camila. I was told she used to hang out here."

One of the dancers, dragging hard on a cigarette, nodded tentatively. She blew smoke away from him. "Are you a cop?"

"No, I knew her father. I'm trying to find her, to help her."

"Honey," the girl said, "I worked with her a year ago. Goes by the working name Gigi. Haven't seen her for a while."

"Gigi?"

"Yeah, that's what I knew her as. Gigi Cortez? Real sweet."

"You know where she went?"

The dancer was coy, as if struggling to remember. "Gigi . . . Let me think . . ."

Reznick pulled out a fifty-dollar bill. "She's the daughter of a close friend of mine. I just want to make sure that she's okay. Her father recently passed away."

The girl took the fifty-dollar bill, examining it closely to see if it was real. "That's too bad. She moved on."

"Do you know where?"

"She told me she got offered more money."

"Where?"

"VIP hostess at Cabaret Sunset. It's owned by a real sleazeball, Trent Bloch."

Reznick made a mental note. "And she definitely went there?"

"Couple months back. She might be there, I don't know. Things change, day to day, week to week. She might have grown sick of that place too. Believe me, this ain't a long-term career."

"Can you tell me anything else about her?"

"Only that she talked about getting into the business. Wanted to be an actress. But that's most of the girls here. Everyone's working the streets, pursuing their dreams. Bright lights and all that."

Reznick thanked the girl and handed her another fifty-dollar bill. "I appreciate your help."

"Anytime, honey. You take care now."

Reznick got back into his car. He took out his cell phone and found the address for Cabaret Sunset, entering the details into the GPS.

It was a mile farther down the Strip, with a pink neon-lit sign—*Late Night Gentlemen's Club*—over a blacked-out window. He parked in an alleyway behind the club. He had line of sight to the back entrance. He checked his watch. It was just past 2 a.m. The club would be open for another hour. He settled down to watch and wait. Time dragged. A customer exited loudly, drunk, and stumbled down Sunset, weaving a path.

The girls emerged about an hour after closing. Reznick got out of his car and approached them, smiling.

"Fuck off, creep," one of the girls said.

"I'm not a customer. I just want to know if you've seen or worked with a girl called Camila who uses the working name Gigi."

One of them—skinny, wearing a short denim skirt and a Clash T-shirt, chewing gum—nodded. "Yeah, I know her. Gigi. She lasted three nights here. Said she had an audition for some big-shot film guy."

"Where would I be able to find her now?"

"Grove 365 in West Hollywood. Some big tippers up there. Said to me that's where she met him."

"When did she tell you this?"

"We bumped into one another one night. She was a bit strung-out."

Reznick handed the girl a fifty-dollar bill. "So this girl, you know her as Gigi?"

"Yeah, Gigi."

"And now she's working at Grove 365?"

"That's right. And that's where she hoped to hook up with a hot shot in the film industry."

Reznick thought about that.

"Who are you, anyway?" she said. "Are you her dad?"

"No. She's the daughter of a friend of mine. My friend died. I just want to make sure she's okay."

The girl shrugged and rolled her eyes as if she didn't believe what he was saying.

"The last time you saw her, how did she seem?" he asked.

"She seemed okay. But I did warn her that, while they might be big tippers up at Grove, that club has got a dark side. I told her to be careful."

"Careful in what way?"

"I mean, hard, hard drugs. Just last week, a friend of mine was found dead on the freeway. She had been partying hard at Grove with a film guy."

"What was the name of your friend who died?"

"Mirlande Jean-Baptiste. Haitian girl. Beautiful. But she got caught up in that scene. Heard she was raped by the film guy one night."

"Are you serious?"

"This is LA. It's just the sort of bullshit we have to deal with. Say, you like to party?"

Reznick shook his head. "I'm only looking for this girl."

"Well, I hope you find her. Tell her from me to look after herself."

"Tell me about the Haitian girl that died."

"Mirlande? She first hooked up with that film guy at some big party up in Beverly Hills. I think that's where Gigi used to go too. He puts on these sex parties with dozens of girls. He's a total creep. Viagra fuck parties, that's what they are. For all his psycho pals. But Mirlande and Gigi were both crazy about getting into the movies."

"So Mirlande died on the freeway. A car accident?"

"Not exactly. Guy I know said he saw her in the club tripping out of her head on something or other. He said he heard from a bouncer that she fled the club, screaming, freaking out."

"Drugs? Someone spiked her drink?"

"Maybe. She was scared of that film guy, though."

"What do you mean?"

Reznick handed over another fifty-dollar bill to help the girl's memory.

"So, Mirlande told me she woke up one time in this guy's bed. TV was on. It was playing a video of him fucking her as she was passed out."

"He'd raped her?"

"Precisely. But she couldn't remember anything about it."

"Roofies?"

"God knows what. She was young, but she was smart. And she wanted to get the hell away from him, big shot or not. She also said she was having flashbacks. She had a memory of being taken to a party and passed around to different men. But she didn't know when."

"Why didn't she leave that party?"

"I don't know. She was scared, I guess. She had no other options."

"Do you know who this film guy is?"

"She told me his name. He's a director. Old guy. Brett Miller. You heard of him?"

Reznick shook his head. "Can't say I have. Why didn't she go to the police?"

The girl stared at him. "That wasn't ever an option."

"Why not?"

"She was illegal. She'd get deported back to Haiti. She said she'd rather die free on the streets of America than ever go back home. Too bad her wish came true."

Twelve

It was ninety-two degrees as they cruised through the sun-bleached streets of the barrio. Boyle Heights, east of downtown and the Los Angeles River.

Carlos Lopez cranked up the air-conditioning. He sat in the passenger seat of his new Porsche SUV, chewing gum, his henchmen in the back. He looked across at the bleak apartment complex, which still looked the same as when he'd moved into the neighborhood after arriving from Mexico. "I don't recognize the people hanging around now."

His brother in the back seat dragged on a cigarette. "Some tough kids coming up."

Carlos knew most of the up-and-coming gang members. He invariably hired them to work security at his clubs. They would have to prove themselves to Carlos for him to like them. They would have to kill. He instilled in his henchmen a love of money. The dollar was king. The greenback could set you free. Everyone loved money.

He pointed off to the side. "Second right, okay?"

The driver nodded. "Got it, boss."

Carlos and his crew were headed to the home of Mirlande Jean-Baptiste's father in the middle of Boyle Heights. The instructions had come from a private investigator who worked for a leading attorney in the city. Someone was worried the father would talk. It was Lopez's job to ensure the problem went away.

Lopez scanned the rundown homes. He'd moved to the area after arriving in America. He had grown to know the people around here well. His associates, all from gangs south of the border, lorded over this area of LA. The SUV cruised along Cesar E. Chavez Avenue. He remembered when it was called Brooklyn Avenue, when he was growing up, before the city renamed it after the union leader. They drove past kids selling tamales and fresh oranges and apples. Past taco stands, and women pushing strollers in the heat of the sun.

The driver pointed to the low-rise housing project in front of them, Ramona Gardens. "This is it, Carlos, yeah?"

"Farther down, on the right. I know where it is. Chico used to live there, with his mom."

His trusted lieutenant, Chico Valdez, was part of the feared street gang Big Hazard—otherwise known as Hazard Grande—associated with the Mexican Mafia. Carlos knew all the players. They knew him. And he himself was integrated into that world more than anyone knew, apart from his blood brothers.

They pulled up at the square, in a parking lot used for drug dealing. "Wait here while we go inside," he said to the driver. Then Lopez turned around and looked at the three men in the back. "Let's get moving. Anyone talk out of place to you, shoot the fucker in the head. They understand that kind of thing round here."

"Got it, boss," one of them replied.

Lopez got out of the car and walked past a couple of wannabe teenagers who were acting tough. "What the fuck you looking at?" he said.

The kids just shrugged and stepped back as Lopez and his crew headed up a flight of stairs.

Lopez knocked hard on the apartment door.

After a ten count a rheumy-eyed old Haitian guy opened it, cigarette in his mouth. "Yeah?"

Lopez barged past him and his men locked the door behind them.

The old guy suddenly looked scared. "What you want? I ain't got nothing."

"Don't worry, pops. Take a seat. We're here to help you."

Joseph Baptiste sat down, bones creaking, dragging hard on his cigarette. He wheezed, "I have no money. So there's no need to try and hustle me. I got emphysema. I ain't got no money."

Lopez sat down as his men stood by the door. "I heard through the grapevine about your daughter, Mirlande Jean-Baptiste. I'm very sorry for your loss."

Joseph had tears in his eyes. "I don't know who you are. Please leave me alone. I have nothing now. She was all I had. I have no money. I have nothing. My daughter, she's gone. What do you want from me?"

"I want answers. I need to know what the cops are saying about how your daughter died. The circumstances."

"What do you mean? What can they say? Cops say she was high. I told her not to go the same way as her mother. She was a junkie. And she worked the streets. I hated it. But I loved her. I'll always love her."

Lopez reached over and patted Joseph on the back of the hand. "Don't be afraid. I've got a proposition."

"What do you mean, a *proposition*?"

"A friend of mine was saying you're going to sue the club where your daughter was partying."

"Yeah, well, I can't afford lawyers. But someone said it might be an idea. The people that supplied her with the drugs must've been inside."

Lopez stared into Joseph's eyes. "I wouldn't recommend that route."

"Why not?"

"One of two things will happen. Either I'll make sure you're deported, or I'll stab you in the face and neck until you can't take another breath. Am I making myself clear?"

Joseph Baptiste's hand was shaking as he dragged on his cigarette. "I ain't scared of you."

"Are you sure, pops?"

"Don't come into my home and threaten me."

"I can help you with some money. Would that be helpful? Twenty thousand bucks? That's a lot of money. It'll help you with your bills. Maybe you can go on a little vacation."

"Who the hell do you think you are? Fuck you, and fuck your money."

Lopez smiled. "I'm a patient man. And I understand why you would be angry. I would be angry too, if that happened to my daughter. But I can help you out. I just need you to sign a document stating that you won't sue anybody, including the club or its owners."

Joseph spat in Lopez's face. "Go fuck yourself."

Lopez took a handkerchief and wiped off the spittle. He put it back in his pocket. Then he grabbed the old man by his scrawny throat, squeezing hard. "I'm disappointed in you. I could have helped you. I help people. Poor people. I help them every day of my life. You know where I come from?"

Joseph closed his eyes, shaking his head.

"Mexico. A village you'd never have heard of. I understand what it's like. Now, you get one final chance. Are you going to sign the document?"

Joseph opened his eyes and spat again in Lopez's face.

This time Lopez used the sleeve of his shirt to wipe it off. Then he took a knife out of his back pocket.

Joseph began to say a prayer in Creole or French.

Lopez grabbed the old man's gray hair and pulled him close. Slowly, he drew a knife across the man's throat. Warm blood spilled onto his hands.

Joseph Baptiste's eyes were frozen in terror, blood spurting from the veins in his neck.

Lopez grabbed the man's left ear and severed it, stuffing it into the old man's mouth.

Joseph began to choke. He tried to open his mouth to scream but no sound came out, apart from the gurgling of blood.

Lopez dragged him into the middle of the floor. He stared down at the terrified, bloody old man. He gripped the knife tight. He bent over and stabbed him repeatedly in the neck, face, and eyes, again and again—ten, twenty, thirty times. He felt frenzied. The blood pooled on the frayed rug.

Then he looked up at his men, who were watching. "Never forget, this is what I do to people who disappoint me."

Thirteen

A light fog had rolled in overnight. As Reznick walked the Venice boardwalk, his cell phone rang.

He answered. "Yeah, who's this?"

"Jon, it's Captain Frank Garcia. You got a minute?"

"Sure thing."

"We've got a problem."

"What kind of problem?"

"We had a complaint."

"About what?"

"About you, what do you think?"

Reznick stared off at the gray ocean, through the gloom hanging over the beach. He wondered if this was in connection to talking with the girls at the clubs.

"You want me to spell it out?"

"I guess you better."

"You were lurking around a couple clubs on Sunset last night."

"There's no law against that, Frank. Besides, that's outside your jurisdiction, isn't it?"

"I was asked to speak to you."

"Who asked you to speak to me?"

"Never mind that."

"Someone at LAPD HQ?"

"I got a complaint from the West Hollywood Sheriff's Station, if you must know. They have jurisdiction on the Strip. You were hassling some girls on Sunset. Asking questions about Camila Ramos, or Gigi. Is that right?"

"Bullshit. I wasn't hassling anyone—what the hell are you talking about? I'm just trying to find Angel's daughter. That's not illegal."

"Jon, listen to me and listen good. This isn't going to end well. We're investigating Angel's death."

"You mean the homicide? It wasn't a simple death, like a car accident; it was systematic torture and homicide."

"We know what it was. But this is complicated. Some of LAPD's finest detectives are working on the case. They need to interview people. Chase down leads."

"I just want to find her. That's separate from your investigation."

"You're also encroaching on the Los Angeles County Sheriff's patch in West Hollywood. They don't like it."

"I don't give a shit if they like it or not."

"They don't want you getting in the way. We work closely with the Sheriff's Department. They know what they're doing. And I'm going to be frank, you have no investigative skills or background."

"I'm just trying to help."

"I'm trying to cut you some slack. If you really knew about all the stories of lost people, lost individuals, hard-luck stories, broken people, you would go completely insane. You need to be able to cut yourself off from this case before you get sucked too far into it."

Reznick knew exactly what he meant. In his own line of work he compartmentalized the killings. The deletions. Call them whatever you wanted. His brain had learned to keep that stuff in the darkest recesses of his mind. He needed to function, day to day. But he could switch to killing mode whenever he wanted. "I'm not getting sucked into anything." The instant he said the words, he realized they weren't true. He was already getting drawn into the twilight world of bars and clubs. Drawn into an investigation which might in all likelihood lead him down a path to nowhere.

"Just let it go. We can't go on wild-goose chases because of the word of some drug addicts and dancers."

"Shouldn't we listen to them?"

"Sure we can listen to them." Garcia let out a long exhalation. Jon let the silence stretch. "Do yourself a favor. Just head back to Maine and get on with your life. LA is full of crazies."

"What if I don't want to go home? The people that tortured and killed my friend are still here." Reznick stared ahead as some rollerbladers weaved in and out of cones on the boardwalk. "You know what I think happened? I think Angel was trying to find his daughter again. He started asking questions. Angel was an abrasive character. Odds are he pissed off the wrong people."

Garcia was quiet.

"I've been thinking about this, Frank. I believe whoever did this might have been acting on behalf of other people. Angel's murder was a warning to others."

"You have no evidence of that, Jon."

"True . . . But I believe Angel got too close to finding out something he wasn't meant to know. He was asking too many questions. And he paid the price for it. He was silenced. How does that sound?"

"I hear what you're saying. I'll tell you what I'll do. I'll personally pass on your thoughts to the team. In the meantime, go home and try and get back to your old life. It's time to move on."

Fourteen

Reznick figured if he hung around it was just a matter of time before he got arrested. The revelation that the Los Angeles County Sheriff's Department had lodged a complaint about Reznick with the LAPD was a serious setback. He wondered if the club owners rather than the girls had made the complaint.

Reznick sauntered over to Muscle Beach and watched some kids shooting hoops. His gaze was drawn to a long-haired, sixty-something man in a wheelchair, remonstrating with a woman swigging from a bottle of wine. He made his way over to them.

The man was sobbing, tears spilling down his face, cigarette in his hand. He caught Reznick's look. The man in the wheelchair had no legs.

"What the fuck are you looking at?" he said. "That's right, I don't have any fucking legs. Satisfied? Get out of my way."

Reznick stepped aside but still stared at the guy.

"Are you deaf?"

Reznick noticed a Marines tattoo on his forearm. It was another ex-soldier, broken and homeless. "Relax, bro. You a veteran?"

"Yeah, you got a problem with that?"

Reznick shook his head and took a fifty-dollar bill out of his wallet, handing it to the man. "I've got no problem with you, man. I wish you well."

The man studied the money. "Is this for real?"

"It is."

He looked up at Reznick and his face broke out in a leathery smile, exposing nicotine-stained teeth. "You a veteran, man?"

Reznick nodded.

"Where did you serve?"

"All over. Iraq, Afghanistan, Somalia, the Middle East."

"Who were you with?"

"Marines. Delta."

The man dragged hard on his cigarette. "Those are some fucking crazy-shit places, excuse my French."

"What about you?"

"Marines. Iraq. Fucked me up good. Thank you, Uncle Sam, you piece of shit!"

Reznick's mind flashed back to the chaos of Fallujah. "What happened, man?"

"They left a dead dog in the road. They attached explosives inside and detonated it remotely. Blew my legs clean off. In a coma for six months. When I woke up I was at Walter Reed in DC."

"I had a few friends who ended up there."

"That was just the start of my nightmare. Wife left me a year later. Lost the house. Lost my old life. So it wasn't just my legs. I couldn't earn money. I couldn't fuck."

"That's tough, man. I'm really sorry, for what it's worth."

The man cut his eyes toward the woman he'd been arguing with. She was still swigging from her bottle of Thunderbird wine. "You need to go easy on that stuff," he called out. "It'll drive you crazy."

The woman turned and spat. "I do what I do, Mr. Tough Guy." She looked at Reznick. "Who are you? You a cop? LAPD, motherfucker?"

Reznick shook his head. "I'm not a cop."

"So what you hanging around with us bums for?"

"I'm looking for someone. The daughter of a friend of mine, Angel Ramos." He pulled out the photo of Angel. "Have you ever seen this guy around?"

The woman put down the bottle and peered closely at the photograph. "I knew him. This was his spot. What happened to him was un-Christian. Unholy. Whoever did this, they will be punished by almighty God Himself, believe it."

"So you know what happened to the guy in the photo?"

"I heard. People talk. And I also know who did it."

Reznick was taken aback at her tone of certainty. He wondered if she wasn't just making shit up for attention. "How do you know that? Have you told the LAPD?"

The woman laughed. "LAPD? No I have not. You think they listen to people like me? I don't mean anything to them. I'm in the gutter. What we say doesn't matter."

"So who killed my friend?"

"I'll tell you who it was. You ready to hear what I have to say?"

"I'm listening."

"We all know who did it."

"What do you mean?"

"The men who did this to Angel, God rest his soul. These people, if I can call them people, are conducting themselves against God's law. It's sacrilege. The people who did it . . . I know alright."

Reznick was skeptical. He was also getting impatient with her slow and meandering responses to his questions. "Give me a name. Who killed Angel?"

"Everyone knows who did it. Everyone here down the beach. We talk to each other. We talk about some of the bad things that happen. The scary things. But also the men that turn up from time to time."

"The men that turn up from time to time," Reznick parroted. "What men are you talking about? I don't mean any disrespect, but you haven't actually told me anything. You're going round in circles."

The woman lolled her head at the veteran in the wheelchair. "Andy, you know the guys I mean? The ones who killed Angel?"

Andy dragged on his cigarette. "Bad dudes. Heavy-duty. I swear, bro, some heavy shit going down. Mexican Mafia tattoos on some of them. One or two are MS-13. Stay the fuck away from them."

The woman edged closer to Reznick. "They drive around in their fancy trucks after dark. We know who they are. There's one guy I know. The man in charge."

"How do you know him?"

The woman leaned forward, warm liquor breath wafting off her. "I know him because I recognized him. He comes from Mexico, like me."

"The guy who killed Angel?"

"I know it was him. I never forget a face. He's evil. I know him by the name he uses here in LA. I didn't know his real name when he was back in Mexico."

"You think he changed his name?"

The woman handed the bottle of cheap wine to Andy. "Yes, I do."

Reznick was still wary about the story the woman was telling him. "Where in Mexico is this guy from?"

"He's from my home state, Veracruz."

"What's the guy's name?"

95

"The name I know him by is Carlos Lopez."

"Carlos Lopez?"

"We grew up fearing him and his gang. He's a member of the Jalisco Cartel. His brother, too. People who cross them disappear. They torture innocent men, women, and children. They want to spread fear. But let me tell you, I'm not afraid of that bastard." She spat again on the ground.

"Where do I find him?"

"You don't. He finds you."

Reznick handed the woman a fifty-dollar bill as well. "And you're sure the guy goes by the name Carlos Lopez?"

"I swear to God, on the lives of my children . . . he's the same one who terrorized us back in Mexico. What he did to your friend, Angel . . . he did the same thing to others in my community. Eyes . . . he gouges them out, right?"

Reznick wondered how she knew that. "The police haven't revealed the details."

"The man that found him, he told us what he saw. And I knew, I just knew, it could only be one man."

The woman looked at the fifty-dollar bill and put it in her pocket. "Be careful. You ask too many questions around here, you end up dead."

Fifteen

Robert Kassan sipped his usual tipple—a glass of San Pellegrino, ice, and a slice of lemon—at the lavish party, wishing he was somewhere else. He smiled and schmoozed as everyone else got absolutely wasted. He couldn't tell if it was due to the free-flowing booze or the drugs they had ingested prior to the party. But through all the endless *darlings* and *we must do lunch*, he kept his game face on, conversing attentively with everyone. From frustrated actresses moaning about a lack of suitable parts to a film producer who was on the prowl for new talent to fuck. Kassan counted at least eight long-standing clients. They had bought rare art from him for their homes and offices, purchased through their offshore companies.

He studied the super-successful. He was fascinated by the circus. He watched the way they talked faster and louder as the evening wore on, occasional trips to the bathroom for some cocaine seeming to revive them, laughter all around. It would have been the easiest thing in the world to be dazzled by wealth, and its cousins, power and influence, allowing oneself to be consumed with jealousy, envy, and hunger to sell one's soul to prosper in the City of Angels. Many people were.

The men and women around him were dream-makers. Kassan showed them respect. He was deferential. But despite the temptations on offer, he remained disciplined, as he wanted to convey a sense of quiet assurance and integrity. It was his brand identity. He had cultivated a particular image—a man who was soft-spoken, a man who never betrayed a confidence.

He hung around for another hour to glad-hand the liberal elites in the heart of their play kingdom. He talked Jackson Pollocks and rare Roman sculptures he had access to. They loved to hear the talk—not so much about the art, but about the exclusivity, the millions these pieces would cost to buy. Oh yeah, they liked that alright. A few of them insisted on talking about global warming, how their dogs were on a macrobiotic diet, and the rationale for buying a more eco-friendly private jet. Staggering levels of delusion.

He wondered why on earth anyone would care about the words such pampered, coke-snorting uber-capitalists masquerading as activists uttered. It was like a cult. But despite everything, and despite his misgivings about their political leanings—or lack thereof—he smiled as if agreeing with every utterance. After all, he still needed them.

Kassan had to be a good listener in his line of work, and he'd grown well versed in every topic under the sun. Environmentally friendly facelifts, or why guns were so bad (despite his clients being protected, night and day, by armed private security firms and personal bodyguards who patrolled and protected their gated communities).

The more he saw of the vacuous world he was part and parcel of, the less he liked it. It was breathtaking how appalling they were. Raising money for Ukrainian orphans and Venezuelan migrant charities; spending years in therapy for themselves, their kids, and occasionally their chihuahua; flying in Gulfstreams to Davos in Switzerland; lecturing the world on global warming; hiring armies of domestic help from the Third World. They loved talking about how "energizing" and "life-enhancing" it was to adopt children from Mali, or Vietnam. Occasionally, Kassan had to watch a TikTok video one of his clients, invariably the wife, had made with their anxious daughter for their millions of social media followers. And they talked and talked. Bemoaning the denizens of the flyover states, or hawking the lifestyle brands that were paying them handsomely. Bragging about making authorized UN trips to war zones to show how caring they were. It was exhausting being them.

What the hell was it all about?

Kassan had given up trying to understand the city and the rich elites up in the hills. He just played the game. He kept his feelings hidden. The reality was if his clients knew his *true* feelings, which centered around tradition and conservatism with a small *c*, he would be ostracized and out of business. So instead he whispered sweet nothings, told them how kind they were, how beautiful they were, how talented they were. Stroked their egos. *What a stunning documentary on female poverty in Latin America you made*, he would say. *What a fascinating film showing how Russia's war with Ukraine is affecting global warming.* Occasionally Kassan heard himself saying things like *I just loved your take on the action thriller genre by making it so much more inclusive and diverse.* And *that postmodern dystopian feminist arthouse movie absolutely needed to be seen by far more people.*

It was a crock of shit. Their entire world was a crock of shit.

Kassan checked his watch and delivered a few discreet goodbyes just before ten. He got in his car and drove straight to Sloane's, his private members' club in West Hollywood. It was the same sort of crowd. But at least they usually kept to themselves.

He headed to the rooftop terrace, where his brother Daniel—the finance director of their company—was waiting. Kassan hugged him tightly and slumped into the sofa opposite. "Sorry I'm late."

"Robert, are you kidding? I've been waiting for over an hour."

"I'm sorry, man. Pressing the flesh in Malibu. You know how it is."

His brother shook his head. "I've got a life as well. I can't just be waiting around for you to turn up."

"I'm sorry. I'd rather not go to these things. But the hosts . . . they buy big with me."

"I get it, I get it."

Kassan smiled at his brother as he hailed a waiter. "A bottle of your finest Chablis," he said.

"Very good, sir."

Robert unbuttoned his linen jacket. He never drank as a rule when at a social event. It was only in the privacy of his club, away from prying eyes, that he allowed himself to relax just a little.

The waiter returned with the wine. "I made sure that you got the 2020 Grand Cru," he said. "Fantastic vintage for Chablis."

Kassan tipped him heavily. "Thank you, Enrique."

"Very kind, sir. Enjoy your drinks."

Kassan took a small sip as he stared out the window. "I love this city. The people are crazy. But I still love it."

His brother picked up his glass, taking a large gulp. "Whatever . . ."

"You not happy?"

"You know I'm not. I want to go home."

"This is our home."

His brother shook his head. "I don't feel like this is home."

"You've got the sun. You have a nice house."

"It's not home, okay?"

Kassan put down his glass and smiled. "You worry too much."

"My job is to worry. I'm an accountant. That's what we do. Which reminds me, how did your meeting go earlier?"

Kassan shrugged. He had meetings all the time.

"The meeting with Jerry Levinson, remember?"

Kassan snapped his fingers. He leaned toward his brother. "Sorry. So, I heard he has two more private clients, one a billionaire, both of whom are seriously interested in items from our latest catalog. Roy Lichtenstein, and a Henry Moore sculpture. Can you liaise with Jerry to set that up?"

"I'll call him in the morning."

Kassan's art dealership was built on exclusivity, discretion and privacy. He would buy a particular artwork, which occasionally got stored in a high-security storage facility. He had access to one in Geneva, one in Zurich, and one in Berne. And then, with the artwork not moving an inch, he would sell to a third party—invariably a super-wealthy friend of Jerry Levinson or one of his contacts. Owners of the artworks stored there didn't have to pay import taxes. The art was viewed as in transit. A hundred-million-dollar painting bought at auction in Manhattan would have an eight-million-dollar sales tax bill. But when stored at a freeport, the tax wasn't payable until the painting left the facility. A lot of the time, his clients just kept the valuable painting where it was, in storage, as it accrued in value, tax free. Jerry estimated, with his twenty percent commission charged to his clients, he had earned the better part of a hundred and forty-five million euros over the years.

"Jerry liaised with his client to explain how we work. They're excited to get such rare artifacts, and the commission oils the wheels, so to speak."

His brother smiled. "You're incorrigible."

Kassan's other major ruse was receiving hard cash from clients in Mexico or Latin America. He then dissipated the money discreetly through diplomatic pouches at LAX, to be deposited on arrival into accounts dotted across the Middle East.

He knew it came from drug cartels. He would be stupid if he didn't know that. But the Mexican cartels had expertise that they were only too happy to share. Quid pro quo.

"The names of these two new clients?"

"No idea."

"How much we talking about?"

"Thirty million apiece. But that's just for starters."

His brother raised his glass and toasted Robert. "Nice work. Good health, brother. To freedom and art."

"And money."

Sixteen

The traffic slowed down to a crawl as Reznick edged along West Pico, driving through downtown LA. His cell phone rang.

The voice of Trevelle Williams, ex-NSA cybersecurity genius and close friend of Reznick, boomed out of the car speaker. He relied on Trevelle's technical brilliance to access the intelligence files of individuals and organizations across the world.

"Hey, Jon, you wanted to know more about Carlos Lopez?"

"You got anything?"

"Carlos Lopez is a badass. Certified psychopath. Former Mexican special forces."

Reznick wondered if Trevelle had the right guy. But his hacker pal had never let him down before. Not once, since he had been introduced a decade earlier by ex-Delta operator Pete Dorfman down in Miami. "Are you sure about that?"

"Affirmative. I've confirmed through scanning records in Mexico. In particular, CNI records."

Reznick knew Trevelle was referring to the Centro Nacional de Inteligencia, Mexico's main intelligence agency. "And you managed to access their files?"

"Not at first. It was far trickier than I thought. But I got in. Backdoor trojan I developed."

"Spill the beans."

"According to his file, the man we know as Carlos Lopez has committed dozens of murders of political opponents of the Mexican government or, on his own time, members of other drug cartels. Never served any time. The most dangerous rap sheet you've ever seen."

"So how the hell is he in this country?"

"State Department wrote a letter to Immigration saying they believe he fits the bill, would be a productive and hard-working citizen. He had assets of more than eight million dollars at the time so they were satisfied he could look after himself."

"Eight million US dollars?"

"That's what it says."

"How come?"

"He's clearly linked to the Jalisco drug cartel."

Reznick drove on. The old woman had named the same cartel. "What was the State Department thinking? Did they think he was going to become a useful citizen and get a job at Walmart?"

"Good point. They knew he had these crimes against him. But the letter states that the allegations, according to the State Department, were 'malicious.' He never appeared on trial for any charges. Nothing."

"So they just let him in?"

"Just like that."

"That's bullshit. Any allegations of that nature would be investigated before they even let him apply for a green card. No way. Not buying it."

Trevelle remained silent.

"And what did you mean when you said 'the man we know as Carlos Lopez'?"

"Here's the kicker. His real name is Diego Hernandez."

"Carlos Lopez is a pseudonym?"

"You got it."

Reznick accelerated as the traffic began to clear. "Goddamn it, the old woman on Venice Beach called it. She said she believed Lopez went by another name when he was in Mexico. She couldn't remember it."

"Diego Hernandez."

"And he goes by the name Carlos Lopez here in Los Angeles? We're sure about that?"

"Affirmative. I have all the classified intel on him now."

"Send it to me, with end-to-end encryption."

"You'll need to be extra careful, Jon. This guy, from what I'm reading in the file, is a nightmare. There's a whole bunch of other stuff that has been attributed to him and rogue elements of the special forces that served under him."

"Like what?"

"You really want to hear it?"

"Some dark shit, right?"

"Drownings. Hangings. Rapes. Torturing children. Killing human-rights workers. His gang marauded around rural Mexico, a law unto themselves. And that's before they decided to start working with a cartel. Very profitable. Killers all."

Reznick wondered what he was going to do with this intel. He felt a dark rage building inside him. "Get me more on him. Address, any businesses, associates, I want it all."

"Will do."

"His properties or companies will be registered under other names, probably."

"I'll check it out. I need a bit more time to dig it all up."

Reznick saw a sign and got onto the I-10, the traffic moving well. "Do what you can. I think Carlos Lopez might be the key to finding Angel's daughter."

"I'm on it."

Reznick ended the call and navigated his way through the next intersection.

As he drove back to Venice Beach, he realized he was nearing the location where Angel Ramos's body had been found. He wondered if it would be useful to get a visual on where the body had been dumped. Were there cameras? Had the cops missed something?

He parked the car on a narrow road a block from the boardwalk, close to a wall adorned with a huge mural. He got out of his car and walked over to the corner of Breeze Court and Speedway. The black graffitied dumpster was nestled under a telephone pole, adjacent to the bright-orange garage door Danny had mentioned.

He stared at the dumpster. He felt an emptiness gnawing at him. He felt sad that such a brave, tough man had ended up enduring such a shocking death, and that he had been forgotten by society, forgotten by former comrades like Reznick. Discarded and left to rot, under piles of garbage.

Reznick felt raw guilt that he hadn't kept in touch with Angel. Work commitments had always seemed to get in the way. The only time he saw his ex-Delta buddies these days was at funerals.

He peered down the alley. The area was affluent—he spotted the rear entrances to some upmarket beach houses and apartments. His eyes were drawn to a surveillance camera fixed to the rear of a building overlooking the alley. He took out his cell phone and took a few photos of the location. It was the only camera he could see in the vicinity. But there it was, plain as day.

He remembered what Garcia had said. This was a live, ongoing homicide investigation. He needed to stay away.

He assumed the LAPD had seen the camera. It was perfectly positioned, up high, set to capture anything. He scanned again for any other cameras overlooking the alley, ideally close to the dumpster. But he could only see that one solitary camera.

Reznick assumed where there were fancy apartments and beach houses, however, there had to be other surveillance cameras, dotted in and around Speedway and also farther down Breeze. Usually there were hidden cameras as well.

Reznick walked down the alley. He counted three additional cameras. All clearly visible on that block. He took photos of these too. Surely one of the cameras had to have captured something.

He needed to speak to Captain Frank Garcia again.

Seventeen

Jerry Levinson strode up the eighteenth fairway of the exclusive Riviera Country Club golf course in Pacific Palisades. He finished the round with his closest friends, ahead of a special private function in the clubhouse to raise funds for a police welfare charity. After a few pats on the back, he showered, changed into a fresh set of clothes, and headed into the dining room. Servers brought round drinks and canapés for the two hundred specially invited guests.

He picked up a glass of champagne as he made small talk with some old lawyer friends. A short while later, the group was joined by the perma-tanned Governor of California, Gary Clarkson, along with the LAPD Chief of Police, and Commissioner Lee Drexel.

Jerry was in his element with the great and the good of the city of Los Angeles. His law firm were hosting and paying for the whole event, raising a few million dollars for a good cause. He knew the importance of this annual social event. The informal chats with the movers and shakers of Los Angeles were invaluable—pressing the flesh with aspiring young politicians, top LAPD cops, a few chief executives of charities, leaders in LA's African American business community, whoever was on the rise. It was far more beneficial for making connections than just turning up at the offices of said individuals, trying to make a deal on a client's behalf.

The top issue for Jerry at present was the murky matter of Mirlande Jean-Baptiste, the Haitian girl who had been killed on the freeway after partying with his client Brett Miller. And here was a perfect nexus of police and politicians for him to reach out to informally on that issue.

Jerry had played the game many times before. He knew the rules. He knew how to win. Nothing else mattered.

Clarkson shook hands jovially with Jerry. He introduced him to the widow of a police captain, and they all got their photo taken. After she walked away, Jerry turned to him. "Thanks so much for coming out here, Governor."

Clarkson grinned the whitest smile he'd ever seen. "Absolutely love it out here. Great work you're doing, Jerry."

"I love this city."

"Gotta go," the Governor said. "Catching a flight to Aspen. Economic conference."

Jerry patted Clarkson on the back as the Governor's aides hustled him away, and he was off. He'd had no more than ten minutes of the Governor's time. But Jerry was due to have lunch with Clarkson in a month. Then he'd have the opportunity to talk with him about all manner of topics.

Jerry walked over to the LAPD Chief of Police Sonny Jackson and introduced himself.

"Mr. Levinson, nice to see you again."

"Appreciate your support."

"Wouldn't miss it for the world. Wonderful cause."

Jackson began to talk and open up. Jerry nodded patiently. He was a great listener. It was one of the secrets of being a successful lawyer—the importance of hearing what the other person wanted or needed. The Chief began to talk about golf and gave a rather rambling and detailed account of a trip to the home of golf in St. Andrews, Scotland.

Jerry tilted his head, smiling, while Jackson monologued about the appalling Scottish weather in midsummer, but also the wonderful hospitality he had encountered.

The Chief was in his element. Jerry had been a couple of times himself to the home of golf, staying in Edinburgh and driving out to play a few championship links courses in East Lothian. Muirfield, Dunbar, North Berwick. "It's a phenomenal experience. Now those are golf courses, am I right?"

"When the wind starts to blow over there, that's what sorts out the bluffers from the real golfers, Jerry."

"You got that right."

Jerry watched as Jackson surveyed the room. "You a member here?" asked the Chief.

"Ten years," Jerry replied. "Very fortunate."

"So true."

"But days like this are what it's all about. Raising money for a charity close to my heart. The brave men and women in blue. My father was a cop."

Jackson smiled. He liked that line.

Jerry sipped his champagne as the Chief droned on about his workload. Jerry had already hired a private investigator, a former LAPD detective, to draw up a detailed file on LA's police chief. His likes and dislikes. He liked basketball—was a big Lakers fan. Jerry had already secured courtside seats for the next few games. He'd learned that the Chief had a lot of outgoings. A costly divorce from his first wife and three college-age kids had put a strain on his finances. Jerry knew all this. But he also knew that the top cop was a social climber. Status was important to him.

Jackson leaned in close. "Jerry, can I ask you something . . . ?"

Jerry sensed Jackson was getting to the point he wanted to make. "Sure thing. Anything."

"This club, membership. I like it here. How much does it cost?"

"A lot. But it's great, isn't it? You live nearby."

"Ten-minute drive."

"Is that right? Well, I'll tell you what I'd like to do, in the spirit of cooperation. I'd be delighted to discreetly nominate you for application."

The Chief winced. "My problem at this current juncture would be the initiation fee. Would that be problematic?"

Jerry could barely wipe the grin off his face. "Forget about that. I can deal with that, and you'd end up with very modest annual fees. I'll get you a ninety percent discount for the next three years."

Jackson flushed. "My wife says I don't get enough downtime."

"She's right! I'll take care of all that. We'd love to have you here as a member. You get amazing opportunities to play golf in Scotland, Portugal, the South of France. Elite courses."

"I'm interested."

Jerry had reeled him in. "Tell me, how is the family? How's your wife?"

"Working hard. Too hard. We're like ships in the night."

"I remember the last time we talked, you said one of your sons is at college in New York, right?"

Jackson beamed widely. "Columbia. He gets his brains from his mother."

Jerry laughed, right on cue. "I love New York. He's a smart kid, he'll do great there." He caught the eye of LAPD Commissioner Drexel, who joined them. The three of them made small talk for a few minutes before Drexel said, "Can I borrow you for a minute, Jerry?"

"Of course. What's on your mind?" Jerry shook Jackson's hand. "Leave the details to me. I'll be in touch, Chief."

Jerry followed Drexel to the far end of the room for greater privacy. "Great turnout," he said.

Drexel smiled. "Appreciate you working so hard on this project. I'm hearing this event and your company's generous donation and fundraising could take us to three million dollars."

"I just want to help. The police have a tough job. We need to look after them."

Drexel cleared his throat. "Amen . . . Jerry, bit of business. You asked me yesterday about a client of yours. Brett Miller."

"Oh yeah," Jerry said, appearing to be disinterested. "How did that go?"

"I'm hearing the detective leading the investigation has a real problem with Miller. Got a real thing for him. He doesn't like him."

"And why's that?"

"Says he's dealt with Brett Miller in the past. And he's not going to allow what he describes as a 'low-life predator' to continue with his flamboyant social life, abusing vulnerable young girls."

"I don't think that's a fair assessment."

"Jerry, the cops are going to nail him this time."

"What about our Chief of Police? He seems like a smart man."

Drexel lowered his voice. "He's a political animal. He knows how these things work. He's usually noncommittal. But he listens to me."

Jerry leaned in close, his own voice barely a whisper. "I've got a couple points you might want to bear in mind."

"Jerry, don't pull that stuff with me."

"What are you talking about? I'm just talking in confidence, right?"

Drexel sipped his champagne, shaking his head. "Go on."

"I've got a proposition."

"I'm listening."

Jerry scrutinized the room to make sure no one was eavesdropping on their conversation. "If you pursue my client, I can guarantee that your department is looking at devastating negative headlines."

"Gimme a break, Jerry. Fuck off."

"I talk to people. They tell me things. I just think it's important we look at this from a position of mutual understanding. Cooperation. You know I'm a stand-up guy, right?"

"Spit it out!"

Jerry leaned in close and whispered in Drexel's ear. "The wife of our esteemed Chief of Police . . ."

"What about her?"

"I'm hearing from a source in City Planning that the wife's company is relying on handouts from the city for contracts. Her only contracts are with the city. Otherwise she would be bankrupt."

"That's not illegal."

"It's not. But it's the optics. How does that look?"

"Seriously? You're going to pull that shit on me?"

"Secondly, the Chief's eldest son. Lovely kid, Ryan. A client of mine told me some stuff about Ryan."

Drexel shook his head. "Don't go there, Jerry."

"I have it on good authority that when Ryan returned home for Thanksgiving last year, he was photographed by a security guy banging a hooker—I swear to God—in an alley behind a strip club on Sunset. Like I said, the optics . . . not good. But I can make both those stories go away, never to see the light of day."

Drexel shook his head. "What do you suggest happens?"

"My client denies any involvement in the death of this young woman. Out of the goodness of his heart he agrees to donate one million dollars to the Los Angeles Police Relief and Assistance Foundation. His grandfather was a cop and he values the service and sacrifices of all police, both serving and retired."

"And it all goes away?"

"Like it never happened."

Drexel smiled and patted Jerry on the back.

"How does that sound?"

"It sounds like you're trying to fuck me over, Jerry."

"I do deals. That's my thing. Why not have a private chat with the Chief?"

Drexel nodded.

"When? I want reassurances that this can be dealt with very quick."

"I've invited the Chief over for dinner at my place tonight. A few drinks. Let me deal with him. And that will hopefully get this all cleared up."

Jerry shook Drexel's clammy hand. "Make sure it is."

Eighteen

Reznick walked along the canals of Venice Beach and back to the police station, hoping to hear that there had been progress in the homicide case. He wondered if the forensics team were studying frame-by-frame footage. He knew there had to be something from one of the cameras.

He entered the station and walked up to the guy behind the desk.

"I'd like to see Captain Frank Garcia. Name's Jon Reznick."

The cop picked up his phone and relayed the news. A short time later—enough to demonstrate that taking him back was a decision to be made—the cop showed him through into the captain's office.

Reznick shut the door behind him.

Garcia was sitting on the other side of his paper-strewn desk. "Jon, pull up a seat."

"I'm sorry about dropping in on you like—"

"That's not a problem, Jon. But I've got to be honest, I'm surprised to see you still here. I thought I told you we're doing all we can. We're on it. I couldn't have been any clearer."

"I'm pleased to hear it. Just looking for an update."

"Why are you still hanging around, Jon?"

"I'm looking for answers."

"From who?"

"Just talking to people, getting a feel for the place where Angel lived his last few years. It's an interesting, eclectic part of town. It's pretty messed-up too."

"I don't disagree with you on that." Garcia shook his head.

"I just keep on turning this thing round in my mind. I still don't know the first thing about who killed him. I thought you guys might've had a breakthrough by now."

"You're getting in the fucking way, Jon."

"Frank, I don't want to be involved in your work. I just want to help you in any way I can."

"Do you think we're sitting on our fat asses all day eating donuts?"

"No, I don't. Just hear me out. First thing, the dumpster where Angel was found . . ."

"What about it?"

"I went there, looking around."

Garcia slammed his hand on the desk. "You are interfering in an active homicide investigation. I've tried to cut you some slack—"

"I'm assuming you know there are cameras around there, in that alley. Breeze Court?"

"Who told you the location? We haven't released that yet. Was it the medical examiner?"

"I talked to people. On the beach. I've been asking if they knew Angel. People there knew him, liked him."

"Don't give me this rose-tinted view of your old Delta buddy. He once put one of my guys in the hospital. Did you know that?"

"No, I did not."

"Your pal headbutted a rookie officer on the beach, then punched him out when Angel refused to move on."

116

"You don't have to tell me what he was like. He was an angry man. It came in handy in our line of work. He was aggressive, violent, I know all that. And I also know that when he was drinking, he was dangerous."

"So what the fuck are you saying?"

"Can I talk about what I saw?"

Garcia shrugged. "Why not?"

Reznick took out his cell phone, pulling up the photos of the surveillance cameras. He handed the phone to Garcia.

Garcia scanned the pictures carefully.

"As you can see, one of the cameras is pointed directly at the dumpster. There are, I counted, three other surveillance cameras trained on various areas of Breeze Court. Have those cameras been checked?"

Garcia handed the phone back to Reznick. "Who the hell do you think you're talking to? You're not a cop, Jon."

"I didn't say I was. I'm just asking a simple question. I'm assuming the footage from these cameras has been retrieved and analyzed."

"Of course we fucking checked. Every camera, not only along Breeze, but Speedway. And beyond."

"Every camera?"

"Every camera . . ."

Reznick sighed. "And what did you find?"

"Nothing."

Reznick shook his head. "That doesn't make sense, Frank. There are cameras all over the place and they didn't record anything?"

"Jon, listen—"

"The camera closest was pointed straight at the fucking dumpster. So don't say they didn't pick anything up."

"The camera you're referring to was incorrectly installed by the homeowner, an old man. He has cataracts. He didn't follow the instructions properly."

"And the rest of the cameras?"

"Some were working, some weren't. But none of them pulled up anything of note."

Reznick looked at him, incredulous. "You drew a blank?"

"It's frustrating; I get it."

Reznick shook his head.

"That's what I'm trying to tell you. Police work is frustrating. It's not like the movies. Shit like this happens all the time. Chasing down leads that go nowhere. It's slow. There are dead ends. Sometimes we get lucky. But we're still working this case, trust me."

Reznick felt deflated. "So what now? It's still a homicide investigation, right?"

"Of course it is. We're investigating other avenues."

He stared at Garcia. "Can you tell me what those avenues are?"

"No. I'm sorry to disappoint you on the surveillance cameras. It's a bitch, I know."

Reznick sighed.

Garcia looked at his watch. "Look, I've got a meeting downtown. I need to get going."

"There's something else I want to talk to you about."

Garcia groaned. "Make it quick."

"I've been given a name. The person who might be responsible. I wanted to pass this intel on to you and your team."

"Who gave you a name?"

"As I said, I've been speaking to people in and around Venice."

Garcia grimaced and motioned dismissively with his hand. "Most of these poor bastards, God help them, are burnout cases. Whatever they said, you can take it from me that it's bullshit."

"Is it?"

Garcia went quiet.

"The woman I spoke to, she said she knows who killed Angel."

"The woman? Was she a drunk, a junkie, a prostitute, or all three?"

"Quite possibly. She was definitely under the influence. But this woman, she told me that the man who did this to Angel is one of those men who drive around in fancy trucks after dark. Gang members. She saw them. One in particular. She gave me his name, or at least the name he goes by here in LA."

Garcia smiled.

"What's so funny?"

"I'm sorry, Jon, I've been doing this job for a couple decades. You don't strike me as a naïve person. Quite the opposite. But these people you say you've been speaking to . . . I swear to God they talk bullshit from dawn till dusk."

"I don't think she was lying. She was very specific. She said the guy was from the same part of Mexico she was."

"That's what she said?"

"That's what she said."

"A word to the wise. They're very good at telling you what you want to hear."

Reznick shrugged off Garcia's indifference. "I believe her. And I can give you the name in good faith. Do you want me to do that?"

"Shoot."

"Have you heard of Carlos Lopez? Does that name mean anything to you?"

Garcia stared at him long and hard.

"Are you going to write it down?"

"No, because it's bullshit."

Reznick picked up a pen from the desk and scribbled it down on a yellow Post-it so there was no misunderstanding. "Carlos Lopez."

"I deal with facts. Not stories and half-truths. Let us do our job. And get the hell out of here."

Nineteen

It was a beautiful place to die.

Just after midnight, on a black lake located high up in the mountains of Ventura County, a motorized boat edged out into the darkness.

Carlos Lopez steered the craft across Lake Piru. At his feet, a gagged and blindfolded Charlotte Orton struggled, weeping, naked, her hands tied behind her back. She was flanked in the boat by his son, Mateo, and one of his men, Diego Cortegna, a hitman friend from his home village back in Mexico. "I hear you like to go swimming," Lopez said. "You like to go skinny-dipping with the rich and famous?" He laughed and kicked her in the face. "Well, this is one swim you won't forget. This is a little surprise for you."

The woman struggled, trussed up tight like a hog. Her muffled voice said, "Please, I'm begging you! I'll do anything you say. Don't kill me. I have a family."

"You lying bitch!" Mateo slapped the woman hard around the side of the head. "Shut up, slut."

She whimpered and shook with fear.

Carlos stared down at the restrained, terrified woman. "It didn't have to be like this, lady. Why'd you make so much trouble? The guy paid you and he fucked you. What's the problem?"

Charlotte wailed. "I'm scared. I have a family. Please let me go. I won't say a thing."

"You could have walked away—and with money. But you didn't."

"I'm a mother!"

"You're a prostitute. But you need to learn this lesson: learn to shut the fuck up, lady. Besides, you like swimming, right? You're going to show us how to swim."

The woman struggled again, biting at the gag, shaking her head.

"You see, no one will ever know what happened to you. It'll be like you just disappeared. And if some miracle happens, and they find you, one day—in a few months, probably years—you will just be a collection of bones. The fishes will have chewed everything away, including your fucking eyes."

The woman wailed through the gag.

Mateo grabbed her hair, punching her in the face until she passed out. "She's nice and quiet now!"

Carlos nodded. "At last, peace! A man doesn't want to hear some bitch screaming like that. Unless we're fucking her, right?"

Mateo and the enforcer laughed.

Carlos turned off the engine. Darkness all around, stars in the sky, bearing witness to what was about to happen. He thought he could hear his heart beating. But he felt nothing. He had no interest in her feelings or anguish. He was immune to it all. But he did feel a frisson of excitement when he heard fear in a person's voice. He got off on that. "We do it here."

Mateo and the enforcer trussed her up with nylon ropes, heavy bell plates and additional weights.

Carlos pointed at the feet. "Make sure that's where the weights are!"

Mateo attached the weights with duct tape to her ankles and her bound wrists.

Carlos had already tortured her with cigarettes, burning her face at an isolated cabin a couple of miles away. It was always good to get the victim in the right frame of mind. Then he had bundled her into a waiting car which drove up to the lake where she was loaded onto the waiting boat.

His orders had been clear. She needed to be "disappeared." He disappeared people all the time. He had specialized in disappearances when he was in Mexico. Besides, it wasn't as if she hadn't been warned. She had contacted a lawyer saying she had been drugged and then gang-raped by Brett Miller and his coked-up friends at a party in Bel Air. When he was alerted to this through the private investigator, Lopez knew what needed to be done. This was his specialty. He made problems disappear.

His men had retrieved all Charlotte Orton's vital electronics. Cell phone, iPad, and a laptop, along with an iMac computer at her home where she had started work on a book about the incident a few months earlier. They had wiped all digital traces and saved copies. Carlos would be paid half a million for one night's work.

Carlos closed his eyes as he said the Lord's prayer in Spanish, part of a sick ritual he did before killing each and every victim, as if he might atone for his sins. He looked around the inky black waters of the reservoir. No lights. No sign of life.

"Careful," he instructed. "Lift her, and then drop her nice and soft, quiet as you can."

Charlotte Orton was still unconscious after being beaten. Mateo and Diego carefully lifted her. Then they rolled her unconscious body into the water. She disappeared below the surface, into the dark depths of the lake, out of sight forever.

There was silence as they watched and waited to see if she would manage to break free. One minute. Two minutes. Three minutes.

She would never be found again. She would never again threaten anyone with blackmail. He hoped she had come to underwater. He wondered if her last moments had been pure terror, trying to escape. The thought made him happy. The bitch was dead, unable to escape the bindings.

"God rest her soul," Carlos said.

Mateo and Diego crossed themselves.

Carlos started up the engine again and edged the boat slowly back to shore. A few minutes later, they were back on dry land. He took the boat's rope and tied it to a tree stump.

The trio got back in the SUV. It was as if nothing had happened.

Diego switched on the headlights and drove them away from the reservoir. Twenty minutes later, they were on the freeway and passing Santa Clarita, headed back to the city.

Carlos took out his cell phone and called a number he knew by heart. The number for private investigator and ex-cop Jay Johnson.

"What's happening?" Johnson said.

"It's done. Your client can sleep safely." He ended the call.

"Is that it for tonight, boss?" asked Diego.

"No. We get back to the city, clean up, and we've got a delivery to a friend of mine around dawn. No rest for the wicked, huh?"

Twenty

The call came at 2:03 a.m.

Reznick was sitting in a late-night diner in West Hollywood, enjoying a burger and fries, pepped up with some Dexedrine and strong coffee. He noticed he had been grinding his teeth.

"Yeah, what's happening, Trevelle? I thought you would have called before now."

"Gimme a break, Jon."

"Relax, it's just the way I am."

"And how's that?"

"Impatient. Demanding. A pain in the ass."

Trevelle laughed. "Now that I can absolutely verify is correct."

"Talking of verification, anything else on Lopez?"

"I began by cross-checking names, addresses, telephone numbers, businesses."

"Any luck?"

"Get this. Lopez is the boss of a nightclub. Razor, I kid you not. He owns a few. It's on the corner of Yucca Street and Ivar, not far from his penthouse on Hollywood Boulevard."

"He's got a penthouse?"

"A nice one, too. But from the security cameras I've checked, he was last there a couple months back. Draw your own conclusions from that."

"I'm guessing he's always on the move, never in one place for very long. The apartment might be more of an investment."

"True."

"What about cars?"

Trevelle gave him two license plate numbers for a black BMW SUV and a silver Mercedes SUV belonging to Carlos Lopez. He waited for further instructions, but Jon was silent. Finally, Trevelle asked, "What's the plan?"

"Well, if he's never at the penthouse, it's a waste of time trying to access that."

"So what are you saying?"

"I need more, Trevelle. A lot more."

"I'm doing the best I can."

"I get it. But I need to know who this guy really is. I've got a partial picture. But I want you to give me a fuller picture on him and his associates. Who does he know? Who does he spend time with?"

Trevelle clicked his tongue. "It'll take some time."

"Get me what you can."

"I'll get back on it."

Reznick sensed that Trevelle wasn't happy having to do a deep dive into the life of Carlos Lopez.

"Trevelle?"

"What?"

"I appreciate what you do. I know I don't say it enough. But I couldn't do what I do without your input."

"Anytime, man. In the meantime, while I'm trying to find out more on Lopez, what's the next step for you, Jon?"

"The nightclub on Yucca sounds like a good place to start."

"Be careful, man. This guy is dangerous."

"He's not the only one," Reznick said.

Reznick ended the call and left the diner, then drove down Sunset to the nightclub on a decidedly sketchy, not well-lit part of Yucca. He parked down the street, in the line of sight of the club's entrance, outside a twenty-four-seven storage facility located behind a high fence, surveillance cameras sweeping the entire block. He sat in his car and watched the scantily clad girls being dropped off and escorted into the club by the bouncers.

Reznick yawned. Time dragged as he watched and waited. Limos arrived and departed, picking up and dropping off girls and flashy guys. Security stood vaping, smoking, and chatting with more scantily clad girls. The minutes dragged. The minutes became an hour. And then two hours.

He felt waves of tiredness washing over him. He took another couple of Dexedrine. A few minutes later his senses began to rouse. He felt sharper.

More girls poured into the club. He couldn't imagine his daughter flitting in and out of sketchy nightclubs.

An SUV passed by Reznick. The license plate matched one of Carlos Lopez's cars. Reznick sat up and took notice. He took out the telephoto lens he had packed into a backpack, double-checking that he had the correct details. Reznick watched as the vehicle pulled up outside the nightclub. It was just before four in the morning. He snapped some pictures as three fearsome-looking Mexican dudes headed into the club. Then took more pictures as they glanced around at the sound of a police siren in the distance. Tough, heavily inked—the real deal. A tattoo on one of their necks was of an eagle and a snake above a flaming circle and crossed knives.

On their way into the club, a bouncer patted them on the back as if welcoming old friends.

Reznick scrolled through the photos on the camera's viewfinder before sending them to Trevelle via the camera's built-in Wi-Fi function.

An hour later and the party finally seemed to be winding down. The last of the clubgoers, girls, and security had all left by five, heading into waiting taxis, limos, and cars. But there was absolutely no sign of the tattooed guys who had arrived in Lopez's vehicle.

Reznick sat in his car, watching and waiting. It was just after six in the morning when the SUV pulled up again. A few beats later a man swaggered out alone, carrying a backpack. Reznick recognized the features immediately. The scars on the face. The tattoos across his neck and forehead. It was Lopez.

Reznick picked up his camera and fired off more shots, sending those to Trevelle as well. He waited until the SUV pulled away before he set off behind it, trying to keep a safe distance. The SUV headed along Sunset Strip, through Holmby Hills in the direction of the Westside.

Dawn was breaking now, the sky a burnt orange.

Mile after mile of headlights on the early-morning freeway, the traffic relatively light, as the SUV headed west. Then a turnoff into an upscale neighborhood. Past huge mansions, winding through a verdant paradise on the Westside.

Reznick drove on as the SUV pulled up outside a house shielded from view by huge hedges, at least thirty feet high, guarded by a wrought-iron gate. The GPS told Reznick he was in Brentwood.

He slowed down as he caught a glimpse of Lopez getting out of the car, backpack slung over his shoulder. Lopez disappeared inside through a huge wooden door. Reznick drove past as the SUV's lights switched off.

Reznick drove farther along the road in the ritzy neighborhood, not wanting to attract attention. He turned around after about a mile, then headed straight back the way he had come. He parked a couple of hundred yards down a straight road with a perfect line of sight. Then he picked up his camera and telephoto lens, observing from a safe distance.

A few minutes later, Lopez walked out, no backpack. The SUV lights came on and the car pulled away.

Reznick wasn't going after him. He had already tailed him once. If he reappeared in the rearview mirror an observant driver would see there was a tail. He sent over the latest photos. Then he pulled out his cell phone and called Trevelle.

"Hey, man, don't you sleep?" Trevelle said.

"I was going to ask you the same thing."

"What do you need?"

"I'm in Brentwood."

"Very nice. I was reading that Ben Affleck lives in that hood."

"I like it. I want you to check out an address."

"Copy that."

"Who owns number 822 North Kenter Avenue?"

"The house is owned by an art dealer. Robert Kassan."

Reznick made a mental note as he wondered what the connection was.

"I'm assuming the photos you sent are Lopez and his merry gang."

"Run face recognition to ensure that I've got the right guy. I need to be a million percent sure."

"Leave it to me. And stay safe. This guy kills for fun."

Twenty-One

Robert Kassan drank his morning coffee in his kitchen in Brentwood, enjoying classical music on the stereo. Sun streamed through the floor-to-ceiling windows. But he still hadn't opened the backpack delivered by Lopez.

The backpack sat atop the Carrara marble countertop.

Kassan would have preferred the exchange to have been carried out away from his home. He had suggested a digital transaction. Ideally in Bitcoin. But Lopez said his "friends" back in Mexico—meaning the Jalisco Cartel—insisted on the old-school methods. It had been this way for nearly three years. He had asked Lopez to reconsider the method of payment delivery. But Lopez had replied that his boss across the border liked it this way.

Kassan didn't want to argue. He could see that Lopez was not a man to get into a negotiation with. He'd agreed to the terms and that was that.

He was in deep. He did not enjoy the sometimes-weekly visits from Carlos Lopez with payments for services Kassan rendered. Lopez was the trusted point man for all the Mexican cartels in LA.

Kassan had used his expertise in money laundering to develop friendships in Mexico and across Central America. The Mexicans liked hard cash—American dollars, Swiss francs, British sterling, and South African gold. These were the usual payment methods for the rare artworks Lopez bought on their behalf. The paintings would not move, stored in a secure warehouse in Switzerland for months. Away from the IRS. Away from the FBI.

Lopez's presence was a sharp reminder that if the Mexicans were double-crossed, they knew where Robert lived. A way of instilling fear without lifting a finger.

Kassan picked up a remote control and pressed a button; all the blinds in the kitchen closed. He picked up the large backpack and unzipped it, looking inside. Thick wads of one hundred-dollar bills wrapped in elastic bands. Probably hundreds of thousands of dollars. But there were other assets the Mexicans had "acquired" in bank raids, home invasions, and extortions of industrialists in Mexico. Those were in the bag too, in the form of Swiss francs, half a dozen gold bars—each worth one million dollars—plastic bags of gold coins, and dozens of Krugerrands.

He pulled up the calculator on his iPhone and did a quick calculation. He estimated that, at today's currency rates, it all amounted to fifteen million dollars. It was a typical amount, sometimes delivered once a week. There was an annual budget of one hundred and fifteen million dollars each year, give or take ten million, for him to buy fine art, ancient artifacts, and also property in Dubai for his Mexican clients. He knew he was just one of perhaps half a dozen money launderers operating on behalf of the cartels across the States.

Kassan zipped up the bag. He would later call his brother, who would arrive with a laundry truck. His brother would come into the house, carefully place the backpack into a laundry basket, cover it with towels and clothes, then carry it out to the truck. He would drive away to a facility near the airport, placing the bag in a secure locker and changing the code. Then, a few hours later, a friend of his brother—a "sleeper" for the cartel—would take the backpack out and send it in an official Mexican diplomatic bag to a lawyer in the Caymans, who would do the rest.

This method enabled his shadowy clients to maintain their anonymity. The Mexicans would get a work of art—a hard asset—purchased through a shell company they controlled, tax free until it was sold. Kassan took the risk in exchange for a hefty commission.

It was a system they had used for years.

Kassan's offshore accounts were where his personal wealth was, tied up in overseas shell companies. His money-laundering fees and commission amounted to twenty percent of the takings. So a ten-million-dollar haul would net him a cool two million dollars. The cash never stopped rolling in. And he could check his myriad accounts on his cell phone from anywhere in the world.

Kassan picked up the bag and headed to his office. A latch in the bookcase revealed a sliding door into a secret room, and he locked the door behind him. He placed the bag in a biometric fireproof safe, careful to lock it afterward. Then he left the room and walked out onto the deck, the sun peeking through the tall palm trees shrouding his property.

Kassan pulled out his cell phone and called his brother.

"It's laundry day," he said.

"I'll be there by nine."

Kassan closed his eyes, the sun already warming his skin. It was going to be another beautiful day in LA.

Twenty-Two

Jerry Levinson was enjoying a rare breakfast with his family when his cell phone rang. He checked the caller ID and looked across at his wife. "Honey, sorry . . . I need to take this."

"Really, Jerry?"

"Client of mine."

His wife just shrugged as if annoyed.

Jerry headed up the stairs to his office, shutting the door behind him. He sat down at his desk. "Brett, how are you?"

"We got a problem."

Levinson closed his eyes. He wondered if there had ever been a more demanding client. "I'm dealing with this, Brett."

"I thought you said you were dealing with the photographer, Jerry?"

Levinson thought back to his conversation with Commissioner Lee Drexel and his private chats with the photo agencies. He had also gotten an informal agreement from the British photographer, Heidi Stratton, that the snaps could not be published or there would be legal action.

Brett stressed again, "Did you or did you not say you would clear that up?"

"Let's start again, Brett. What exactly are you talking about? Just so we're clear."

"I'll tell you what I'm talking about. You remember the chick in the club? The photographer?"

"You mentioned her, yes. As I said, this was dealt with."

"Think again."

"What?"

"So, according to Jimmy Gatz, I'm hearing that the photographer chick is talking privately about selling the photos of me in the club with the Haitian girl to a third party. I thought this was taken care of, Jerry!"

"My associates have already spoken with Heidi Stratton, and her lawyer has agreed to reach a deal with us. The photographs won't see the light of day anywhere in America or the English-speaking world, as well as Europe."

"Well, I don't want to piss on your party, but I think she's not going away and she wants to cash in big."

"Give me the details."

"Jimmy, who's a very good friend of mine, said he had heard that she would sell the copyright of the photographs to an agency in Berlin, and they would syndicate it around the world, earning her millions. What am I paying you for if you can't make this sort of shit go away!"

Jerry closed his eyes. He had grown used to Brett going off as he harangued whatever minion was working for him. It didn't matter if they were a top LA lawyer or a pool boy who was giving him some lip—Brett never let anything go. He always had to take it to the edge. It was almost like Brett enjoyed confrontation. It was just his aggressive nature. But if what Brett was saying was true, then they did have a problem.

"Listen to me carefully, Brett."

"I'm here. I'm focused."

"You heard this firsthand from Jimmy Gatz?"

"Jimmy is a close friend of mine. He's solid. We move in the same circles. He's respectful, too. I like that."

"Respectful . . . You know him well?"

"We go way back. We're both from the same neighborhood in Brooklyn. Borough Park."

"I understand. Did Jimmy hear this firsthand from the photographer? And if so, why would she tell him?"

"She never told Jimmy this directly."

"So this came secondhand to Jimmy?"

"Right."

Jerry leaned back in his seat, getting frustrated with Brett, his attitude, and his perpetual problems. He was exhausting. "So, next question: who told Jimmy?"

"A picture editor at a photo agency in Berlin."

"Do you have the name of the agency?"

"No. You need to understand how Jimmy and some of these paparazzi operate in Hollywood. Jimmy might take a photo of Stallone or one of the Kardashians going to or from the gym or a restaurant."

"Got it."

"Jimmy is the point man in LA for this German agency. He sends them photographs throughout the year—Hollywood parties, premieres, drug busts, new babies. Going on a coffee run with a new girlfriend . . ."

Jerry felt tension tighten up his shoulder blades. It sounded to his ears like Brett was coked out of his mind. He was talking incessantly.

"So, Jimmy and this German guy got talking about photos he had seen of me—big-shot American movie director, right? Anyway, the German dude says he had lunch earlier this week with his editor. And he said he had seen photos of me, snorting cocaine off this Haitian chick's breasts or something, inside a booth at the club. I don't know if she had a hidden camera or what. But it's pretty fucking crazy. I can't seem to catch a break. Do you understand my concerns, Jerry? I'm not making this shit up. And neither is Jimmy. I believe Jimmy."

"The message we sent to Heidi Stratton and her lawyer— verbally, in person—was crystal clear. She got the message. We were assured the photos would not see the light of day. In exchange, we sent fifty thousand dollars to her lawyer."

"And that was to ensure compliance? Her silence?" said Miller.

"Correct. But this changes everything, if what you're saying is true."

"Clearly."

Jerry's mind turned to Jay Johnson. The private investigator who worked in the shadows. He knew gangbangers and assassins who could be hired. They made problems disappear. They made people disappear. "Here's what I think. I know someone who can sort this out once and for all. I'll deal with the Berlin end. And an associate of mine will deal with the LA side of things. And I assure you, that will be the end of the matter. How does that sound?"

"Make it go away. Make her go away. And those photographs. I don't care how it happens. But you need to make this go away. There are rules in my world, Jerry. She's breaking cardinal rules. I can't have that."

The line went dead.

Twenty-Three

It was early afternoon, blazing hot, when Reznick emerged from his hotel room, blinking into the light. He had tried to get a few hours of sleep. But his racing mind, thinking only of Carlos Lopez, could not drift off. The psycho had exited the club at dawn and then headed up to Brentwood. He had been carrying a bag. And he had ditched the bag at that house.

Reznick went for a jog in the ninety-degree heat, dripping sweat. He always felt better when the endorphins kicked in. When he returned, he showered and changed. He grabbed a bite to eat at a boardwalk diner. Then he walked. He had walked for miles every day since arriving in Venice. Up and down the by-now familiar side streets. Past swanky beach homes and townhouses, which sat adjacent to sketchy-looking alleys. A gentrified neighborhood mostly. But the forgotten, the homeless—huddled under blankets smoking crack pipes, a few lighting fires, some drinking cheap wine, some hawking bags of pills on street corners—were still there. And all the while, convertibles sped down the sun-baked streets, music blasting.

Reznick watched a panhandler collapse in slow motion in the middle of the street. He ran over to the man, kneeling over him, one hand calling 911, the other trying to feel a pulse. But he couldn't feel a thing.

A passing motorist, who turned out to be a nurse, stopped and gave the guy some water as he slowly revived, and they waited with him for the paramedics.

The guy's eyes were vacant as he sat up. "Who are you?"

"Just relax. You seem to have collapsed. You're going to be fine," said Reznick.

The nurse was checking the man's pulse. "Do you have low sugar levels, sir?"

The man nodded. "I'm diabetic."

Reznick took out a candy bar from his pocket and unwrapped it. He handed it to the man, who greedily ate it.

"Medication. I need medication."

The sound of sirens in the distance. "They're coming, pal. They'll figure it out. Just take it easy. You just had a fright."

The man fixed his gaze on Reznick. "You got any weed?"

Reznick grinned. "Drink your water and eat the candy. It'll do you good."

The poor guy nodded as onlookers filmed the scene with their cell phones. "I feel like I'm in a fucking zoo."

Reznick knew what he meant. He waited with the guy until the paramedics were right there. "Take care, my friend."

The guy stared up at the paramedics. "Anyone got any weed? I'm dying for a smoke."

The rest of the sweltering afternoon dragged. Fierce, hot sunshine had rollerbladers, skateboarders, tourists, and the homeless trying to find some shade, the breeze off the sea unable to cool down the boardwalk.

Reznick stopped for a beer at the Whaler beach bar on Washington. He sat by himself, watching a Dodgers game on the big screen, lost in his thoughts. *Carlos fucking Lopez.* He sensed that bastard had been instrumental in Angel's death. He had to assume that the police were dragging their heels for a reason. He wondered who Lopez worked for.

A burly, bearded guy holding a bottle of beer in his hand cocked his head. "You enjoying the game?"

Reznick nodded.

"Dodgers fan?"

"Red Sox. My daughter occasionally drags me to a Yankees game."

The guy grinned. "You on vacation?"

"Just a bit of business in LA. Then headed home."

The guy finished his beer and ordered two more. He shook Reznick's hand. "Chuck Rollins." Then he handed Reznick a bottle of beer.

"Jon Reznick. Nice to meet you, Chuck."

Chuck leaned in close. "I don't want to pry . . . but Reznick, you say?"

He nodded, wondering where the conversation was headed. "Yeah, Jon Reznick."

"I'm friends with most of the guys at LAPD Pacific Division. I keep my ear to the ground. And I've heard your name mentioned."

Reznick gulped some beer. "Is that right?"

"Yes, sir."

"You mind me asking how you're friends with the cops down here?"

"I got out two years ago. Shot in the abdomen. Early retirement." The guy pulled up his T-shirt, showing the eight-inch scar on his huge gut. "Gangbanger. You believe that?"

"When you say you heard my name mentioned—"

"I'm not prying. Your name just stuck in my head. Your friend was murdered down by the beach, right?"

"Correct."

"Sorry about that, man. Angel Ramos. Am I right?"

Reznick nodded.

"I knew Angel. He used to work VIP security. I was based in Hollywood at the time."

"You knew him?"

"I knew him quite well. I worked undercover—Vice. He was a good guy in the early days. But then his life went on the slide. We lost touch. And it turns out he ended up down on the beach. Horrible end."

Reznick knocked back his beer and ordered two more, handing one to Chuck. "You live around here?"

"I do. It's a tiny studio. Me and my wife divorced. I used to live in Simi Valley. A lot of my friends in the LAPD lived nearby. But I wanted a different life. So, now I'm a beach bum."

Reznick smiled. "Can I ask you a question?"

"Sure thing."

"Angel's murder. You say you keep your ear to the ground. Let me ask you something. That was no ordinary murder, right? The level of violence seemed off the scale."

Rollins pointed to a corner table, away from the bar, and walked toward it. "Bit more private," he said.

Reznick sat down at the table, opposite Chuck. "What can you tell me?"

"I can tell you the LAPD are under pressure."

"Pressure to find the killers?"

"I heard that things are a bit . . . How can I put this? A bit strange."

"What do you mean?"

"They say they have no leads. But I know this area. There are surveillance cameras covering the crime scene."

"I saw that. I took photos of the cameras. But I was told they showed nothing. Incorrectly installed surveillance camera, and the other cameras didn't catch a thing."

"Bullshit."

Reznick tilted back his beer. "That's what I was told."

"I know a guy in Forensics. Friend of mine. You know what he said?"

"What?"

"He said—no lie—the footage got seized, then that footage was erased."

"Fuck off."

Chuck shrugged, shaking his head. "So when they told you there was no footage, it was the truth. Up to a point."

"What the hell does that mean?"

"Internal investigation. Heads might roll. But no one knows how it happened. They used video recovery software or something, but there was not one second of footage."

"What do they think happened?"

"One of the techs mentioned a remote wipe. Apparently you can delete any files or data. Overwrite the stored data as well, preventing someone from recovering it. The surveillance cameras that were hooked up to a computer at their lab had been returned to factory settings. Meaning professional bleach job."

"And nothing's been recovered? Not one byte of data?"

"Nothing. FBI called in too. They got nothing. So whoever did this is no amateur."

"Who had access to the footage?"

"A forensics guy is under investigation, that's all I know."

Reznick took another sip of his beer. "Chuck, this is ridiculous."

"It is what it is."

"Are you saying the forensics guy at the lab might have been responsible?"

"I don't know. It's possible, if someone leaned on this guy, threatening his family. Or he got bribed, who knows?"

"It's very elaborate. Very unusual."

"It's not the first time weird shit has happened with evidence. The same thing happened once before, at least that I know of. A break-in at a film star's home by an ex-lover. But the footage there was mysteriously erased too. You see what I'm getting at?"

"So when a captain I spoke to said there was nothing, he was telling the truth."

"Frank Garcia?"

Reznick sipped his beer, not confirming or denying.

"I know Frank. He's a good guy. He knows how things work in LA, and especially in Hollywood."

"Meaning?"

"There are powerful people in this city. People with money. With influence. And that makes them potentially dangerous. They can get things done. You pay a high enough price, you can get away with murder."

Reznick leaned in close. "Everything we're saying . . . off the record, of course?"

"Right."

"So, if I asked you, man to man, without any dog in the fight, how could this happen?"

"I would say that there are people in this town who can fix problems. You want people disappeared, that can be done. You want forensic evidence to be corrupted, I know a guy who knows a guy. It all comes down to serious money. But if you've got money, you can do anything."

"I was given a name. I passed on that name. But Frank didn't seem too interested."

"Let me guess. Carlos Lopez?"

Reznick nodded. "You know him?"

"He's a cast-iron psychopath. A kid who worked for him started hanging out with a black girl. Nice girl, apparently. This went against Carlos's 'business ethos.'"

"What happened?"

"No one knows. He went missing. Lopez and his crew were interviewed. Not a thing."

"What do you think happened?"

"Killed him, chopped him up, and fed the body parts to the pigs. That's what an informer told me. But I couldn't prove a thing."

"That's revolting."

"He's a revolting man. Stay away from him and his crew."

"Do the LAPD have Lopez in the frame?"

"They do. But there's no proof, it's all hearsay. From what I heard, they tried to triangulate the cell phone signals of his devices and that of his crew, to see if they could be linked to Angel's murder, but they were all in a club on Sunset at the time."

"That's a sophisticated alibi."

"You better believe it."

"So if the cops think Lopez and his crew killed Angel, do they know why?"

"Now that's the six-million-dollar question. Who wanted Angel Ramos dead? Was it Lopez himself? Did Angel cross Lopez at one point?"

"What do you think?" Reznick asked.

"My hunch? Lopez is a crime boss. He runs a gang of enforcers. He's also a hitman. That's what he did for the Jalisco Cartel down in Mexico. Now he's in LA, he deals drugs, moves them from Mexico. Traffics people, mostly for prostitution. I don't think he'd be killing a homeless guy just for the sake of it."

"So what are you saying? Carlos Lopez was ordered to carry out a hit by a third party?"

"That would make sense. He would be paid a sizeable sum, and a problem would disappear for someone."

Reznick finished his beer and got another two.

"I gotta warn you, man," Rollins said. "If you go after Lopez or dig deeper into this case, it won't end well."

"That's what Frank said."

"He's right."

Twenty-Four

Reznick left the bar. The conversation with Chuck Rollins had left him feeling empty, anger gnawing away at him. He did have a better handle on the situation, though. He knew he wasn't just up against a psychopathic killer. And the data on the surveillance cameras had been remotely wiped by a cybersecurity professional. He wondered if Lopez was part of a wider network in LA. Had the malign influence of Carlos Lopez and those he worked with reached as far as the LAPD? It was a chilling thought.

Reznick wanted answers. He felt as if he had lost his moorings, pursuing loose ends and long shots as he tried to get closer to the truth. Talking to Rollins had confirmed his worst fears that Lopez was acting with impunity. But where did this power originate from? Was he just a killer acting in his own interests? Or was he a terrifying enforcer called in to maim and kill by wealthy and powerful people, as Rollins had suggested? Probably it was a combination of both.

Reznick walked for an hour or two, just mulling over his thoughts. When he felt a wave of tiredness wash over him, he headed back to his hotel room, climbed into bed, and fell into a fitful sleep.

◆ ◆ ◆

When he woke up, his cell phone was ringing. He checked his watch, bleary-eyed. It was only midnight.

Reznick picked up, switching on the bedside light as he did.

"Jon, it's Trevelle. You enjoying some downtime?"

Reznick groaned. "Hardly. Just catching up on some much-needed sleep. Don't you ever sleep?"

"I just got up. It's three in the morning here in Florida. Category 2 hurricane on its way. So, you any farther along?"

"More questions than answers. Carlos Lopez is the main man, I suspect. But I seem to be going around in circles. Where you at?"

"I'm still doing a deep dive on Lopez and his associates. What I can tell you from the photographs you sent me from outside the club is that it's not just him, it's three of his associates in Los Angeles. All Mexicans."

"And they're residents here in LA?"

"Identified each of them. They all live here. And all these guys, including the man who now goes by Lopez, have committed shocking human-rights violations and extrajudicial killings. Every one of them."

"Mexican assassins? Guns for hire for the cartels?"

"Yes. And yes. But one other thing."

"What's that?"

"When Carlos Lopez was in the special forces, he and fifteen of his comrades attended the School of the Americas."

"We trained him?"

"Precisely. You know the place?"

"I know it well."

"They renamed it. Now known as the Western Hemisphere Institute for Security Cooperation, right?"

Reznick sat up in bed, throat dry after the booze.

"New name," Trevelle said. "Same place. Overseen by the Pentagon, training elite soldiers as well as the police of South

American and Central American countries. Classes on military tactics, training skills, arms skills. From its inception, it's been aimed primarily at eradicating dissent and controlling the people of these countries."

Reznick knew all about the school. He had been brought in for a month to train soldiers from El Salvador in counterinsurgency. But he hadn't much cared for teaching assassination skills to soldiers from countries outside of the United States of America. All the trainers knew the types of maniacs who frequented the School of the Americas. The aim wasn't effective policing. It wasn't even for anticommunism. It was to train cops and soldiers in Central and South America for the subjugation of the people. The training focus had changed from the red threat in South and Central America to the narco-terrorist threat across the region. He'd decided after a short while that it wasn't for him, expressed his displeasure, and been promptly transferred back to Delta.

"You dig up anything else in Venice about Lopez?" Trevelle asked.

"I had an interesting chat with a retired LAPD cop earlier this evening."

"Yeah?"

Reznick recounted what he'd been told about the surveillance footage being scrubbed.

"You want me to try and see what I can find?"

"I don't think so. From what I was told, they've had the FBI cybersecurity experts examining the devices, but there's zero data. Is that even possible?"

"Remote wipe. Most surveillance cameras have vulnerabilities. If the Feds can't unearth anything, assume it's gone for good."

"So we're no further along. I was told that there's a tech guy in their forensics department who's under investigation."

"Interesting. That would point to him being compromised. I'll look into all of it."

After ending the call, Reznick realized he couldn't sleep. He quickly changed and headed out onto the street, finding his car and heading back to Yucca and Ivar in Hollywood. He saw the distinctive Capitol Records building off to his right. He parked behind another car, concealed but with a line of sight to the club.

A neon sign for a nearby coffee shop caught his eye. He was starving, and ordered a large black coffee and slice of blueberry pie with whipped cream. He ate quickly. He felt better, not having eaten since lunch. He ordered another coffee and took a couple of Dexedrine to keep him going.

Through the coffee shop window he had a perfect view of the side entrance to the club across the street.

He finished his coffee, paid the bill, left a tip, and headed over the crosswalk back to his car. He turned the radio on low—a local station playing some late-night jazz. Melancholic trumpet and piano notes washed over him. A meditative sound. Timeless. Yet it sounded vaguely familiar. He absorbed the music as he watched the comings and goings at the club. When the song ended, the radio presenter announced it was Miles Davis. That's why it had sounded familiar. He remembered his father playing Davis's albums, especially *Kind of Blue*, every time he got loaded. John Coltrane too.

The night dragged on. Reznick watched as more clubgoers headed into Razor. Taxis dropped off girls. It was just after 2 a.m. when a limo and a Bentley pulled up.

Men in suits emerged from the cars alongside a security detail. He took out his camera and telephoto lens and photographed the men. He did not recognize Lopez among them. Time passed. There was the sound of wailing cop car sirens in the distance. Then blue lights, speeding patrol cars heading fast along Yucca, lights and sirens blaring.

He watched one of the bouncers talking to a cop, pointing over in Reznick's direction.

Fuck.

Reznick knew they had seen him observing the club. He switched on the ignition. He was checking his mirror, about to reverse out of his parking spot. A cop car, lights on, pulled up tight behind him, blocking him in. He got out of his vehicle, hands on his head. "Easy, guys," he said.

Two cops emerged from the patrol car, guns drawn. "Get on the fucking ground!"

Twenty-Five

The cop car had headed downtown until it reached a glass and limestone building—the headquarters of the Los Angeles Police Department.

Reznick was guided from the back seat, handcuffed, and escorted to an interview room on the seventh floor.

A cop said, "Take a seat."

Reznick did as he was told. He stared at his reflection in the mirror on the other side of the table. He assumed they were watching him. His gaze wandered around the room, to a surveillance camera positioned high up on a steel bracket, recording his every move.

The minutes became hours.

Reznick sat alone, staring at himself. He took this low-grade psychological pressure in his stride. He yawned, showing how bored he was.

A cop came into the room. "You okay, buddy?"

Reznick grinned. "Can't beat a bit of solitary time, right?"

The man shrugged. "I guess. Can I get you something?"

"Coffee and a cheese sandwich out of the question?"

"Not at all. Back in a few."

The cop returned fifteen minutes later with a tray. Cheese on fresh rye, and scalding-hot black coffee. He unlocked Reznick's handcuffs. "Enjoy."

Reznick devoured the food, then sipped the coffee from the Styrofoam cup. He felt rejuvenated. The door opened and a female officer wearing forensic gloves walked in. She picked up the plate, cup, and tray, and walked out of the room. He wondered if they were getting his prints or his DNA.

◆　◆　◆

The first tinges of burnt-orange light flooded the room from the small windows below the ceiling.

Reznick stretched. The door opened slowly. A couple of detectives came in. An Asian cop led the way, followed by a heavyset white officer, both clean-shaven, wearing crisp white shirts, suits, guns visible in their shoulder holsters, badges hanging from their belts.

The Asian detective sat down first. He opened up a file, leafing through some papers. He scribbled a few notes as the white officer sat down, fixing his attention on Reznick. The first detective stared across the desk at Reznick and smiled. "How are you?"

Reznick shrugged.

"My name is Detective Andy Chow of the LAPD," he said, putting down his pen. "This is my colleague, Detective Gregg Dorman."

Reznick thought it best under the circumstances to appear cooperative and compliant. "How can I help you?"

Chow smiled. "We were hoping you would say that. We've got a few questions for you."

"Do you mind explaining why I've been arrested?"

"We're asking the questions, Mr. Reznick, but to answer yours, you haven't been arrested. You are being detained pending questioning."

"What do you want to know?"

"I guess I'd like to know why're you still hanging around Los Angeles."

"I'm free to travel wherever I like."

"Yes, you are."

"I'm a free man. I can go wherever I want. That's not illegal in California, is it?"

Chow shifted in his seat, as if slightly uncomfortable. "The problem starts, Jon, when you begin interfering in things that don't concern you. For example, we have evidence you have been monitoring various premises over the last few days. You've also spoken to an officer in Venice Beach, Captain Garcia, regarding an ongoing homicide investigation, am I correct?"

Reznick folded his arms and shrugged.

"I've been reading your file. Some pretty heavy-duty stuff you've been involved in, Jon. You served your country?"

"Yes, I did."

"Where?"

"Overseas. War zones, that kind of thing. Behind enemy lines. Classified."

"That's right. And Delta Force, no less."

Reznick sat in silence.

"I have intel that you might have also worked for the CIA at one time. And also for the FBI under an Assistant Director Martha Meyerstein?"

"I don't think it's technically correct that I worked under the Assistant Director. I guess I consulted on several investigations. I did not work for them. I was a consultant."

"Consultant . . . Right. You've got a very interesting backstory. You get around. So can you help me out, Jon? Why exactly are you still here?"

"It's simple really. I came to LA after I was informed that a friend of mine had died."

The other detective began writing in his notepad. "Who was that?" he asked.

"I'm sure you've got that information already."

"Can you tell me the name of the friend that died?"

"Angel Ramos."

Reznick watched as Dorman noted down the name.

"Angel was found tortured, then killed, in a dumpster off the boardwalk in Venice. Breeze Court."

Chow nodded. "We're aware of this case. We're investigating this, Jon. We have protocols we adhere to. We don't allow ad-hoc interference in cases. From anyone. Period."

"I'm trying to help."

"You're not, Jon. You're getting in the way. And you have been spoken to by Captain Garcia about this interference."

Reznick batted this away. "He's a good guy. I was only asking questions of people on the beach, hanging around. I get it, cops do the investigations."

"So why haven't you taken Garcia's advice and gone back to Maine? Your friend's funeral has taken place; you have no other business in LA."

Reznick leaned back in his seat, arms folded. "You don't have any suspects, right?"

"We haven't revealed if we have any suspects or not."

"So you do have a suspect?"

Chow sat in silence, not taking the bait.

Then he finally answered, "You don't know what intel we have. And we can't divulge what we know. It's very straightforward."

Dorman smiled. "Jon, we don't have any beef with you. We just want you to understand that, in this city, people don't take kindly to outsiders—no matter how well meaning or qualified—trying to get involved."

"I haven't broken any laws . . ."

"That's debatable. You've come to the attention of a businessman whose club you were seen outside of on a couple occasions."

"A businessman . . ."

"He has spoken to an attorney, who is talking of threats and harassment toward his client's business. *Intimidation* is the term he keeps using. We have to take these concerns seriously."

Reznick smiled. "Let's cut the bullshit, gentlemen. Are you talking about Carlos Lopez? If you are, I might be able to help you out. Does the LAPD want to know his real name? I'm assuming you must."

Chow shook his head. "Jon, this is what I'm talking about. You're acting as if you're a cop. But you're not." He turned and exchanged a look with Dorman.

"My friend was horrifically murdered. I want answers. And another thing—you haven't answered my question: does the LAPD know Lopez's real name?"

"We're telling you only what we can divulge."

"Which is precisely nothing. I'm not against the LAPD or the Los Angeles Sheriff's Department."

"We don't need your help."

"I want to give you intel that you may or may not have. That's all."

Chow cleared his throat. "What intel?"

"Lopez, I have reason to believe, is former Mexican special forces. American trained."

"What do you mean by that?"

"He graduated from the Western Hemisphere Institute for Security Cooperation. America taught him all he knows. He is a highly dangerous individual."

"We have information on that."

"Well, now we're getting somewhere. His real name is Diego Hernandez."

Dorman scribbled down the details. "How do you know all that, Jon?"

"I just do. Check out what I'm saying. He lives and works in LA. But he's part of a powerful Mexican cartel operating in the city. I've heard that human-rights organizations in Mexico are aware of extrajudicial killings, torture, disappearances. Diego Hernandez was a critical element of those."

Dorman set down his pen. "How does Angel Ramos fit into all this?"

"I believe Angel was trying to find out where his daughter was. He was worried about her being involved in prostitution. He came across Carlos Lopez and his crew as he tried to find his daughter."

Chow pinched the bridge of his nose. "It's an interesting hypothesis."

"I think if you test it, you'll find it's correct."

Dorman leaned back in his seat and smiled. "Let's assume that we investigate all leads, Jon. Which, by the way, we do."

"I'll take your word for it. I'd like to know what progress you've made. Tell me something to allay my fears that this homicide won't be investigated thoroughly."

"Jon, I'm going to give you some advice. The same advice you were given by Captain Garcia."

"And what's that?"

"Go home, and we'll be in touch."

"I'd like nothing more. When I see some progress, then I'll think about going home. Make an arrest. Show me you're serious."

Chow shook his head. "That's not how this works. Let me ask you a question. Why are you photographing the patrons of the Razor nightclub?"

"It's pretty simple. Who owns that club? Who owns Heaven nightclub? I believe that Angel's daughter is either working in a club like that or she's involved in prostitution. Angel Ramos was trying to save her from that world."

"Has she got a name?"

"Camila Ramos. She might be going by the working name Gigi Cortez in the bars or clubs."

"And you think you'll find her by just randomly turning up at a club?"

"What concerns me now is that something might happen to her. She hasn't got anyone to look out for her."

"You said she goes by the name Gigi Cortez?" asked Dorman.

"That's what I've heard. She might be working the bars and clubs as a hostess, an escort, or on the streets as a prostitute."

"We have no evidence at this stage that Angel Ramos had a daughter," said Chow. "We've checked. There is no family to speak of."

"She came into his life when she was a teenager. She didn't take his name originally."

"We've checked, Jon. There is no girl. Someone is feeding you bad intel, and you need to get the hell out of here."

Twenty-Six

It was late when Carlos Lopez arrived at one of his clubs, an old, abandoned warehouse on West Pico Boulevard and Bronson. He liked to make sure his staff weren't dipping into the cash behind the bar. But as he walked through the doors, past security, his mind drifted back to another night. A night etched on his memory. The first night he spoke to Gigi Cortez. A girl he introduced to the Hollywood scene. He remembered she worked at his club. A stunning beauty. She was cute. He recalled the club was packed, bass reverberating off the walls. He could still see her face carved into the darkest recesses of his mind. The dark, brown, alluring eyes. He remembered her smell. It all began to flood back. It was just after midnight . . .

The sound of pulsating disco music boomed from huge speakers on the ceiling. The smell of sweat and booze, cut with a whiff of perfume, hung like mist in the clammy air. He brushed past security and picked his way through the crowd. Big screens were showing seventies porn, and the music got louder the farther he got into the club. He headed past a group of girls waiting for some customers. "Everything okay, girls?" he said. "You look nice."

"We're fine, Carlos," one of them shouted above the din. "We like it here."

"Keep the dudes rolling in, and we'll all be happy."

The girls laughed as he headed up a flight of stairs, past a VIP room where a twenty-something English actor was fucking a girl from Finland.

Lopez walked down the hall and headed into the last booth.

A young girl, one of his new employees he had never met, sat on a sofa, hands clasped on her lap. She wore a short plaid skirt, a tight top, and high heels. She was cute. Super-cute. Beautiful, even. The girl looked vaguely Mexican, like him. Her name was Gigi Cortez.

Lopez pulled up a chair and sat down opposite her. He had been told that she wanted to talk to him. "So, here we are."

The girl smiled, her teeth perfect—straight, as if she'd had work done.

"I haven't noticed you before," he told her. That was a lie. He noticed every girl that worked for him. He took an interest in every one of them. But he had taken a special interest in her. "You enjoying your work?"

"I am."

"Glad to hear it. Where you from?"

"Denver."

Lopez knew that was a lie. "Nice city. Let me see your arms."

The girl rolled up her sleeves, exposing her honey-brown skin.

Lopez ran his finger across the front and back of her arms and wrists. "No track marks. That's good. My clients don't want to see that sort of shit. So, you're not an intravenous drug user?"

"No, sir."

"You smoking the brown? You like heroin? You chase the dragon?"

The girl shook her head. "No, sir."

"What do you use to get you through the nights?"

"A bit of coke. A bit of speed."

Lopez smiled. "I like your style. That's okay. That's allowed."

The girl seemed coy.

Lopez smiled at her and began to stroke her silky brown hair. "You seem like a sharp girl."

"Thank you."

"I'm assuming you worked a few bars, a couple strip joints in West Hollywood, before you joined us?"

"A few clubs."

"So you happy here?"

"I'm happy. But I want to move on."

"Move on? Move on where?"

"I don't know . . . I guess I want to make some decent money."

"Ambition is good."

"I also want to meet better people. I'm enjoying my time here. But I'd like to be introduced to some big names. I heard you can open doors for girls."

He smiled. The girl wasn't shy. "What do you mean?"

"I was hoping you could help me. I've spoken to a couple of the girls here and they say you're a good guy to know. You have connections."

Lopez inhaled deeply, breathing in her cheap perfume. "Maybe I do. Maybe I don't."

"If you do, I'd like to be introduced. I have a lot to offer."

"What kind of introductions you looking for? Be more specific."

The girl smiled. "I want to move up in the world. I want to be in the movies."

"You want to be in the movies? What kind of movies?"

"I want to star in a big-budget blockbuster. You see, I've been taking acting classes."

"Good for you."

"I can do this. I just need a chance. A chance to prove myself."

"Everyone in this fucking town wants to be in the movies. And I mean everyone."

"Can you help me? I do good business here."

Lopez liked her straightforward manner. He liked her curves. He liked her face. He liked her mouth. "Maybe."

"I think I've got an awful lot to offer."

"I believe you do too. I like you. You seem like a regular kind of girl. But a fun girl, right?"

"I like parties."

"You enjoy performing?"

The girl flashed a million-dollar smile. "Yes, I do."

Lopez knew a bunch of people in the industry who would love to get their hands on her. "How long you worked here?"

"A little while."

Lopez handed her a wad of notes.

"What's this for?"

"A little bonus. Don't tell anyone. I give favors to close friends of mine. But I have to know that I can trust you."

"You can trust me. I'll do whatever you want."

Lopez caressed her hair again. "A friend of mine knows a guy. This guy is well known in the film community. He's a director. Big, big name. And I heard, through my sources, that he's looking for a girl who looks exactly like you."

"Really?"

"Yeah . . . But he's demanding. He'll ask you to do all sorts of weird shit. It's Hollywood. You need to understand that."

"I know how it works."

"I heard he likes to audition girls. Beautiful girls. He'll want to fuck you."

"What's his name?"

"Brett Miller."

"I've attended his parties before. I know what he's all about. But I would love a personal audition."

"Leave it to me and we'll talk tomorrow or the day after. You need anything else?"

"Please make this happen."

Lopez got off on using girls like Gigi to bargain with Hollywood types higher up the food chain. He winked at her and tossed her a small bag of coke. "Enjoy your evening. But don't tell a soul. It's our little secret."

When he was satisfied that the takings were up on the previous night's, by a cool fifteen hundred and fifteen dollars, Lopez left the club through a back door. He was picked up and driven away by his men to a rundown section of East 5th Street in downtown LA—the heart of Skid Row.

The SUV pulled up at the side entrance of an abandoned auto repair shop, where a light shone on the second floor.

Lopez looked up. "Looks like she's home, guys." He pulled on a pair of forensic gloves, got out of the vehicle along with Juan, a childhood friend, brushed past an old wino who was drinking from a bottle of vodka, and approached the video intercom.

Juan buzzed. Lopez waited, tapping his foot.

A woman's voice came over the video intercom. "Yeah, who's this?"

Juan flashed a fake LAPD badge. "LAPD, I'm looking to speak to Heidi Stratton."

"That's me. What's this about? It's very late."

"We've been made aware of an ongoing threat to your life. We need to talk."

"What?"

"This is urgent, ma'am. Let us in. Right away. Can you let us in?"

"Sure. I'm on the second floor."

Juan was buzzed in. Lopez followed close behind as they headed upstairs.

A pretty white woman cracked open the door, the chain still on.

Juan kicked the door in, breaking the chain. He grabbed the terrified woman and dragged her across the floor of her dimly lit studio, a huge hand across her mouth.

Lopez buzzed in the other men. Soon, they were all inside.

He locked the door and watched as one of his men shut all the blinds and switched on the stereo, turning up the volume. Foo Fighters. He fucking loved them. Juan took out his cell phone and began to film what was happening.

Juan threw Heidi Stratton to the floor and began to throttle her, hands around her neck. She was choked out to the point of unconsciousness. He then trussed her up with duct tape and rope.

Lopez waited until his men had recovered the woman's computer and iPad. Juan handed him her iPhone.

Heidi was tightly bound and struggling, awake now, her eyes wide with terror.

Lopez pulled up a chair and sat down beside her, staring down at her. "I love this latest iPhone, don't you? So, tell me your six-digit code for this shiny new iPhone."

"9-3-2-4-1-8," she shouted.

"Very good, thank you." He logged into her iPhone and checked her emails, which showed communication with a photo agency in Berlin. A cursory check, and he saw a folder with thirty RAW photo files entitled *Brett Miller inside Razor club.*

"Please don't hurt me."

Lopez smiled. "Trust me, we're not going to hurt you. We just need the photos. So, I can see the folder with the thirty photos. That's all there is? Backups? Where do you keep them?"

"They're backed up to my iCloud if you want them. Just don't hurt me."

"That's good to know. What about Dropbox?"

"Just iCloud. You can check."

"Trust me, we will."

Lopez handed the cell phone to Juan, who had placed all her other electronic equipment in a backpack. Two cameras were also retrieved with memory cards inside. "So you wouldn't be holding any negatives or prints?"

"Nothing. I promise."

He could smell her perfume and fear. "I don't like liars. If I find out you've been lying to me, I will get angry."

"Don't touch me!"

Lopez laughed, seeing how afraid she was. "You know how that works? First, I find your mother, father, and the rest of your family, and then slowly, very slowly, we torture them to death. One after the other. Heightens the fear."

"Please . . . I don't know what else you want."

Lopez leaned in closer. "Now, just so we're clear, you don't have any other prints that you've forgotten about, here in the house? Because if I find something, I won't be happy. And your mother, father, and younger brother will all die. I believe they live in a nice part of West London?"

"I'm sorry, I remember now . . . Prints in my safe, behind the mirror, in my bedroom, next door. I swear, that's all I have."

"Code?"

"1-9-2-5."

Lopez signaled for one of his men to go retrieve the photos. He returned holding a folder of black-and-white prints showing Brett Miller inside the club, snorting cocaine off a girl's chest. "You definitely have great talent. You should be very proud of yourself. Do you do weddings? You see, a nephew of mine is going to get married. He still has to arrange a photographer. Are you available?"

Heidi Stratton began to sob. "Please . . . leave me alone!"

"You should do weddings. That's a very lucrative market."

The woman wet herself with fear and closed her eyes. "I'm sorry. I'm scared."

Lopez looked over the photos again. "Nice work. Now, you're not forgetting anything else, are you? You haven't shared any photos online? I'll find out. One last chance to tell me."

"That's everything."

"Nothing saved to a Dropbox?"

"I told you I only use iCloud for secure backup. Just please, leave me alone. I have a heart condition."

Lopez laughed and began to stroke her hair. His eyes lazily strolled over the high ceilings of the old auto shop. Wood and iron beams and girders spanned the ceiling. "It shouldn't have come to this. I think I would have liked to have gotten to know you so much better. It's a shame."

She was sobbing.

Lopez comforted her. "Cry it out. That's right. Don't worry. The worst is over." He looked over at Juan. "Get me a chair for the lady."

Juan went through to the kitchen and brought out a wooden chair. He exchanged a look with Lopez, who knew what was going to happen.

Heidi Stratton struggled, shaking her head uncontrollably, trying to escape.

Juan pulled out a length of rope from his backpack and threw one end over the wooden beams, fixing it to an iron hook on the wall. The other end of the rope he tied into a noose. He lifted up her head and placed the noose around her neck. Then he pulled the noose tight, constricting her throat.

The woman was weeping, her body shaking, as she was lifted onto the chair. "Please! I've given you everything you want! Please! What in God's name are you doing?"

Lopez shrugged as he took out his cell phone. He began to film the terrified young photographer standing, quaking, whimpering. "Any last requests?"

"I'm begging you, I don't know who you are. Please, stop."

Lopez kicked away the chair and she dropped. Her neck cracked.

Juan filmed the whole thing. He stood close to her, her legs still twitching in her death throes. He checked his watch. She stopped moving after twelve seconds.

Three minutes later, they had turned off the music, and bagged up all the electronic equipment and photographic prints. Then they carefully exited the studio, switched off the lights, made their way down the stairs, and crossed the street to their car, laughing and joking as they went.

Twenty-Seven

When Reznick was finally released by the police, he went immediately back to Venice Beach. He bought a cup of coffee from a food truck adjacent to Muscle Beach. He felt deflated. The LAPD had not played ball at all. And he was stuck—no closer to tracking down Camila Ramos. He drank his coffee, then tossed the Styrofoam cup into a trash can.

He wondered, not for the first time, if there was any point in sticking around. He was attracting heat. Besides, he had already spent almost two weeks in and around the city, looking for clues. The days and nights were merging into one. He wasn't sleeping well, wired on Dexedrine and caffeine. He had seriously considered returning home to Maine on a couple of occasions. It would be the easiest option. Perhaps it would be for the best. Leave the investigation to the professionals. He figured that he could still call or email Garcia or Chow to get updates. But the longer Reznick spent exploring the seedier side of LA, the more he felt himself getting drawn into that twilight world. He couldn't let it go.

It was as if the ghost of Angel Ramos was all around Venice Beach, watching over him. He imagined Angel begging for money, for booze. And he wondered if Angel had also begged for his life, right up until he drew his last breath.

Reznick had been warned by the LAPD to go home. He was on their radar. But he figured that he was also on the radar of Carlos Lopez. The Mexican clearly had the wherewithal to neutralize threats. Reznick was walking a razor-thin line. But it wasn't in his nature to just walk away and turn the other cheek.

He knew how to play the game. It was important that he didn't make the LAPD turn against him entirely. He needed them. But he sensed he was close to more dangerous, unknown territory. The same sort of territory Angel had crossed into.

He wished Angel had reached out to him. He'd had Reznick's number after all, hidden in his tattered sneakers. But Angel was just too proud. Too stubborn. Too pigheaded. Reznick could have helped him find a place. He could have helped him out with money. Even gotten him a job. And if everything had broken right, Reznick would have been able to help him find his daughter.

Reznick realized he needed more help. A team of people to investigate and track down Angel's elusive daughter. He wondered if he should reach out to his contacts within the FBI. He could even put a call in to former Assistant Director Martha Meyerstein, despite her having left the Bureau. But all of this assumed that Camila was still alive. What if she wasn't?

There was another matter that he understood all too well. If the people who'd done this to Angel were still hanging around—that put Reznick in their crosshairs. He had been detained by the cops. He had spoken to the Venice Beach police. He had even watched and photographed the comings and goings at several sleazy Hollywood clubs owned by Carlos Lopez. He had drawn attention to himself. He was no longer operating under the radar. People had noticed.

Reznick's cell phone rang, snapping him out of his dark thoughts.

"Hey, Jon, back at the beach I see." The voice of Trevelle.

"Problem is, I'm no further along. I need to catch a break. And quick."

"I've been doing quite a lot of digging on a guy Carlos Lopez visited."

"Up in the hills?"

"That's right. It may or may not be of interest. Remember Lopez dropped off a backpack at the house in Brentwood?"

"Yeah."

"I'm sorry it's taken me a while to piece this together."

"Don't sweat it. You got a name?"

"Robert Kassan."

"Okay. So what's the connection between Robert Kassan and Carlos Lopez?"

"Here's the thing. At first I couldn't figure it out."

"Tell me about the homeowner."

"Kassan is highly educated. The Sorbonne in Paris, Cambridge University in England, Yale. He's an art expert. He runs a successful high-end gallery in Beverly Hills."

"A highly educated man who runs a gallery and a psychotic killer in league with Mexican drug cartels . . ."

"Bingo. A strange meeting of the minds, if ever there was one."

"Tell me more."

"Wealthy clients across Hollywood who want rare paintings, ancient sculptures, medieval artifacts—collectors' items."

"I don't get it. Doesn't sound like a natural friendship with an animal like Lopez. They're not lovers, are they?"

Trevelle hummed. "That I don't know. But I don't think that's where it's at."

"So is this Robert Kassan an American citizen?"

"Dual citizenship. Greece and the US."

"Where he was born?"

"This is where it gets a bit more interesting. Kassan was born in Lebanon."

Reznick remembered, as a child, that his father had shown him the Marines memorial in Arlington, dedicated to the two hundred and forty-one US service members who had died in the 1983 truck bombing of the Marines barracks in Beirut. "Kassan's family fled the Lebanese civil war when he was a baby, like a million others. And they started a new life in Europe. Greece, to be exact. Robert was exceptionally bright and he won a scholarship to Yale to study History of Art. And hence his introduction to America."

"Interesting backstory. So far so good. But why would Lopez visit this Kassan dude?"

"All in good time, Jon."

Reznick got to his feet and began to walk. He felt himself smile. "You have something, don't you?"

"I'm getting to that. But you're right—what has brought these two disparate personalities into the same orbit?"

"What've you got?"

"I managed to access files from the FBI, CIA, State Department, and myriad contractors who work at the Pentagon. Classified files."

"About this Robert Kassan?"

"Oh yeah. And this is where it gets real interesting. About a decade ago, the IRS and FBI were investigating Kassan. It never came to anything. A Special Agent in Charge in Los Angeles, Liam McArdle, found no evidence of crimes being committed pertaining to tax evasion or the forgery of works of art."

"I guess investigations run their course. So the file was closed on Robert?"

"No, it's no longer an active investigation, but the case remains open, unresolved."

"Tell me more about these concerns."

"The investigation centered on Kassan channeling some of the proceeds from the sale of valuable artworks—some believed to have been stolen—to controlled bank accounts in the Middle East, including banks in Beirut."

"You kidding me?"

"Swear to God. Sometimes the artworks never moved from facilities in Switzerland. Bought for five million by Robert, sold by Robert for eight million to another buyer. Money steered to Lebanon."

"To private individuals? Family or friends?"

"In a way, yes."

"Lebanon to me means . . . Hezbollah?"

"Very perceptive. Robert Kassan was on the FBI's radar. A file was opened for money laundering. An informer said that Robert was a 'significant' source of external funds for the terror group."

"I can't believe this. Still not seeing the tie between Lopez and Kassan though."

"This is where my digging paid off. There's mutual interest."

"Doesn't seem like a natural fit. Hezbollah and Mexican drug gangs?"

"That's where you're wrong. Lopez—real name Diego Hernandez—is part of a Mexican cartel cell operating on the West Coast of America. We know that. Cash from robberies, gold, anything stolen, is used to buy art. You see where this is going?"

"Motherfucker!" Reznick's mind was racing. "So a cute way of money laundering for the cartels?"

"Bingo! Cartels are smart. Rare art doesn't lose value. If anything, its scarcity makes it even more valuable, and it's a good investment in the medium to long term. And once they've bought the art, through an offshore company in the Caymans for instance, the art can be resold, sometimes back into the European market."

"So the backpack may be . . . hard cash? Something like that—as payment for legitimate art?"

"Could be. I don't know."

"But I'm guessing this has been impossible to prove . . . at least so far."

"Check out what else I uncovered. The CIA station in Mexico City sent a cable which I unearthed from the records. It's linked to Hernandez's file. The CIA had two separate sources detailing North Korean help and tunnelling expertise given to Hezbollah. Hundreds of miles of tunnels crisscrossing Lebanon. Into Israel. Deep into the Gaza Strip. But the CIA said in the cable that Hezbollah are actively sharing that advanced tunnelling intel with Mexican cartels, allowing trafficking routes to open up under the border and into the American market. So that's the connection. Art, money, tunnelling expertise. Quid pro quo."

Reznick walked on along the Venice boardwalk, cell phone tight to his ear. "I'm speculating here, but I wonder if Carlos Lopez is the point man linking the cartel with Hezbollah's money-laundering guy in Los Angeles?"

"It makes sense. The FBI described Robert Kassan, when he first came on their radar, as potentially being the nexus for Hezbollah on the West Coast."

"It's crazy stuff. An art dealer?"

"Ultimately it allows the Mexican cartels to get their product onto the streets of America, rake in the huge profits, and launder the money. It's big-time stuff."

Reznick stopped and stared at the guys and women lifting weights on the beach. "This changes everything. But . . ."

"But?"

"The problem is, I'm no closer to finding Camila Ramos."

"That's the other reason I'm calling. I might have something. I checked way back—immigration records, health records, dental records, Camila does exist. That is her name."

"So where the hell is she?" Reznick asked. "She's working in Los Angeles. We know that."

"She's been in rehab centers multiple times," said Trevelle. "She was known as Camila Ramos for a short while, probably when she first moved to the city, but she has since been known as Gigi Cortez."

"You got an address?"

"She gave her address to a drug center in Pasadena."

"Give it to me."

"It's way up in the Hollywood Hills."

"The other stuff can wait. I want to find her. Only then can I consider heading home."

Twenty-Eight

The sun dipped over the horizon in Malibu, bathing the ocean in a dreamy tangerine glow.

Robert Kassan was schmoozing inside Audrey Roscoff's modernist beach home. She was a valued client, and through Kassan she had bought many great works of modern art to adorn her beautiful home. Sculptures by Jeff Koons, a rare gelatin print by Man Ray, a painting by Andy Warhol, a David Hockney print, and a Roy Lichtenstein painting from 1964.

He stole glances out of the floor-to-ceiling windows, watching the sunset. He often wondered if he should move down to the beach. He knew dozens of clients who lived in and around Malibu.

Satisfied, he turned and mingled with this group of super-wealthy friends: producers, directors, actors, artists, screenwriters, who bought their art exclusively from him. He felt the cool air on his skin from the new air-conditioning system installed by a German company.

Kassan caught his reflection in a mirror. He was lean, the same weight he had been for nearly ten years. He loved his new lightweight navy virgin wool suit from Savile Row in London. The cut was impeccable, showing off his classic titanium Hublot chronograph watch. He moved in circles where such details mattered. His clients noticed what he wore. The way someone appeared before them, how they carried themselves, and the vibe they gave off was important.

The hostess sidled up to him, holding a glass of champagne, doing the classic double kiss on the cheeks. "Robert, can you spare a few moments of your time?"

"Audrey, for you, anything!"

Audrey Roscoff smiled, as she always did. Her smile lit up rooms. She was a successful producer of low-budget indie films that did spectacularly at the box office. Films about mothers and daughters, and estranged fathers finding love. He followed her as she stepped out of her fabulous Malibu home, down the creaky wooden steps to the beach. The waves crashed onto the shore.

"It's impossible not to be inspired here," she said. "I love the ocean. I grew up on the ocean in Montauk."

"Oh my goodness, I love Montauk. I remember a party that Gore Vidal gave all those years ago. He was such outrageous fun." Kassan realized he was slowly morphing into everything he hated about Hollywood.

Audrey laughed along, the genial host as always. "So, what do you think of the house?"

"What do I think? It's gorgeous. As are you. You have impeccable taste."

Audrey blushed, sipping some champagne. "Thank you, Robert. You're very kind."

"It's a divine property. I've been admiring how the glass catches and reflects the light, especially at the end of the day."

"My darling," she gushed, "stop it! We're very fortunate. My last film made a ton of money on the back end. Twenty percent on the gross, if you must know."

Robert smiled. She was talking about her slice of the film's gross profits. He'd read that the global box office on her last film,

My Mother, was three hundred and forty million dollars. And that would mean she would rake in a cool sixty-eight million. An insane return. "Let me tell you, I saw the film—"

"Did you?"

"I did. The second night it was out, I went and saw it. Phenomenal. Smart. Punchy. So you. Really quite a smash. And yes, I cried. My God, I cried. Darling, I'm thrilled for you."

"Honey, you're too kind."

Kassan sidled up to her, sensing she wanted to talk some more. Probably share some Hollywood gossip.

"Robert, I was wondering if you could do me a favor?"

"For you, anything."

"My daughter, Jenny, she's studying History of Art at the University of St. Andrews in Scotland. She'll be home for a month. And I was wondering—"

"If I can help out, I'll help out. But don't you dare utter a word about this. The whole humanities faculty of UCLA will be looking for the same thing."

Audrey laughed, tucking her hair behind her ear. "I knew I could rely on you. She would really benefit from an internship at a prestigious gallery. Yours is the best on the West Coast."

Robert smiled. "It's the best in the west! I should really have that on the door. Consider it done. Tell your daughter to report to Marcia. She's fabulous. I'll let her know to expect Jenny."

"You're the best. Hey, we've got a jazz band playing in an hour in the lounge. I hope you're staying."

"I'd love to, Audrey. But I've got an appointment with a client who flew in from Germany this evening. I hope you understand."

"Of course, darling."

"I've had a beautiful evening. And thank you so much for the invite. And tell Jenny I can't wait to meet her."

A short while later, Kassan made his excuses and left the party, relieved to be out of the stultifying atmosphere of the righteousness and moral certitude of the wealthy guests.

He got in his car and drove from Malibu along the Pacific Coast Highway, getting off on the freeway, ending up in West Hollywood. He left the car in the underground parking garage of his private members' club. He took the elevator to the sixth floor and met up with his brother.

The attraction of the club was that mobile phones were switched off, and tapping away on laptops, fielding calls, or doing business of any sort was strictly not allowed. He had been a member for the last five years. In all that time, he had only twice bumped into clients: an actor who was stoned and didn't recognize him, and a famous director who'd been hand-in-hand with a pretty intern, who didn't seem to recognize him either, which was fine.

Membership was a mixture of creatives in and around Hollywood—a few Bel Air producers, Beverly Hills directors, screenwriters, a smattering of gallery owners, a few documentary makers, and a load of Netflix executives and media people.

"How was Malibu?" his brother asked, handing him a glass of single malt.

Kassan took a sip. "Ghastly!"

"Tell me the truth."

"Same as ever. Fabulous. But it was still ghastly."

His brother smiled and knocked back his Scotch and ordered two more. "No gossip?"

"I did hear someone talking about a well-known actress who's in the middle of medically transitioning."

"Damn." His brother groaned. "You need to name names!"

Kassan shook his head. He might later, when they were out of earshot of any passing waitresses. "Another thing, we'll be having an intern for a month. Jenny Roscoff, daughter of Audrey."

"Oh Christ, must we?"

"She's a great client. What does it cost us?"

"True."

A waiter returned with two tumblers of single malt. "Gentlemen," he said.

Kassan tipped him fifty bucks.

"Thank you, sir. Enjoy your evening."

His brother waited until the guy was out of earshot. "What about you? You said earlier you had some news."

"I was talking to a friend of Brett Miller."

"Brett? Okay . . ."

"Remember the veteran that was hanging around the gallery a month or so back?" Robert said. "Angel something. Whack job."

"Angel Ramos?"

Robert leaned in close, his voice barely a whisper. "Right. Remember the guy who picked up a wine bottle and threatened me one night in front of my clients? Saying I was fucking his underage daughter? Remember, I met her at one of Brett's soirees?"

His brother stared back at him. "I remember only too well."

Robert's mind flashed back to the terrifying encounter, the painful memories flooding back.

"I thought Angel Ramos was taken care of?" his brother said.

"I was assured he was. But . . . I've got an update. I was told through the grapevine that the cops have told Jerry Levinson, who represents Brett, to be aware that there's a guy in town. He's asking questions."

"Questions about what?"

"Aren't you listening? He's asking questions about the guy, Ramos, who was hanging around the gallery. Threatening to expose my relationship with his child."

His brother stared at him as if dumbstruck.

Robert looked around the club, taking in the other members laughing and joking, relaxing, eating out on the deck overlooking the lights of Hollywood.

"Where is this going? I mean, what does this mean? You say a guy is asking questions?"

"I just think it's important we're aware this guy is around," Robert said.

"You think he'll come and see us?"

"The homeless guy . . . he won't bother us again. But this guy—he's a friend of the homeless guy, I've been told."

"I don't like this. Not one bit."

Robert felt the same. He was a private person. He prided himself on keeping his life far from prying eyes.

"What do we know about him?" said his brother.

"His name is Reznick."

"Reznick?"

"Former special forces."

"Holy shit."

"He's been down in Venice for a couple weeks. Spotted outside a couple nightclubs in West Hollywood. I'm worried."

"Keep me abreast of anything, Robert. I've got a bad feeling about this guy."

Twenty-Nine

The diner was an American classic, located on the corner of Sunset and Gower in the heart of Hollywood.

Reznick walked in and sat down in a booth. He looked up at the clock on the wall. Three minutes after midnight. A Cure song—a favorite of his daughter Lauren's—was playing quietly in the background. He looked over at a tattooed young woman wearing a red Billie Eilish T-shirt, rocking her baby back and forth in a stroller. A guy wearing dark glasses, eating fries, was muttering to himself.

A server strolled up, beaming. "Good evening, sir, what can we get you?"

Reznick looked over the menu and ordered blueberry pancakes and maple syrup, with a strong black coffee.

"Coming right up, sir," the girl said.

Reznick waited until his coffee had arrived before he knocked back another couple of Dexedrine. Whenever he felt he was about to hit the wall, he reached for the amphetamines. It was a terrible habit. His sleeping patterns were non-existent. When he did sleep it was only for an hour or two at a time. It wasn't good for him at his age. He wasn't a guy in his twenties, behind enemy lines in

Somalia, crunching Dexedrine for fun to keep him wide awake. He didn't need to do this anymore. So why did he? Was he in denial about his drug habit from his Delta days?

When the waitress returned with his food, she said, "You need anything else, just let me know."

"Appreciate that, thank you."

"You're very welcome."

Reznick was famished. He watched as a group of what looked like Japanese tourists arrived at the diner. The waitress headed over to greet them, unfailingly polite and good-natured. Not an easy job, dealing with tourists late at night.

Reznick ate his pancakes, grateful to get some sustenance. Outside on Sunset snaked a trail of headlights. The nighttime traffic crawling through the neighborhood kept a steady glow coming through the windows. He heard the sound of police sirens in the distance. He drank his coffee as he contemplated where he was at.

Earlier that day he had drawn a blank when he'd visited the last-known address for Camila Ramos. No one had answered the door. There was no car outside. He'd thought of leaving a note for the person living there to give him a call, but he'd decided against it. He would head up there again at first light. Six hours from now. He figured it would probably be the best time to catch her if she worked nights as a bar girl or escort.

His cell phone rang, interrupting his thoughts. He checked the caller ID. A number he didn't recognize.

"Dad?" The beautiful voice of his daughter.

Reznick's heart swelled. He hadn't heard from her in a while. "Lauren? Is that really you?"

"It's me, Dad."

"So lovely to hear from you, honey."

"You too. Dad, are you okay to talk?"

Reznick felt thrilled to hear his daughter's voice. "Of course. How are you? How's Jakarta?" He dropped his voice down to a whisper. "And how's life in the Agency?"

"Interesting, that's for sure."

"I bet. I can't remember the last time you called."

"I'm sorry. You know how it is."

Reznick smiled. He knew exactly how it was. It was easy to get caught up in work, especially when working abroad for months at a time. "So talk to me. How are you?"

"So where are you?"

"Sunny LA."

"Seriously?"

"Well, not so sunny as it's after midnight."

"I hope I didn't wake you."

"No chance of that, honey. Have you ever been to LA?"

"No, I have not."

"I'll arrange a trip the next time you're home. Just the two of us."

"Sounds like a plan. Are you on vacation?"

"Not quite."

"So are you working?"

"Sort of. I'm doing a bit of this and that."

"A bit of this and that," she parroted. "Be careful, whatever you're up to."

"Don't worry about me. So when you coming home, kid?"

"That's why I'm calling . . . They extended my time here by another year."

"That's great for your career, right?"

"It wasn't what I planned. But it's fine, Dad."

Reznick detected tension in her voice. "Well, as long as you're fine with that. Are you enjoying your stint in Jakarta? It's not exactly Midcoast Maine."

"The job, the city, it's . . . I guess it's good. A lot to take in." There was the sound of a phone ringing in the background. "Dad, I'm sorry, that's my boss. I don't think there are enough hours in the day."

"Take it easy, honey. And call your old dad more often!"

"Love you, Dad."

"Love you too."

Reznick felt as if a little piece of him had died hearing his daughter's voice from so, so far away. He missed her badly, hadn't thought he would. He looked forward to when she came home to visit. She used to come back to Rockland once a month to see him. He'd go to see her when she was in New York, working for the FBI. She was great company. He missed her presence in his life.

He wondered if she'd met a guy overseas. But Lauren kept her personal life very private, which was fine. He just wanted her to be happy. She sounded quite hesitant. But he knew better than anyone the toll foreign assignments took on a person.

Reznick drove back to Venice and grabbed a couple of hours' sleep in his room. When he awoke, dawn was breaking over the beach, the sun streaming through the blinds. He quickly freshened up, splashing cold water on his face, then drove all the way back to the Hollywood Hills. He drove higher and higher, along winding, narrow roads. Eventually, he reached the address. The same address he had visited the previous afternoon.

Reznick pulled up at the tiny, secluded cottage on Ivarene Avenue. There was the fresh scent of jasmine bushes, and the overhanging palm trees cast shade across the road. A small, dirty Honda, spattered in dried mud, was parked outside. It hadn't been there when he had visited yesterday.

Reznick's gaze was drawn to a curtain at a weird angle, as if it needed to be hung properly. He got out of his vehicle and knocked on the front door. He wondered if someone would be in this time. He knocked three more times.

Slowly, very slowly, the door cracked open.

A bleary-eyed young woman, wearing only her dressing gown, was yawning, squinting against the morning sun. "Yeah?"

"I'm looking for Camila Ramos."

"Who are you? You a cop?"

Reznick shook his head. "Camila is the daughter of a friend of mine. A friend who passed away recently."

"You're a friend of Camila's dad?"

"Yeah."

"That's weird. I didn't know she had a dad. She said she didn't have a family."

Reznick looked past the girl and down the hallway. "Do you mind if I come in? I've got a few more questions."

The young woman winced. "I don't know. How do I know you're not going to kill me?"

"Relax," Reznick said, showing his ID. "My name is Jon Reznick. Camila's father served with me in special forces—Delta. I heard she wanted to meet him and that's why she moved to LA. She also tried to help her dad with his addictions. But I believe she got drawn into a life of . . . how can I put it? Bad choices."

"Yeah, tell me about it. And you're not going to kill me?"

Reznick smiled. "I'm not. I've just got a few questions."

"Stay right there. I'm going to get some clothes first." The young woman shut and locked the door. A few minutes later she opened the door again wearing a gray Nike tracksuit. "Sorry about the mess. Come in."

Reznick followed her down the hallway and into a small, sun-filled room overlooking the canyon below. "Nice views up here."

"Yeah, it's better than the shithole I was in downtown, let me tell you. Neighbors are nice too up here. A cardiologist to my left. A graphic artist and his wife to my right. Cool crowd."

"Sorry, what's your name?"

"Flo Jackson."

Reznick sat on a chintzy sofa, next to an armchair, both saturated with the smell of stale cigarettes. "So, Camila . . . does she live here still, or has she moved out?"

"She took all her stuff a little while ago."

Reznick's heart sank. He could see this lead was another dead end. "Do you know where she went?"

"I don't. I lost her number. But she calls me occasionally, caller ID withheld."

"She does . . . Do you mind me asking what she calls you about?"

"She's lonely. She's lost. And she wants someone to talk to."

"Is she still on drugs? I heard she had a problem."

"You sure you're not a cop?"

Reznick shook his head.

"She's scared. That's the truth. Strung-out and frightened."

"What's she scared of?"

"More like who is she scared of? She has mood swings. One day she's super-happy, the next day she's freaking out."

"Who is she scared of?"

"She's scared after recently hooking up with a fucking bullshit rich boyfriend."

"Rich boyfriend? Is that not a good thing?"

Flo shook her head, dragging hard on the cigarette. "Nope. He's got a bad reputation in this town. Very controlling. Says he loves her. Promises her the moon. Then fucks her."

Reznick winced. "You got a name for this rich boyfriend?"

"Don't say where you got the name, right?"

"I swear."

"Brett Miller. He's an old guy. Easily in his seventies."

"His seventies? What?"

"It's disgusting if you ask me. Viagra grandpa. She told me she attended a few of his drug and sex parties last summer, up at his house in Bel Air. She was just a piece of ass for him and his friends. And yes, before you ask, he's already fucking her, along with everyone else in town, I've heard. Has multiple girlfriends. Complete slut. Has had more sexually transmitted diseases than anyone! I'm worried for her."

Reznick texted Trevelle. *Get a fix on Brett Miller.*

He tried to exude a sense of calm. "This name, Brett Miller, this name has cropped up before. Can you tell me a bit about him?"

"You don't know Brett Miller?"

"Not a lot."

"You honestly haven't heard of him?"

Reznick shook his head. "Not much. Sorry, I don't know the players in the city, the big shots. I'm not familiar with the business either."

"He's a super-successful director. He promised to get her in his next film. But that's his line with a million girls. He fucks them, then he *fucks* them. Promises made, promises broken."

"He sounds like a charmer."

"Sleazeball of the highest order."

"What else can you tell me about their relationship?"

"Well, I heard that he set her up with an apartment in the West Hills. But she won't give me the address. Scared she'll lose her material things and all that bullshit."

"Interesting. Let me ask you something. When she's not waiting for him, what does she do usually?"

"When she was here, before she hooked up with her big-shot grandpa, she was working for tips. Dancing, stripping, bars and clubs on Sunset. She was pretty wild, hanging out at Hollywood parties. Always wanted to get into the movies."

"When was the last time you spoke to her?"

"Last night. She sounded really wasted. She said she was scared of him. I told her to leave him."

"And did she?"

"Camila is a mess. A drug-abusing mess. She's used to doing tricks for fifty bucks. She worked as a bottle girl. An escort. Stripping. But she doesn't want to go back to that life. She thinks this guy is her best option. But it's her worst option. She doesn't listen."

Reznick sat in silence, absorbing the details of this monumental mess of a life.

"I've told her she'll wind up dead. Either he'll kill her or she'll die of an overdose."

"I think you're probably right."

Flo began playing with her hair, as if she was a little girl self-soothing. "You know what really freaked me out?"

"What?"

"She said that he threatened to have her killed if she told anyone about their relationship."

"Brett Miller threatened her?"

"Swear to God, that's what she told me."

Reznick felt a rage burning inside him. "I need to find her."

"I told her to get the hell out of that situation. It's bad juju, that's for sure."

"You got any paper?"

The girl pointed to a yellow notepad.

Reznick ripped off one piece and scribbled down his cell phone number. He handed it to her. "My number is on that. If you hear from her, if you see her, don't hesitate. Just give me a call."

Thirty

The offices of Jerry Levinson's law firm were located on the fourteenth floor of a glass tower in downtown Los Angeles. He could look out and see the sprawling, sun-drenched city from every angle. He had found himself, however, working a couple of days each week from his home in Pacific Palisades. He needed to be close to his wife, Andrea, who was still recovering from a major operation to remove some cancerous tissue. But today, Jerry sat behind his desk, working away on finalizing transactional contracts for two of his highest-earning clients. Every so often he glanced at his phone, waiting for an important call.

When it came, Jerry picked up right away.

The gruff voice on the other end of the line started with "I might have something for you."

Levinson leaned back in his seat. The abrasive Jay Johnson, retired LAPD homicide detective turned private investigator. The guy was completely discreet. He was a man who made problems disappear, partly by subcontracting work out to highly dangerous individuals. Men like Carlos Lopez. Johnson knew that when a lawyer with a stellar client list contacted him, it was to silence or neutralize a threat. It might be blackmail. It might be the threat of violence. But sometimes, and Levinson was well aware of this,

Johnson gave the go-ahead for the execution of individuals. Some took a fall from a high building. Some were dropped in the sea. Levinson was breaking every law, as a conspirator. That didn't sit well with him. But his firm was the pinnacle of Hollywood representation. He had grown up in a trailer with his mother and two brothers. He had vowed he would never be poor again. He paid significant fees for his mother to live in a gated community in Florida. He had backed his brothers in their failed business ventures. The bottom line? There was no going back. Even if he wanted to. He was in too deep.

The cutthroat nature of Hollywood legal representation meant that firms could not afford to lose A-list clients. He knew two other law firms in Los Angeles were now using the off-the-book services of Johnson as well. No questions asked. Jerry's firm had been working with Johnson in the last year. But the results for his clients, despite the steep price that Johnson charged, more than made up for it.

The shadowy relationship had begun when Jerry was given Johnson's card by a fellow lawyer. He had reached out to Johnson for help on a case; it involved surveillance of a little-known actress who was blackmailing Brett Miller. And it had snowballed from there.

"Hey, Jay. Something important?"

"I would say so. It might be best if we meet in person."

"You got anywhere in mind?"

"You know the Frolic Room?"

Levinson knew the bar on Hollywood Boulevard. "Sure. What time?"

"I'll see you at eight. Oh . . . don't bring your cell phone. And don't wear a smartwatch."

Levinson carried his cell phone at all times. He needed to be contacted by clients. Especially people like Brett Miller. "That might be a problem. I need to be reachable."

"Take it or leave it. That's the deal."

"Very well. I understand. No electronics."

The line went dead.

The bar was two doors down from the Pantages Theater in Hollywood.

Levinson walked in already feeling out of place as the thumping rock music hit him. The Stones on the jukebox. The red lighting created a moody vibe. Three girls in skimpy dresses were drinking cocktails with a couple of guys.

Levinson walked to the far end of the bar and sat down.

The bartender was wiping down the counter. "What you having?"

"Scotch on the rocks."

"Coming up."

He was given his drink and he sat, nursing the strong Scotch. He felt naked without his cell phone in his hand or on his person. He was always at the beck and call of his rich, famous, and demanding clients. It felt strange knowing they couldn't contact him, at least while he was in the bar.

Johnson walked in. He wore jeans with a gray sweatshirt. He sat down on a stool beside Levinson.

Levinson turned to him. "What are you drinking?"

"Double Scotch on the rocks."

Levinson ordered two doubles.

"No cell phone?"

"Left it in the car."

"Let me see your wrists."

Levinson showed Johnson his traditional, mechanical Rolex. "There's no smart technology on this model. It was my father's, back in the day."

Johnson nodded as the barman served up the doubles. He picked up the drinks and cocked his head. "Follow me."

Levinson followed Johnson to a table in the far corner of the bar, away from the other drinkers. Virtually out of sight.

Johnson sat down and sipped his Scotch. "Damn, that's good."

"Twenty-year-old single malt."

"Now we're talking."

Levinson took a small sip of his drink. "That is good."

"How are you?" Johnson said.

"You know how it is. Working morning, noon, and night."

"You got any vacations coming up, Jerry?"

"Wife wants to go on a cruise to the Caribbean."

"You into that?"

"Fuck no. Stuck on a boat with five thousand other miserable fuckers. I'd rather fly to St. Barts, kick back."

"There we go, I can dig that." Johnson sipped his drink.

"So, what've you got for me?"

Johnson leaned in closer, his voice a whisper. "You inquired about the guy pulled in for surveillance of the Razor nightclub."

"Yup."

"How does this interest your client?"

"Someone told me, a friend of mine in the commissioner's office, that some guy was showing a marked interest in several locations across town. My client's name was mentioned. I can't have that. He values his privacy."

"Has your client got a name?"

"Jay, it's strictly confidential."

The investigator sipped his Scotch, swirling the glass around. "Ten like the last time?"

"Ten big ones. How do you want it this time?"

"However you like," Johnson said. "Bitcoin?"

Levinson smiled. "Not a problem. I never figured ex-cops to be so fond of crypto."

Johnson handed Levinson a piece of paper with a bitcoin address.

"So, who's the guy that was pulled in?" Levinson asked.

"Special forces type."

"And this club that he was observing?"

"The Razor is a dark, crazy place—prostitutes, maniacs, sex fiends, you name it, they all hang out there. What I know is that guy who was sniffing around this club has been seen scoping out a few places up in the hills. He's a serious guy. Some of the places he's looking at are owned by Carlos Lopez's company. You know the guy I'm talking about?"

Levinson sipped his drink. He knew full well that Lopez was one of the "contractors" Johnson used.

"So this guy, from out of town—the LAPD are on to him," Johnson said.

"Name?"

"Jon Reznick. Spelled R-E-Z-N-I-C-K. Former Delta, I've heard."

"Who's he working for? What does he want?"

"He's not working for anyone. A friend of his got murdered. Angel Ramos down on Venice Beach. His friend was a homeless bum. But he wound up being tortured and killed."

Levinson was aware of the killing of the homeless bum. He hadn't asked for the guy to be neutralized. But he had been plaguing people he knew in and around Beverly Hills as well as trying to contact Brett. "I'm assuming this Ramos guy pissed off someone else."

"Exactly. He was sniffing around your client at one time. His daughter attended one of Brett's fuck parties last year, which enraged this guy."

Levinson knew not to ask who had asked for the homeless guy to be killed. He felt sick. He always did when he realized the nefarious aspect of his practice. But he rationalized that bad things happened to people in big cities. "So, this Reznick guy . . . he has it in his head that Carlos Lopez might be responsible?"

Johnson nodded. "Absolutely."

Levinson stared blankly into his drink. He knew that there was a connection of sorts between Lopez, who was on Reznick's radar, and himself. An indirect association.

"What I'm telling you," Johnson said, "is that, as myself and Carlos Lopez have a business relationship, it was important to bring this to your attention."

"I know."

"I don't want any heat he's getting to disturb you."

"I appreciate the heads-up. But I pay you for problems to disappear."

"I understand. And I can deal with whatever is required if and when that happens. We're not at that stage."

"What do you suggest?"

"I suggest you sit tight and don't sweat it," said Johnson. "That's my honest advice. I think this Reznick guy who's running around asking questions . . . he'll focus his energy on Lopez. In that respect, that's not a bad thing. Lopez and his guys can deal with anything."

"Just to be clear. This Jon Reznick, he's not looking anywhere else?"

"Just Lopez. For the time being. That's the guy he has in his sights. I hear he's also looking for the daughter of Angel Ramos."

"Who's she?" said Levinson.

"No one. Working the streets, escorting."

"And the daughter is in LA?"

"Reznick seems to think so. My advice to your client? Stay out of trouble. Stay out of clubs. Stay away from hookers. And this will all go away."

"But what if it doesn't? What if this guy hangs around? What then?"

"We deal with things if and when they occur. Don't sweat it."

"Is Lopez aware of this guy?"

"He's well aware," said Johnson. "This guy Reznick is a marked man."

Levinson's mood was low. He felt anxious. The shadowy world of Lopez might be exposed. He knew that if push came to shove, every man had a price. A tipping point. Lopez would be no different. Levinson feared that Lopez might lead all the way to Brett Miller and, ultimately, to Levinson. He needed to play it cool. He had a duty to let his top client know. It didn't fill him with excitement knowing what the response from Brett Miller would be.

He got in his car and headed up to Beverly Hills, along Mulholland, toward his client's fabulous estate—secluded, exclusive, and a million miles away from the psycho Lopez.

Fuck.

He knew all about Lopez and how he, in a roundabout way, fitted into Brett Miller's seedy existence. It was a loose connection. But a connection all the same. A thread. A link.

Brett Miller was oblivious to all this. He frequented clubs operated by or owned by Lopez. He was not a friend of Lopez. But occasionally they moved, unbeknownst to one another, in the same circles.

Brett was a libertine. A man who lived for pleasure. A man who was selfish to his very core. But he lived life on his terms. He didn't care if you judged him or not.

He was oblivious. He was a great client. He would pay his invoice from Levinson's firm the day it landed on his accountant's desk. A cool two thousand dollars an hour added up. Levinson estimated that in the last six months Brett had racked up nearly two million dollars in legal fees.

Levinson wasn't just negotiating contracts pertaining to entertainment law, his specialty. He also worked the darker side of the equation. The bribes, the coercion of the police—which amounted to blackmail. This was how Levinson operated. So clients like Brett could live their lives without any repercussions. It was the Hollywood way. No matter how fucked-up the talent, they had to be protected at all costs. Rapes, serious assaults, even murders. The talent knew the greenbacks spoke. Pay a price, and all the bad stuff would magically go away.

Levinson negotiated a tight bend as his mind drifted. He hadn't started out this way. He had begun his legal career straight out of Harvard as an idealist. But decades later, it was crazy to see how he'd ended up. How would he look back on his life and career in ten years' time, when he had retired? He wasn't a religious man, but he wondered if he would pay for his sins in another life.

Levinson questioned, from time to time, why he had taken the path he had. It broke every law, legal code, and ethic expected of an attorney. But the truth, the hard truth, was that he had significant obligations. He had three ex-wives, alimony, five kids going through college—he needed to keep the big bucks rolling in.

The problem Levinson had now was that it wasn't just Brett Miller who had indirect links to Lopez, through fraternizing at his clubs and bars. Levinson knew of Lopez through Jay Johnson. And he was worried that Jon Reznick's one-man surveillance operation on Lopez and his clubs might bring trouble to either Brett or himself, further down the line.

Levinson pulled up outside Miller's palatial mansion. He leaned out of his car window and spoke into the video intercom. "It's Jerry." He was buzzed through the huge gates and drove up to the house. He walked inside and headed through the marble masterpiece of an interior. Greek columns, frescos on the wall, modern art, Roman statuettes Brett had bought through Robert Kassan's gallery.

Miller was sitting by the pool, drinking a cocktail, watching as a young girl swam. He turned around, grinning like a madman. Eyes wide, bloodshot. He was out of his mind. "Hey, Jerry, what a surprise. You should have called."

"I needed to speak face-to-face. It's urgent. Hope you don't mind."

"Why the fuck would I mind? We're in the middle of setting up my latest film. It's all coming together great."

Levinson pulled up a seat as Brett slumped down on a sofa. His client seemed oblivious to his own mood swings. One day he would be screaming bloody murder that he was in trouble, the next, everything was golden. It was exhausting being his attorney. "The deal is coming together nicely," said Levinson. "I hope we'll have it all tied up, contract signed, by the end of the month."

Brett leaned in close. "I meant to say sorry for my behavior the last time you saw me. I was a bit stressed, you know, with that girl's death on the freeway. You understand, right?"

"Onward and upward, Brett!"

Brett smiled.

"I'll tell you why I'm here, Brett. You're my client. My number one client. And I love you."

Miller leaned over and hugged Levinson tight. "And I love you too, man. Can I fix you a drink?" He looked around, unable to stay still.

"I'm fine, thanks." Levinson was about to tell him about the guy pulled in by the LAPD. But he could see Brett was distracted, his eyes drawn to the young Latino woman doing lengths in the swimming pool. "Who's she?"

"In the pool? Just a girl."

"Just a girl—is that right? Who is she?"

"I'm thinking about casting her in my new film. She's a real beautiful girl. A peach."

Levinson felt uncomfortable. The girl was clearly underage. "How old is she, Brett?"

"Does it matter?"

"How old?"

"She's nearly seventeen."

"So she's sixteen? Are you kidding me?"

"She's a sweet kid. This is Hollywood. Everyone deserves one shot at the big time, right?"

"Are you fucking her?" The words came out of Jerry's mouth before he could stop himself.

"Jerry . . . come on, man, don't get so angry. What's the matter with you?"

Levinson had daughters the same age. "Well? Are you?"

"No."

"Tell me the fucking truth."

"What can I tell you? She's a nice kid."

"Brett, I don't have to remind you that you could be charged with statutory rape if you're having sex with her."

"I'm not fucking her."

Levinson didn't believe him. "As your attorney, I think you need to be very, very careful."

"I hear you."

"What's her name, as a matter of interest?"

"Her name? Camila Ramos. Likes to be called Gigi Cortez. Don't you love that name?"

Thirty-One

The red neon sign for the Whisky a Go Go club flashed bright, cutting through the dark.

Reznick was driving past, thinking of his next meal, when he got the feeling he was being tailed. He looked in his rearview mirror. A black Suburban was indeed following him. He called Trevelle and relayed the license plate.

"Two minutes, man," Trevelle said.

Reznick checked his mirror again and noticed the vehicle was now three cars behind him. It had dropped back, as if trying to be discreet. He drove on a couple of miles through the heart of West Hollywood. Trevelle's voice came back through the car speakers.

"Jon, you got Feds on your tail."

"Those are Feds?"

"One hundred percent. Assigned to the LA field office. You need anything else?"

Reznick glanced in the mirror again. The SUV was still hanging in there. "Probably a good lawyer at this rate."

Trevelle laughed. "Man, you are attracting some serious heat in LA."

"I'll be in touch."

"Stay safe."

Reznick kept going, waiting to see what the Feds would do next. He got his answer when the Suburban accelerated, overtook him, blue lights on, and then veered in front, blocking him in. He pulled up sharp.

A couple of Feds got out of the SUV and approached his car, guns drawn and pointed through his window.

"Jon Reznick?"

He put his hands up. "That's me."

"You need to come with us. Right now."

The FBI's Los Angeles field office was located in a modern building in Westwood. Reznick was escorted into the building in handcuffs and into an elevator. He thought it a tad excessive. But such were the ways of the FBI.

The ride to the seventeenth floor seemed to take a lifetime, hemmed in as he was by surly special agents.

When the elevator door finally opened, Reznick was escorted down a series of corridors until he came to a gray interview room. A desk and three chairs. Two more special agents—a woman and a man—were already sitting to one side, sifting through some papers.

"Pull up a chair, Jon," the female agent said. The ID card on the lanyard around her neck identified her as Olivia Rodriguez. The male agent was Tom Blake.

Reznick sat down and held up his wrists. They jangled. "Do you mind uncuffing me?"

Rodriguez motioned to one of the agents behind Reznick. Reznick was uncuffed. "That'll be all. We'll take it from here," she said to the agents who had escorted Reznick into the building.

The door was shut and locked behind them.

Reznick rubbed his wrists. "That was a bit over the top, wasn't it?"

"We weren't sure how you were going to react," she replied. "Besides, it's better to be prepared for the worst, right?"

He shifted in his seat. "Sometimes, yeah."

Rodriguez leafed through a few pages of the file in front of her. "I was sorry to hear about the death of your friend."

"Appreciate that."

"We've got a problem, though . . ."

"What's that?"

"I'm having trouble understanding why a smart, capable, and highly knowledgeable operator like you seems to be acting oblivious to the risks involved here."

Reznick sat in silence.

"I suppose I'm wondering why on earth you're still hanging around after your friend's funeral. Why aren't you back in Maine?"

Reznick shrugged. "I have my reasons."

"And what are those?"

He said nothing.

"Look, we're trying to help," Rodriguez said.

"Are you?"

"Jon, we know who you've been seeing," she said. "Our patience is not infinite. I know all about you, and I respect it. What you've done. I know you've worked with the FBI on numerous operations. I know your history. And that's why I've been playing this low-key."

Reznick stayed quiet, focusing on the drab walls.

"But that was then. This is now. Do you know that the obstruction of a federal investigation carries severe penalties?"

"So it's not just the LAPD?"

Rodriguez fixed her steely glare on him.

"So now we're getting somewhere. You're investigating something which I may have inadvertently gotten involved with, right? Must be pretty big, for the Feds to be muscling in," he said.

Rodriguez scribbled a few notes before looking up. "Don't fuck with us, Jon. We know about your friend that died. His background. But you need to know it is the jurisdiction and responsibility of the LAPD to investigate your friend's death."

"I'm well aware of that. So why is the FBI hauling my ass in?"

"Let me give you an update, to assuage your fears that nothing is happening. That's not the case. The FBI is now actively involved. We have launched an investigation into the people who may be linked to your friend's death."

"You haven't answered my question. Why are the Feds involved?"

Blake cleared his throat. "Jon, we were brought in because of the nature of the homicide. A former American soldier, but no ordinary soldier. A military operator, like yourself, who was involved in classified operations. And that's why we were brought in."

Reznick contemplated that development. "Do you believe a foreign element may be responsible? Transnational, so to speak?"

Blake nodded.

"I appreciate your candor on that. I have my own thoughts. You mind me asking you another question?"

"Sure."

"Does one of the people you're investigating go by the name Carlos Lopez?"

A flash of anger in Rodriguez's eyes. "Where did you get that name?"

Reznick sat in silence. He stared at Blake, who averted his eyes. He was onto something.

"What do you know about Carlos Lopez?" Rodriguez said. "Is that why you were scoping out several businesses in West Hollywood?"

"Let's cut the crap. I've been given a name."

"By who?"

"Not going there. The name I've been given is Carlos Lopez. But that's not his real name, is it."

Rodriguez stared back at him, shaking her head. "A couple people are accusing you of harassing them. Stalking them. The joint investigation by the LAPD, the LA County Sheriff's Office, and the FBI could be jeopardized by your involvement. Do you understand that?"

"I've worked with the FBI in the past. I have no problem with the FBI. But I am not the enemy. The enemy is in plain sight. So if you want to charge me, charge me. Let's not beat around the bush. You charge me, fine. But that will not stop me from trying to determine who not only killed Angel Ramos, but also from finding out who ordered his killing."

"You're taking this very personally, Jon," Blake said.

"Damn right it's personal."

"Why are you fixated on this ex-Delta pal of yours? The guy had fallen on hard times. He died."

"He was murdered! Get it right. Angel may have ended up in a bad place. But to me, my memories of him are very different. He was the bravest man I ever knew. I owe it to his memory."

"Rest assured, we are doing our utmost," Blake said. "We're pulling every resource into this. We will find the person responsible."

Reznick folded his arms, his head bowed.

"I know it's hard, Jon. We are on this. And we won't let up. We thank you for passing on what you have. But I think it's time for you to let us get on with our job, and bring the person responsible to justice."

"Can I say something?"

Rodriguez stared at him. "Is it relevant to the case?"

"Most certainly."

"What's on your mind?"

"I believe that Angel's murder has all the hallmarks of a punishment killing. The hallmarks of a death squad, I would venture. A torture gang."

"That is pure conjecture," said Rodriguez.

"I heard how he died."

"How did you hear that?"

"He had holes drilled through his fucking eyes, head, neck. Horrific. I know what punishment killings look like. It's not pretty. And that's why this Carlos Lopez fellow is so important."

Rodriguez turned and looked at her colleague.

Blake glanced at his notes before sizing up Reznick. "We seem to be going around in circles. Can you give us your word that you'll head back home and leave us to it?"

"No can do."

"You don't seem to be reading the tea leaves too well, Jon. We assumed, as did the LAPD, that you would have gone home by now. Now we're asking you nicely, please let us work this out."

Reznick shook his head.

"Fair enough. So, as you are not willingly going back home, it's my duty to bring to your attention the main reason we've brought you in."

"It wasn't because I was monitoring Lopez's clubs?"

"That wasn't it."

"So what is it?"

"We're worried that your life is in danger. And we have decided to put this through the traditional channels."

Reznick wondered where Blake was going with this.

"Jon Reznick, we are warning you that we have credible intelligence which indicates there is a specific threat to your life. This is a requirement of our Duty to Warn. We want you to know that there are serious ongoing threats to kill you in Los Angeles. Do you understand what I have said?"

Reznick's mind raced as he absorbed the information. He knew that Duty to Warn notifications from the FBI were rare and very serious. "I hear you. Loud and clear."

"Do you understand fully what a Duty to Warn entails?"

"Yes."

"I'll say again, Jon, we believe your life is in danger if you remain in Los Angeles. We thought about emailing you this warning, but we deemed it more appropriate to speak face-to-face on the matter."

Reznick processed the gravity of the situation. He knew they weren't bluffing.

Rodriguez noted the time and scribbled some more notes on her legal pad. "I'll ask again, do you understand why we believe your presence and involvement in this case is viewed as such a serious matter?"

"Yes. And thanks for passing on the warning."

"The FBI has a solemn duty and responsibility to notify persons of threats to their life. But also of threats that may result in serious bodily injury. We also have a duty to notify other law enforcement agencies, which we have done. This includes the LAPD."

"I've already spoken to them. Venice Beach and LAPD headquarters."

"We know. But we are reiterating, Jon, that we believe . . . in fact, I'll go further, we *know* these are credible threats to end your life. If you continue this investigation into the death of your friend, it could very well get you killed. I can't make it any clearer than that."

"No, you cannot," Reznick agreed.

"Think very carefully about what we've said. Take this threat seriously. Our best advice would be to leave Los Angeles right away. Not in twenty-four hours. Go right now."

"Can you compel me?"

Blake shrugged. "It's an advisory notice. But make no mistake, when the FBI issues a Duty to Warn notice to an individual, you need to wise up and get out of town. The intel we have suggests your name is known. And it's not just one person who has a reason to kill you. Take this warning seriously . . . otherwise, Jon, I'm afraid you'll wind up on the mortuary slab next."

Thirty-Two

It was the dead of night as the headlights of his SUV illuminated the road ahead, up through the Hollywood Hills.

Carlos Lopez drove alone, yawning as the sultry voice of the GPS guided him to his destination along Mulholland's winding bends. The overlook was on the north side of the road, just west of Laurel Canyon.

Lopez pulled up beside a Buick truck that was already parked, lights off. The driver was silhouetted, staring ahead at the San Fernando Valley. Carlos switched his lights off. Down below, the countless lights of Los Angeles seemed to extend to the horizon.

The driver in the Buick was still staring straight ahead. Lopez got out of his car and walked around to the driver's side to speak to the man.

The guy was smoking a cigarette. "You're late. What kept you?"

"Tying up loose ends," Lopez said.

"So . . . you dealt with the photographer chick as I requested. Nice work."

Carlos cleared his throat. "Your client won't be hearing from her again."

"Photographs? Laptops?"

"Bleached the backup files on the cloud. Destroyed the rest."

"And she's gone—no trace of any incriminating photos or messages?"

"Oh yeah, it's done," Carlos said. "I heard you wanted to see me."

The man dragged hard on the cigarette, blowing the smoke out of the side of his mouth. "You heard right."

"You got a name for me?"

"Jon Reznick. He's staying down in Venice, I heard. Not far from where his pal was found."

Lopez tried to place the name. "Reznick . . . Where's he from?"

"Maine."

"He's a fucking long way from home."

"So are you, buddy."

Lopez felt his fists tighten. He wanted to strangle the racist fucker with his bare hands. But he had learned to deal with guys like this. He knew the guy was a former cop who wouldn't think twice about killing him. He was that sort of guy. Besides, he didn't want to fuck with people who could get him deported, or worse. "Who are you?" said Lopez. "I don't know much about you."

"Probably for the best. You don't need to know the details. What I can say is that I'm a middleman. I work for important people. I'm a cutout, if you will."

"I know what a fucking cutout is. Who you working for?"

"That would be telling. So, you did good work on the Angel Ramos homeless dude, Reznick's friend. Did all the money go through okay?"

"Nice and clean."

"I keep my promises."

"So do I."

"You the one that took care of Reznick's friend? Or one of your crew?"

Lopez smiled but didn't answer.

"Anyway, doesn't matter, my client has accepted my recommendation that Reznick is becoming a problem. And he agrees that he needs to be neutralized."

"You white boys love using words like that."

"And you *beaners* don't?"

Lopez felt triggered by the guy's race-baiting. It had been a while since he'd heard the slur from someone he didn't execute a little while later. "I'm listening."

"I advised my client that Reznick wasn't to be killed. At least not yet."

"Why not?"

"I'll get to that. But I do want you to deal with him. He needs a serious warning."

"Depends what you mean by *warning*?"

"I mean beat the shit out of him. Until he's unconscious."

"Why?"

"Why what?"

"Why is he to be targeted? Because he's snooping around?"

"Precisely. He's asking a lot of questions. And he's popping up around town, including your clubs."

Lopez nodded. He had planned to find and kill Reznick. But that wasn't the order.

"So, on the Reznick issue, our interests align."

"What about the girl I recommended to that Hollywood film big shot a few weeks back?"

"Very nice bit of ass. The big shot is a close friend of my client's. And I'm told he's enjoying her."

Lopez grinned. "I bet he is. Dirty gringo."

"However, there's a problem. This chick you sent him, Gigi, has apparently been messaging a friend of hers, Florence Jackson."

"I think I've heard of her."

The guy dragged hard on his cigarette, blew smoke away from Lopez's face. "Gigi and this girl used to share an apartment together. On Ivarene Avenue. Nine-two-five-seven. And lo and behold, Jon Reznick was knocking on her door. And that's not a metaphor."

"No idea what you're fucking talking about sometimes, man. You want me to deal with Florence Jackson, too?"

"Yes. You deal with Florence."

"And this Reznick guy? He's becoming a major pain in the ass."

"He is. But on reflection, we don't want you to kill another Delta veteran in LA."

"He's Delta too?"

"He *was* in Delta Force. Killing a second one of them would attract attention. We thought about it. But it's too high-risk. It'd draw serious heat. However, we want you to speak to Reznick. And leave him in no doubt of what will happen if he doesn't get the hell out of town."

Lopez felt himself beginning to smile. "What about the girl up in the hills?"

"Florence Jackson?"

"Yeah, what exactly do we do with that chick?"

"What would you like to do with her?"

Lopez smiled. "I'd like to do a lot of things."

"Then you shall. First, go to Florence's apartment and secure any electronic devices, phones, computers."

"Then what?"

"She's fully expendable. Have a little fun. You Mexicans like fun, right? Really go to town."

Lopez grinned. "We'll give her the special treatment."

Thirty-Three

Reznick floated in darkness on a dark, blood-red river. The stars in the inky sky were like white pinpricks. He sensed someone was close. He turned his head in the water. Corpses, headless corpses, floating past. The acrid smell of smoke in the distance. Minarets, collapsing in flames; rockets firing into the night sky. Tracer fire all around. Bombs being dropped by fighter jets swooping low. The ground erupting. Flames burning everything in sight. The smell of kerosene as the water caught fire. The flames spreading. He began to scream.

He awoke, bolt upright, in a cold sweat. He could hear his heart racing. He took a few moments to get his bearings. He reached over and switched on the light on his nightstand. It was 11 p.m. He had slept throughout the night and day. His body had been drained, running on adrenaline and Dexedrine. But it had all caught up with him and he had crashed.

He went into the bathroom and splashed some cold water on his face. It quickly revived him. His stomach growled; he was starving, not having eaten since yesterday. But that could wait. He needed to clear his head.

He decided to go for a run. He pulled on his jogging clothes and sneakers and headed out into the hubbub of Venice Beach. He walked over to the boardwalk and did some stretching exercises for his calves. Then he set off along the beachfront toward Santa Monica.

He ran hard, picking up speed, his heart rate hiking up a few notches. Sweat stuck his T-shirt to his skin. On and on, farther and farther. Past the homeless people, the alcoholics weaving up and down the boardwalk, the skateboarders smoking weed, the cops on bikes trying to keep an eye on everyone who was out and about.

Reznick thought back to his meeting with the FBI the day before. Their warning that his life was in danger had been unexpected. He knew it wasn't something he should ignore, but as he reflected on the risks he faced, he also wondered if he had really taken the investigation as far as he could. He couldn't be blasé about what they'd told him. But he wasn't afraid of unknown threats. He assumed Lopez and his psychotic thugs had him in their crosshairs. But it didn't matter who it was. He wasn't afraid of reprisal.

What did concern him, as a father, was the impact it would have on Lauren if he were killed. He needed to be aware of that. It wasn't all about him—about his quest for justice for Angel's daughter.

Reznick figured his death would also impact Elisabeth, the wife he thought had died on 9/11. It was true that he had been deceived by her, along with the CIA, who had used the terror attack on New York as a pretext for her to set up a new identity and life as a spy in Switzerland. It was a miracle he had found her again. But now she was back in America, ensconced in a safe house somewhere in New England, living under an alias. Reznick had been told she could visit him and Lauren once a year. But he hadn't heard anything since.

The bottom line? His daughter and his estranged wife, Elisabeth, would be impacted by his death.

Reznick ran on. He had been chasing shadows since he had embarked on this mission to track down Angel's killers. But he had also become sidetracked as he tried to find the whereabouts of his friend's daughter. He wondered if the FBI warning was the line in the sand he shouldn't cross. The smart thing would be to get back to his hotel room, pack, get in his rental car, and drive straight to LAX before boarding a flight back home in the morning.

What more could he legally do?

Reznick was sorely tempted to leave the cops and the Feds to figure it all out. He knew a long vacation in Europe—taking in the sunshine of the Amalfi Coast or the charms of the sun-kissed skies of Mallorca—would do him a world of good. It would rejuvenate him. And the Feds and cops could get on with their investigation.

He knew deep down in his soul that it was time to walk away. Forget everything. Swimming in the Mediterranean Sea, early-morning runs in the summer heat, glasses of red wine at a restaurant overlooking the water—it sounded idyllic.

The problem was Reznick wasn't very good at walking away and leaving a problem unresolved. It wasn't in his nature. No matter how alluring a vacation sounded, something, maybe his conscience, would still gnaw away at him. He'd hold a feeling in his gut that Angel's daughter, if she was even still alive, needed to be saved from her toxic lifestyle. How could he, in all good conscience, turn his back on the daughter of one of his closest comrades in Delta?

He not only couldn't, he wouldn't turn his back on her. He didn't know her. But she existed. He knew it. She was out there somewhere. The problem was, where?

Up ahead, Reznick saw the lights of the Ferris wheel on the Santa Monica Pier. The lights a beacon in the darkness. It was at that point that he jumped down onto the beach and vowed to stick around to the end, no matter what. It wouldn't be easy. But he had a sense of honor. A sense of duty. He wanted to find Angel's girl. It would inevitably take time. But that was something he had plenty of.

Reznick jogged back to his hotel. It was just after midnight. He showered and changed before heading out again, finally grabbing a bite to eat at a late-night taco truck. He picked up his rental car, which had been helpfully dropped off behind the hotel by the Feds. He was soon driving on South Centinela Avenue and onto the freeway, the glare of oncoming headlights as far as the eye could see. The traffic, even at this time of night, was down to a crawl all the way to West Hollywood.

Reznick's cell phone rang.

"You still there?"

"Yeah, I'm still here."

"I hadn't heard from you for a while. I thought something had gone wrong."

"I'm fine. What's on your mind tonight, Trevelle?"

"I see you're on the move. You know someone else who's on the move tonight?"

"Lopez?"

"Big Hollywood player . . . Brett Miller."

"The director?"

"Right. He's an elusive fucker, Jon, let me tell you. I don't know how many cell phones he has. It's ridiculous. But I managed to get a fix on one. And I've got a fix on his current movements in real time."

"Where's this guy live?"

"Very fancy. Up in the hills. He lives in a big house in a compound on Perugia Way, in ritzy Bel Air."

"He's there now?"

"Negative."

"So where is he?"

"You're going to love this. As of right now, he's at a nightclub on Sunset." Trevelle gave an address which Reznick punched into the GPS. "You're a couple miles away. Club Taurus."

"Perfect. Thank you, Trevelle."

"What are you going to do?"

"Improvise. Let's see where that takes us."

Reznick ended the call and drove over to the club. Revelers were lined up for half a block to get in, security checking bags. He sharked around the block, looking for a vantage point, before he found one, driving down an alley with a line of sight to the club entrance.

He pulled up and turned off the engine. He needed to get into the club. The chance might never appear again. The girl might be with Miller.

Reznick got out of his car, carefully locking the doors. He stretched his legs; he'd been stuck in traffic for way too long.

He waited for a few minutes. He sensed there were people behind him.

Reznick turned around. He saw three heavyset, tattooed Latino men. Toughs. Tight tops showing off rippling, inked biceps. He studied them quickly. The biggest of the three was a huge slab of a guy, tattoos across his neck, face, hands, and arms. Gang tattoos. He saw one particular tattoo, two letters marked on his brow. The letters *MS* . . . short for the fearsome Salvadoran gang Mara Salvatrucha, or MS-13. He knew the gang had originated in Los Angeles but had links with various Mexican cartels.

The guy with the *MS* tattoo stepped forward as he pulled out a knife. "You got a light, white boy?"

Reznick shook his head as he walked up to the guy and quickly kicked the knife out of his hand. He sidestepped a punch and slammed his elbow into the man's flabby throat. He went down, out cold. The impact on the carotid arteries had knocked him unconscious as blood momentarily stopped flowing to the brain.

The other two pulled knives. Bigger knives. One looked like a machete.

"Who's next?"

The pair of musclebound hoods rushed him.

Reznick took a step sideways and slammed his fist into the side of one of their heads. The knife fell from the stunned man's right hand. Reznick stepped forward and rabbit-punched the man on the back of his head. The guy crumpled to the ground, lights out.

The third man took a step forward. "I'm gonna fuck you up bad, dude."

Reznick signaled him forward. He watched the man's quick hand movements, switching the machete expertly between his right and left hands. The guy hissed, exposing a gold grill on his teeth. Reznick waited for the right moment, wanting him to make a move.

The guy lunged forward, machete in the air, swinging down at Reznick's head. Reznick deftly stepped aside, kicking away the man's legs. He fell to the ground and Reznick stomped down on his wrist. The guy screamed, and the machete was loosened from his grip. Reznick kicked it away.

Reznick stood over him and stomped down hard on the guy's jaw. Heel hard into the mouth with the grill, multiple times. A crack as the guy's jaw and teeth broke. His eyes rolled back in his head until he was out of it too. Three goons lying prone in the alley, two knives and a machete lying unused.

He rifled in each of the men's pockets for ID. Nothing. Only a cell phone on the last guy. No guns. No wallets. That was strange in itself.

Reznick grabbed the phone and put it in his front pocket. Groans emerged from the first thug, blood pouring from his mouth. The big lunk was coming to.

Reznick grabbed him by the hair and dragged him farther into the alley, away from the two other unconscious men. He grabbed his throat, pressing hard on the carotid artery. "Who sent you, fat boy? Who's paying you?"

The guy grimaced, eyes shut tight, as Reznick exerted pressure on his neck.

"You don't answer, I'll send you for a long sleep. You know what I mean?"

"Carlos Lopez. He's the one. He sent us."

Reznick released his grip. Stared down at the man on the ground. He stepped forward and kicked the guy in the side of the head and the thug went unconscious again.

Three heavies sent to harm Reznick. They wouldn't be trying that again.

Reznick brushed himself off and walked around the corner to the club. Security eyed him up as he waited in line. He paid fifty dollars in cash, had the back of his hand stamped by a shaven-headed dude and got waved into the club.

He went to the bar and ordered a double Scotch. The music was disco. Seventies music. He hated that shit.

He picked up his tumbler and took a large gulp. He felt the amber nectar warm his chest. Then the liquor hit his head. It felt good. His gaze wandered around the booths and the dancers on the floor of the club.

Reznick finished his drink. Ordered another. He fixed his gaze on a perma-tanned man he recognized as Brett Miller from the photos he had studied. The film director was sitting beside a smartly dressed man in a gray suit. Both were deep in conversation.

He stared at Miller's reflection in the mirror behind the bar. The guy was animated, laughing loudly, chewing gum, sipping champagne.

Reznick just quietly observed the pair for the better part of an hour. He watched as a trio of pretty girls sat down beside Miller and his friend. More champagne and vodka shots were ordered.

Reznick studied the faces of the girls. One African American and two white girls. No Hispanic girl who might be Camila Ramos. It had been a long shot, hoping that she would be sitting alongside Brett Miller.

The problem was that even if she was here, he didn't know what she looked like. He regretted not asking Florence if she had a photo of Camila.

Reznick watched as a blonde girl sat on Miller's lap for a few minutes and he stuffed dollar bills into her cleavage. He felt sick. He knocked back his single malt and ordered a bottle of Schlitz. The hours dragged as he hung around the sleazy club.

When Miller and the blonde girl left, Reznick stayed seated at the bar, the disco music still blaring, wondering if Camila was even alive.

Thirty-Four

Jerry Levinson was working late into the night on a draft contract for Brett's new five-year, exclusive first-look deal, when his phone rang. He groaned. There was no escape, even in the middle of the night.

He checked his watch. It was 4:11. He wondered who was calling at this ungodly hour. He picked up his phone.

"Jerry?" The voice of Jay Johnson, the private investigator.

"Speaking."

"Man, you're going to work yourself into an early grave."

"Is that right?" Levinson was never eager to talk to Johnson. He was always worried the call was being recorded. His clients were world-famous. Fabulously wealthy. Everyone was ripe for blackmail. His phone could be bugged on whatever charge the Feds wanted to conjure up. He needed to be on guard in case the cops were eavesdropping on his discussions. His clients' legal affairs and private matters had to be zealously guarded. "It'll need to be quick."

"I've just had a rather unsettling conversation with Lopez."

"Everything okay?"

"He's not happy."

"What are you talking about?" Levinson picked up his Montblanc pen and began to write down the details. The time of the conversation, who it was about, and the nature of the call.

"Lopez sent over three of his best guys to give Reznick a warning."

Levinson felt sick. He wondered if Reznick had died. "What happened?"

"All three of his men wound up in the hospital."

"Hang on, are you saying Lopez sent three guys to deal with Reznick and they got fucked-up?"

"Big-time. All three of them. One of them might have brain damage. One has serious internal injuries. The other has a broken jaw and teeth, and his face is smashed in bad. It's a shitshow. And this was all one man. Jon Reznick. This is fucked-up."

Levinson felt as if his head was going to explode. They didn't need any heat from this Reznick character. The guy seemed to be homing in on Lopez and his role in the death of Reznick's friend. It was clear that Reznick was not going away. He wondered how long it would be until Reznick's path crossed Miller's.

Levinson had been up at Brett Miller's Bel Air mansion last night and a naked girl going by the name Gigi Cortez had been there in the flesh. Her age was the first major problem. But the second problem was that the girl's real name, according to Brett, was Camila Ramos. The daughter of Angel Ramos. The girl Reznick was looking for. A girl who had been recommended by Carlos Lopez after she'd been working in one of his sleazy clubs.

"Are you still there?"

Levinson pinched the bridge of his nose, feeling a migraine coming on. "I'm still here."

"I thought you'd want to know. What do you want me to do?"

"Nothing right now. I'll be in touch."

Levinson ended the call. His client was in deep shit if this got out. His career would be over. But that wasn't the only matter. What if this special forces guy, Reznick, tracked down Brett Miller, taking the law into his own hands? He feared for Brett's life if that came to pass.

He sat at his desk, fretting. He messaged his wife and said he'd be home for breakfast.

Levinson waited for a couple of hours, until his personal assistant began her day. He heard her moving around. He buzzed her phone. "Clear my diary for today, Jean," he said.

"Business breakfast?"

"Meeting a new client," he lied.

"You need a vacation, Jerry."

"Tell me about it."

Levinson headed down to the underground garage, got in his car, and drove up to Brett Miller's home in Beverly Hills. Dawn was breaking, and a gorgeous candy-cotton pink sky heralded the new day.

The butler showed him through to the pool area again. No girl this time.

Brett Miller was doing some laps. He stopped and looked up, smiling at his lawyer. "Hey, Jerry, how goes it?"

"I need to talk."

"At this hour? I'm getting in shape. I'm getting my shit together." Brett climbed out of the pool and toweled himself dry before flopping down into a sun lounger. "So, what gives?"

"I just got word that a guy called Jon Reznick, the guy that's snooping around Carlos Lopez, his nightclubs and his strip clubs, has put three of Lopez's guys in hospital. Police are investigating."

"What's your point?"

Levinson shook his head. He didn't want Miller to know that it was his lawyer who had contracted Jay Johnson to instruct Lopez to beat the shit out of Reznick. But he thought it important that Miller knew Reznick was encroaching on his territory. "I wanted you to know."

"You said you thought the Feds were going to run him out of town. Didn't you say that?"

"I did. But I guess that's easier said than done."

"Am I missing something, Jerry? First there was Angel Ramos, a homeless bum who was outside my home, outside my art dealer's gallery, prying into my fucking life. And now we've got this whack job? A friend of his, right? Gimme a break."

Levinson pulled up a seat beside Miller. "Reznick was Angel Ramos's friend, that's true. They were both in Delta Force. He's a badass. So you need to understand what I'm telling you."

"And this guy is still hanging around town? Why can't the Feds deal with it?"

"The FBI issued a warning for him to leave. He didn't."

"So what now? Do I just have to wait until this fuck strangles me one night?"

Levinson shook his head. "Forget about Reznick for now. Tell me, the naked girl that was in your pool the last time I was here, you remember her?"

"Cute, wasn't she?"

"She was underage, right? And her real name was Camila Ramos, right? That's what you said."

"Right."

"So that girl you were fucking was Angel Ramos's daughter. His friend is hanging around trying to find her. That's what I've been told."

"Why didn't anyone say? I didn't know."

"Well, now you do."

"Jerry, this guy Reznick, whoever the fuck he is . . . this is my fucking town. I have ruled this place for twenty fucking years. And I'm not going to allow some cunt to saunter into my world and tell me how to live my life. Okay?"

At that point, Levinson should have just ended their relationship. He had put his entire career in jeopardy for this pedophile. He stared at Brett, who continued to towel his tanned torso.

"You're killing me with this shit," Brett said.

Levinson wanted to pull the plug. He knew he needed to sever the relationship. But, after a few seconds of reflection, knowing how much money he made from Brett Miller, he decided instead to double down on efforts to protect Brett, come what may. "We need to be careful what we do going forward."

"Jerry, let me make it crystal clear to you. Do I have to get someone else to sort this shit out? Do you want me to fire your ass?"

"Brett, there's no need for that. Calm the fuck down. Take some Xanax and drink a glass of Scotch."

"No, I won't calm the fuck down. I don't want anything jeopardizing the films I'm lining up. Can't happen. I want you to sort it out."

"And how do you suggest I do that?"

"Reznick needs to be wiped off the face of the earth."

Levinson weighed up what his client was saying. He understood his meaning, but he needed to be sure.

"Did you hear me?"

"Yes, I did."

"So what are you going to do?"

"What do you want me to do, Brett?"

"I want him taken care of."

"What do you mean by that?"

"I mean, have someone make the guy have an accident. A bad fall. You know people, right? This guy Reznick, he doesn't know who the fuck he's dealing with. I want you to make sure he takes his last breath. Got it?"

"Leave it to me. We're going to put an end to this, once and for all."

Thirty-Five

The near-deserted streets of downtown Los Angeles flew past in a blur. Reznick accelerated hard along the roads, residential and office towers all around. He had been trying to lose the tail for the last five minutes, but with no luck.

He glanced in his rearview mirror, dazzled by headlights. A white van was tucked in tight behind him, twenty yards back. He had pulled a couple of U-turns. Accelerated away. But he still couldn't shake whoever was behind him.

"Who the fuck are you?"

Reznick glanced again in the mirror. The vehicle had been on his tail for a couple of miles. He'd wondered at first if it was the cops, a plainclothes team. Or maybe the Feds. But he sensed that this was nothing official. He had already received a formal warning from the FBI. The cops had pulled him in. He knew the Feds or the LAPD would just pull him over if they wanted.

He looked in the mirror again. The driver was wearing sunglasses and a baseball cap. The other guy, the passenger, was a burly guy, vaguely Hispanic—smoking, arm out the window.

Reznick wondered how he should play this. He figured these might be assassins sent to neutralize him. The beating he had inflicted on the three thugs would have escalated things with Lopez.

He contemplated calling 911 to get the tail to pull away. But he knew the cops would take a few minutes to reach him, if they managed it at all.

Think, goddamn it, think.

A neon sign for a multilevel parking garage on South Figueroa Street up ahead gave him an idea. He turned abruptly into the garage and accelerated hard up the ramp. He reached level five and pulled into a tight space between a pickup truck and an SUV. He switched off his lights and engine.

Reznick opened his door and crouched low as he knelt beside his vehicle, quietly closing the door behind him. He took out his gun and crawled under the adjacent vehicle, ensuring a line of sight to the ramp and the stairwell. He pulled back the slide of his Beretta and flicked off the safety. Then he waited.

He sensed they would follow him in. He lay prone, the heat from the underside of the car warming him. The acrid smell of oil and gasoline filled his nostrils.

Reznick's senses were switched on. He was back in the zone. His body needed to be ready. Sharp. He felt the heavy vibrations as the van approached. A kill switch turned on inside him. His awareness of everything around him was heightened. Every sound. Every movement. Every shadow.

He watched and waited as the white cargo van thundered up the ramp, turning left. A tattooed arm still hung lazily out of the passenger window. He caught a glimpse of the man's features. Short, slick, dark hair, a bull neck, black eyes scanning the parking garage, gang tattoos inked on his neck and forehead.

He felt himself zoning out. He was starting to compartmentalize. He held the gun tight. Not long now. Just the waiting. And then contact.

The van screeched to a halt, the engine still running. The tattooed passenger wound down his window in full. He began to whistle as his hooded eyes looked around the parking garage. The guy finally zeroed in on Reznick's vehicle. He leaned out of the window with an Uzi submachine gun dangling from his hand. The man raked Reznick's car with gunfire, bullets ricocheting as the glass shattered, piercing the metal above him.

Reznick blocked out the deafening noise of gunfire and the car alarms blaring. The acrid smoke bathed the concrete catacomb. He scrunched up his eyes, waiting for the smoke to clear.

The tattooed thug stepped out of the van, his Uzi raised. He walked toward the car in a crouch.

Reznick needed to time this right. He lay perfectly still as his heart raced, thumping in his chest. The legs of the man's tight jeans were all he could see. He held his breath. When the man was at the right distance, Reznick fired off two shots at his right knee. The guy collapsed, screaming, blood pooling onto the concrete. The gunfire was deafening. Reznick's ears rang from the shots echoing around the building.

Reznick had a clear shot of the man's face. The guy who had looked so sure of himself with a cigarette or an Uzi now stared, eyes wide, as he lay writhing, moaning, and crying on the ground. Reznick fired off two more shots at his forehead. Bloody holes. The fucker was dead.

He crawled under the next car for protection as the driver of the van stepped out, his own Uzi in hand.

A female security guard emerged from the stairwell.

The driver reached over and seized the woman by the throat, gun to her head. He looked around, calling, "Hey, white boy, wherever you are, what are you going to do now, huh?" The guy laughed, fury in his face as the woman began to shake and cry. He slapped her before he grabbed her neck again, tight. "Come out, white boy! Let's deal with this, man to man." The guy fired off three shots at Reznick's front fender. One of the bullets ricocheted, hitting the concrete wall behind where Reznick lay.

Reznick realized the man didn't know he was under an adjacent car. The guy fired off more shots. Bullets ricocheted off the walls and support pillars. Reznick spread himself as flat as he could, gun aimed at the man's head. He needed to get this right. He had one chance.

The woman screamed as the guy pulled her closer, his face against hers. "Come out, white boy, or she gets her pretty head blown to shit. You understand?"

Reznick lay motionless as the woman struggled. He wanted a clean shot.

"You want to fuck with me? Because if you—"

Reznick fired once. The bullet drilled into the man's forehead, blood spilling out of the wound, as the guy collapsed on the concrete. The woman screamed, brains and blood splattered all over her face and hair.

Reznick crawled out from underneath the car and walked toward the woman. He yelled at her, "Get out of here!"

"Don't kill me!" she screamed, cowering, on her knees.

Reznick pointed to the stairwell. "Get out of here!"

The woman got up and ran away—terrified, hysterical.

When she was out of sight, Reznick approached the bloody body of the driver first. His eyes were open, blood oozing from his mouth, head, and nose.

The guy was still breathing, bubbles of blood coming from the corners of his mouth.

Reznick bent over him. He fired one shot into the man's right eye. The gunshot tore a massive hole, blood spurting out of the gaping, terrible wound. The sound from his handgun rang around the parking garage.

In the distance was the sound of yelling and sirens. The woman had collapsed behind a car at the far end of the parking garage, screaming uncontrollably.

A couple of cops emerged from the stairwell, guns drawn. "Drop the weapon now!"

Reznick complied.

"Get on your knees, hands on your head!"

Reznick did as he was told, getting one last look at the two dead men.

Thirty-Six

The hours dragged as Reznick sat alone in an interrogation room in an LA police station. An air-conditioning unit on the wall growled in the background. In his mind's eye he relived and relived each man's last bloody seconds.

Reznick had been taken in to Central Division on Skid Row. The precinct was responsible for downtown Los Angeles. He'd been photographed, fingerprinted, and forensic swabs were taken from his gun, hands, and mouth. His clothes had been carefully bagged and he'd been marched into the interview room. He'd been sat down, handcuffed, and left alone with his thoughts. He had crossed a line. But he'd had no options. It had been self-defense.

A uniformed cop eventually came in with a tray. A Styrofoam cup of coffee and a sandwich. "Is there anything else you need?"

"I need to make a call."

"My colleagues will talk to you about that soon."

The cop left, locking the door behind her.

Reznick felt famished. He ate the ham sandwich on rye first and then drank the scalding coffee, burning the back of his throat. Still, it felt good to get sustenance. He looked up at the clock on the wall. It was six thirty in the morning. He had lost all track of time. Days had bled into weeks.

It was another hour before the door was unlocked.

A couple of detectives walked in, sitting down opposite him.

"LAPD Central Division Homicide, Detective Cody Cazalez." The mustachioed cop introduced himself. "This is my colleague, Detective James Francini. Quite a night you're having."

Reznick nodded. "Do you mind taking these cuffs off?"

"You're not going to go crazy on us, are you, Jon?" Cazalez asked.

Reznick shook his head.

Francini walked around the table and took out a set of keys, unlocking the steel handcuffs. He placed them on the table. "You okay?"

Reznick nodded.

Cazalez leaned back in his seat. "We're not going to be recording this. We're not videotaping this. Just so you know."

Reznick wondered why protocol was not being followed.

Cazalez smiled. "You're probably wondering why, right?"

He shrugged. "It had entered my head."

"It's your lucky day. You got anything to say?"

Reznick sat in silence.

"You're free to go. Your attorney is waiting for you in the next room."

"My attorney?"

"Straight up, man. You're free."

Reznick was not easily shocked, but he was more than slightly taken aback that he had been freed within hours of gunning down the two thugs. He walked out of the interview room, through the door, and into the adjacent room.

Waiting for him was a blonde woman wearing an impeccably cut black suit. She shook his hand. "Nice to meet you, Jon. Samantha Isaac. I'm your attorney."

Reznick felt as if the whole thing was a big setup. "Is that right?"

"Before we go any further, I just want to acknowledge that I know exactly what you're thinking."

"And what's that?"

"You're thinking when did I become your attorney? You didn't appoint me, right?"

"I guess so."

"I'll explain everything. Let's get out of here first."

Reznick wasn't arguing with that. He followed his lawyer out to the parking lot. She pulled out her keys and opened a midnight-blue BMW.

"Hop in," she said.

Reznick waited until she'd gotten behind the wheel before he climbed in.

She said gently, "Don't be nervous."

"Why should I be nervous?"

"No reason at all."

The lawyer edged toward the electronic gates of the police station. The steel gates opened slowly. She drove out of the station, past the neighborhood's homeless tent city.

"Seen better days, huh?" he said.

"Yeah, ain't that the truth." The lawyer accelerated onto the I-10, before veering over to South Robertson Boulevard. Then north into the Hollywood Hills, and on past manicured neighborhoods, finally reaching Beverly Hills.

She turned into an underground parking garage. She got out of the car and he followed her to the elevator.

Reznick wondered if this was where her office was. "Do you do this for all your clients?"

"This is a first."

The elevator dropped them at the eleventh floor.

Reznick followed her down a corridor until they reached a black steel door. She pressed her palm against a biometric scanner and the door clicked open.

"Interesting level of security you have here," he remarked.

The lawyer didn't answer. He followed her through an empty open-plan space until they got to a back office.

A man in a navy suit sat behind a desk, staring out of the window at some killer views across the city. "Pull up a seat, Jon," he instructed without looking around.

Reznick sat down, his new lawyer at his side. She smiled at Reznick. "How you feeling? You need any medical treatment?"

"No, I'm good. Thanks."

The man faced Reznick. "Quite a night you had, Jon. You pack a lot in, that's for sure."

Reznick said nothing.

"You're probably trying to figure out who I am."

"I'm trying to figure out when you're going to get to the fucking point."

The man smiled. "They said you'd be like this. I don't mind abrasive. I was expecting it. The file. It mentioned your abrasiveness."

Reznick shifted in his seat.

"Jon, I'm going to answer your questions the best I can," the man said. "Some things I can't answer. But I'll try and keep things on the level."

"I appreciate that."

"My name is Daniel Black. I work for the United States government."

"What agency?"

Black smiled. "Very perceptive, Jon. Would it surprise you if I said I worked for the CIA?"

"Probably not."

"I'm a liaison man. I liaise with other agencies."

Reznick turned and looked at his lawyer. "Do you want to jump in here? You want to explain who appointed you as my lawyer?"

Black intervened. "I did."

Reznick studied the tired, hangdog features on Black's face. "You work for the CIA? And you appointed Samantha Isaac as my attorney? Do I have that right?"

Black nodded. "So far, so good."

"Do you mind explaining—first of all—why I was released by the LAPD? It's very irregular."

Isaac smiled. "It is irregular, I agree."

"Why are both of you involved in this particular case? It strikes me as more than unusual that an attorney and a CIA operative are concerned with what appears to be a simple LAPD matter."

"Nothing is ever simple in LA, Jon," his lawyer intoned.

"Talk to me about jurisdiction."

"We'll get to jurisdiction. First, the reason you were out of there so quick is that we represented you."

Reznick leaned back in his seat, arms folded. "That's not how it works. I gunned down two dudes in a parking garage. I should be in a six-by-four."

"I don't agree. The reason? Self-defense, Jon. That's what it was."

"And the LAPD bought it, and that was that? Just go on your way and all that?"

"Pretty much."

Reznick stared across the table at Black, who was checking his cuticles as if bored. "I'm not buying it."

Isaac smiled. "It is an unusual set of circumstances. But you were faced in the parking garage with a simple matter of self-defense. You would have lost your life. I fast-tracked your case."

Reznick chortled. "Fast-tracked? You must be very persuasive to have gotten me released so quickly."

The lawyer shrugged before exchanging a knowing look with Black, who crossed his arms, seemingly not willing to engage.

"So let me get this straight," Reznick went on. "The use of deadly force is okay as I was in danger of losing my life?"

"There was also the small matter of the woman who was held hostage."

"I think it would be pretty standard operating procedure to call what I did an unlawful killing. That would be the reason behind the charge. Ordinarily I would have faced trial, right?"

Isaac gave it some thought. "Depends on how good the lawyer is. Under the law, there is a thing called affirmative defense. It basically voids a defendant's criminal activity. Self-defense is just one example of an affirmative defense."

Reznick wondered if he really would have been released, even with Samantha's help, after being grilled by the LAPD for several hours, or even a few days. "But I wouldn't have been released without the cops asking me one single question, would I?"

"On that point, you are absolutely correct. This is an unusual case. And we spoke to the Chief of the LAPD and their lawyers, and explained some deep background which they were unaware of."

"Some *deep background*?"

"You've had an interesting career, Jon. The LAPD knew some of it. But they were unaware of your past links to the CIA."

Reznick sat and waited for Black to elaborate.

"As is your daughter. She is also unaware of your past with the Agency."

"What does she have to do with any of this?"

"Just as an exercise, try and imagine if prosecutors learned that your daughter worked for the CIA. The ramifications in the media would be huge."

"What else?"

"Your background involves sensitive areas of national security. You used to work on a case-by-case basis with the FBI, under former Assistant Director Meyerstein, did you not?"

"I did."

"So, with all these factors in play, I don't think, and I'm speaking as your lawyer here, that it would be in the interests of American national security if this all came out at trial. It would get messy."

"Who contacted you?"

Black nodded at Isaac as he chimed in. "Trevelle Williams. He was apparently watching the whole thing at the parking garage play out in real time. And he reached out to me."

"How does he know you?"

"I know a lot of people." Black pointed at Reznick. "There's something else."

"There is?"

"The Agency doesn't have any involvement on American soil. Foreign intelligence service only, right?"

"Go on."

"But occasionally, there is a coming-together. An FBI investigation which overlaps with ours, and vice versa."

"Cross-border?"

Black clapped his hands once. "I knew you would get it immediately. We're still doing some checking, but those two guys you took down?"

Reznick nodded.

"Mexican cartel assassins. Two of their top guys."

Reznick could see the background to the story beginning to make sense. "On the orders of Carlos Lopez?"

Black's eyes became hooded. He sat in silence.

"I'm assuming the drug cartel angle is pertinent to the nature of the CIA's interest?"

Black glanced at the lawyer, who stayed poker-faced.

"Am I missing something here?"

"There's more to this than just Mexican drug cartels. There are other elements, shall we say, at play."

"Elements at play? Elements that played a part in the death of my friend Angel Ramos?"

"Perhaps."

"I'd like an explanation."

"Angel, from what I know, was turning up at doors in Hollywood. The doors of powerful people in the city. Wealthy people. His daughter was an escort," said Black.

"Getting back to your situation, Jon," Isaac interjected. "The surveillance footage from the parking garage of the killings?"

Reznick nodded.

"That has been secured by the CIA."

Black leaned back in his seat. "It's like it didn't happen. Nice work by the way, neutralizing the cartel thugs in the parking garage. But to let you into a little secret, Jon, the instant Angel Ramos was killed, we were expecting you to show up in LA."

The revelation crashed through Reznick's mind like a concrete block. "You've been expecting me?"

"We don't operate on US soil, Jon. You know that."

"I understand. So when did you guys get involved?"

"We spoke to the Feds and, once you touched down at LAX, they let me know. That's when we knew things were going to happen."

"You've been watching me the whole time?"

"I was the point man, Jon, here in Los Angeles. I've been liaising with the Feds, Homeland Security, Immigration, LAPD, all in regards to cartel operatives. We believe Lopez is a senior cartel associate in the city. So I knew we'd have our hands full."

"The FBI hauled me in. Said they had a duty to warn me that folks wanted to kill me."

"And they were right."

"I'm assuming you're going to advise me to get out of town?"

Black held out his hands like he was finishing a magic trick. "We aren't involved, Jon. We don't exist in America."

"Except you do."

Black arched his eyebrows in a sly, noncommittal way. "Do you mind me asking you a question?"

"Sure."

"Is your work done in the city?"

Reznick remained silent.

The lawyer continued, "Jon, we took the liberty of booking you into an apartment—a safe house, some might call it—and have transferred your case and all your clothes, et cetera, to that address. In West Hollywood. We hope you don't mind. That's if you want to stay in the city."

Reznick contemplated the incredible series of events.

"Talk to me, Jon. What's on your mind?" Black inquired.

Reznick smiled as it slowly dawned on him.

"Talk to me," Black said again.

"I'm guessing there are two reasons why you got me off the hook. First, if this went to court, the media would have a field day. Lots of questions. How were these cartel assassins in the city of Los Angeles? And it could all lead to Carlos Lopez further down the line. But that would be problematic for the American government, who actually trained him."

Black sat in silence, his face like stone.

"Second, the reason you want me off the hook is you want me to neutralize Lopez, right? That would put an end to the investigation. Or am I missing something?"

"Do you want me to level with you?" asked Black.

"Please."

"You're right on both counts. Right on the money. Now, we would never, ever admit to what you're saying. You understand the rules of the game, Jon. You know how it works, right?"

Reznick turned to Isaac. "What are you saying?"

"As your lawyer, I'm duty-bound to look out for your best interests. I would strongly advise you to head back home. You might not be so lucky next time."

"You've got a choice, Jon," said Black. "Choose wisely."

"I'm guessing the cartel guys aren't going to take this lying down?"

Black shook his head. "I'd think long and hard about your next move. You need to be very careful, my friend. These people don't play by the rules."

"Neither do I."

Thirty-Seven

The safe house was an apartment on the eleventh floor of a glass building in Shoreham Drive in West Hollywood. Reznick was dropped off by Samantha Isaac and given a key.

He unlocked the door and went inside. Then he carefully locked the door behind him and switched on the lights.

Reznick had a quick look around. His clothes had been carefully hung up or folded neatly in drawers. A handwritten note said, *Be good*. He wondered if this was Black's idea of a joke or a lame attempt at humor. He wanted to crash out. With all the Dexedrine and lack of sleep, he wasn't thinking straight. Dozens of crazy images ran through his brain—images of killing the cartel assassin who'd been holding a gun to the woman's head. Slow-motion, frame by frame. He paced the room, trying to figure it all out. Then he sat down and stared at the walls. He wasn't twenty anymore, able to stay awake for long periods at a time. He felt wiped out by it all.

The late-morning sun cut through the slats in the blinds.

Reznick pulled the curtains shut, nearly blacking out the room. He took off his clothes and flopped onto the bed, not knowing or caring if he would ever wake up again. His eyes felt heavy. Then they closed as he began to dream the same dreams of the past, the unending loop of recurrent nightmares.

The sound of banging at his door snapped him out of his dreams and back to the apartment.

Reznick came to in darkness. The only sound he heard was the low hum of the air-conditioning. He reached for his gun, pointing it to the ground as he approached the door. He looked through the peephole. It was a young woman with towels. He opened the door.

"Sorry, sir, I believe no one left towels for you in your apartment. There you go."

Reznick took the pile and took out his wallet, handing her a twenty-dollar bill. "Many thanks."

"We thought you might want to use the rooftop pool. Hence the towels."

"Rooftop pool?" The CIA, or whoever was footing the bill, didn't skimp.

"Yes, sir. Enjoy your stay."

Reznick shut and locked the door, putting the towels on the bathroom shelf. He checked his watch. It was 9:30 p.m. He had been asleep for nearly ten hours. He took a pair of swim shorts out of his suitcase and headed up to the rooftop pool. He surveyed the empty sun loungers and the views of the city below. It was a pretty, upscale apartment complex they'd put him in. Was this where they put assets on the run? Informants? Either way, it was a cool place to kick back.

The pool was empty. Perfect. The water rippled in the night breeze. He took off his robe, kicked off his slides, and dove into the pool.

The water was cold, taking his breath away. He swam and swam.

Reznick counted off fifty laps. Up and down. Powering through the water. He felt alert. Switched on, endorphins racing through his body. Afterward, he dried himself off and lay back on a lounger, allowing the warm night air to dry him. He closed his eyes.

His mind flashed back again to the parking garage ambush. They had walked into the trap he had laid. A double killing, buried deep inside his other dark memories. It joined a litany of other assassinations. The darkest corners of his mind stored what he had done. He had learned to switch off the replay. He had to. If he didn't, he would go insane at the death and destruction he had wrought. Overwhelmed by it all.

Reznick seemed to have a capacity to just let it go. It was the way he was wired. Something in his psychological makeup. Most likely he was just damaged, and he didn't know it. Wasn't that closer to the truth?

He pushed those thoughts and the corresponding images to the side.

Reznick got up from the lounger and walked over to the edge of the roof. He appreciated the lights of West Hollywood spreading up into the hills. Police sirens blared. And in the night sky, he saw the lights of planes coming in to land at LAX.

He thought of Angel's daughter out there, selling her body and her soul for drugs. The specter of the CIA reaching out to him had thrown him a lifeline. The Agency was clearly aware of the connection between members of the Mexican drug cartels and operations in Los Angeles. But Daniel Black had talked of "other elements" involved in the death of Angel Ramos.

Reznick was intrigued. He wanted to know more. But he knew he was being played. Black had admitted that they had kept him free, out on the streets, expecting Reznick could track down and neutralize Carlos Lopez. It was classic double dealing. He knew the game.

The more he thought through the chain of events, from the first steps he had taken after he'd gotten the call from the LAPD saying a body had been found, the more he wondered what the hell he had got himself into. It was bad enough that he had pissed off the Mexican cartels. They didn't fuck around. If they found him, they would chop him up. If he was lucky, it would be quick. But odds were, knowing what they had done to Angel, for him they would gleefully bring out their bag of tricks. Classic terror tactics.

He considered his next move. He had to think not only of Camila's life, but the impact on Lauren if this investigation of his continued. What if he was neutralized in the same manner Angel had been? She would be devastated. She'd have lost her dad. He still viewed himself as her protector despite Lauren being a grown woman and on the other side of the world. She might be a CIA overseas agent. But she was still his little girl. She always would be.

Black had him thinking that he had only scratched the surface. It was clear there were other aspects to the case that he wasn't aware of. Was Lopez only one part of a complicated picture? Reznick vowed to stay till the bitter end and find out. No matter what happened.

It was the only way he knew.

Thirty-Eight

It was nearly midnight when Reznick watched the NBC news report of the shooting in a parking garage.

"Police sources are saying that it is almost certainly a fallout between rival drug gangs in Los Angeles."

Reznick could see that the fix was in. The coverup of the true nature of the events was underway. It was how awkward problems got handled. But it had a semblance of truth to it. A couple of drug cartel gangbangers had been gunned down in a parking garage. That part was true. But the false part of the equation made Reznick wonder if the LAPD had been leaned on to be economical with the truth. Who benefited from the false narrative? Reznick did, of course. But so did the CIA, whose fingerprints were all over this. Daniel Black deploying the dark arts of media manipulation. A quiet word here, a misdirection there.

The reporter continued: "Critically, police sources say that there was no footage from inside the parking garage due to what is being described as 'technical issues.' But they reassured residents who live nearby that there will be extra patrols operating in the neighborhood, and the community should be reassured that this is an isolated incident."

Reznick's cell phone rang and he answered.

"Jon, can't believe you're still in town," said Trevelle Williams.

Reznick smiled. It was nice to hear his friend's voice. "I believe I owe you one."

"Why?"

"Getting me a lawyer. A great lawyer. Putting in the call."

"Forget it. So, what gives?"

"What gives? I'm still here in crazy Hollywood. I'm starting to wonder if I'm going a little crazy myself, being in this city."

"Got to be honest, Jon. I thought after the parking garage killing you would have hopped on the first plane out of there."

"I'm not going anywhere," Reznick said. "Let me ask you something. Any progress on getting a fix on that Brett Miller guy? Or Camila?"

"Thought you might ask that. And that's why I'm calling. You heard of Sloane's in West Hollywood?"

"What the hell is that?"

"A private members' club. Thirty-five thousand dollars a year for membership, and you have to be nominated by two current members. And the initiation fee is three hundred thousand dollars."

"Who's there?"

"As of right now, Brett Miller. One of those places where Angel Ramos turned up at their door previously. If you open your iPhone, you'll notice I've added an app for Sloane's."

"You signed me up?"

"Precisely. I accessed their membership records. Created a new member by the name of James Adler."

"I'm supposed to be James Adler? And that'll work?"

"I guarantee it. And you won't have to kick down any doors."

Reznick stared at the TV, which was showing police patrolling the parking garage where he had gunned down the two men the previous night. "It's nearby?"

"A mile. Get an Uber. How does that sound?"

Reznick contemplated his plan for heading into the private members' club. It was no use just turning up to confront Brett Miller. He didn't even know if Angel's daughter was still with him. When he'd seen Miller at the nightclub he'd been with a blonde, and Camila had been nowhere in sight. He might no longer be using her.

Reznick needed to play this smart. What was his end goal? It was twofold. He wanted to find Angel's killer. But he also wanted to find Camila Ramos, if she was still in the city, and get her to a place of safety. Nothing more, nothing less. The opportunity to get up close to Miller could be useful. But only if Camila was there.

Miller might not even be there by the time Reznick turned up. But he figured it was worth a shot. Besides, what did he have to lose? "Does this club have a dress code I need to know about?"

"No tracksuits. No beachwear."

"Leather jacket get me in?"

"As long as you're not decked out in beachwear, anything goes. It's a place for creatives, hence why Brett Miller and his ilk are members. Networking, schmoozing, out of the public eye."

Reznick sounded skeptical. "And this app will work?"

"I promise, I've set it up. James Adler. You're on the list."

Half an hour later, after freshening up and catching an Uber to the club, he walked into a marble lobby adorned with modern art.

Reznick strolled casually up to a security guy, who pointed to a digital card reader. He opened the club's app and pressed it to the reader. It pinged, lighting up with a large green tick.

"Very good, Mr. Adler, nice to see you this evening. Enjoy your night."

"Thanks," Reznick replied. A hostess materialized from a door off the lobby. She introduced herself and escorted him into the elevator. It headed toward the rooftop bar and restaurant.

Reznick stepped out and into a mix of people. The chatter and hubbub of eighty or so men and women, some smartly dressed, some casual, some gray-haired, some young model types. A jazz band was playing some cool, late-night, John Coltrane-style jazz.

He saw a good spot and sat down, admiring the phenomenal views of the Hollywood Hills through the wall of windows.

Another hostess approached, smiling. "What can I get you from the bar, Mr. Adler?"

"Single malt with ice and a beer chaser. How does that sound?" Reznick handed her a hundred-dollar cash tip. "Get yourself a drink, too."

The hostess blushed as she took the money. "I haven't seen you in here before, Mr. Adler."

"Recently joined."

"Well, you enjoy your evening, sir. I'll go and get your drinks."

Reznick watched as she headed to the bar. His eyes wandered around the palatial surroundings, taking in the Japanese-inspired prints and paintings on the wall, the wide velvet sofas, bespoke chairs, and fancy marble tables, all lit by huge lamps putting out as little light as possible. It all created an affluent and relaxed European vibe. It was impossible to ignore the expensive watches, glinting under the soft lights, or the diamond-encrusted rings. The smell was mostly expensive perfume cut with even more expensive liquor. Sharply cut suits, no ties, except those worn by the servers. A chill, urbane, city vibe. A few of the men wore T-shirts and nice jeans.

He looked out onto the terrace. He saw a gray-haired man with a deep tan sitting out there. The man was smoking a cigar with one hand, and with the other he was stroking the hair of a very young woman. Reznick couldn't know for certain, but she looked like a teenager.

The man looked to be in his seventies, with stunning white teeth. He wore a pale blue button-down shirt and a chunky watch. The girl sipped a pink cocktail, playing with the little umbrella in her glass. The age gap was striking, even by Hollywood standards.

Reznick took out his cell phone and called Trevelle.

"What can I do for you, man?"

"Rooftop bar of Sloane's, on the terrace outside, there's a couple. Looks like Brett. The girl with him is very, very young. Hispanic, as far as I can tell. I might be wrong. Can you run some face recognition on who that guy is?"

"I'll get on it. It might take a few minutes to get into the system."

"Get on it now. I want to know who this guy is. And more importantly, who the girl is who's with him."

Thirty-Nine

Carlos Lopez paced the back office of one of his clubs in East Los Angeles, seething. He looked at his team, who bowed their heads, slightly sheepish, as if they knew what was coming. He picked up a bottle of whiskey from his desk and threw it against the wall. The glass smashed and liquor dripped down, mixing with the broken glass all over the wooden floor. "Explain to me," he said, pointing at his deputy, Rico, "what happened last night?"

"Boss, listen—"

"Shut the fuck up! I don't want to hear *listen*. Tell me what happened."

"Our two guys—cool guys from Tijuana, we all know them—were tailing Reznick. They're solid operators. Real smart."

"Smart? Are you fucking kidding me, Rico?"

"They followed him into the parking garage. They had him cornered. They drove up to where he parked. But they were lured into a trap. The Reznick dude, he took them out. Both of them."

Lopez grabbed Rico by the throat. "You dumb fuck. We got played."

"I know, boss."

He loosened his grip and shook his head. "I'm sorry, my friend. I know it's not your fault. So what exactly went down?"

"We believe Reznick got out of his car and crawled under the car next to him. When Reznick's car got shot up, our guys assumed he would be hiding inside. But this dude, he's smart. He got Santiago and then his brother, Vicente. The guy did them cold. Brutal, man."

Lopez sighed. "Who was instructing Santiago and Vicente? Who was giving the orders last night?"

"I was."

Lopez took a gun out of his waistband and pressed it to Rico's temple. "What do you think I should do?"

"Boss, please! I swear to God, this guy Reznick . . . this is no ordinary cop or Fed. No cop could've done that. This guy is a bad motherfucker. Boss, I'll fix this."

Lopez turned and looked around at the rest of his men. "Rico says he's going to fix it." Blank faces from the rest of his crew, no one wanting to show any emotion. No one rushing to Rico's defense. "Got quiet all of a sudden, guys. You going to let this fucking gabacho get away with this? No fucking way." He turned and faced Rico. "It looks like this gabacho is smarter than us. What do you think? You think this can be allowed to happen? How do you think that makes me feel?"

Rico shook his head.

"Does that make me a dumb jefe? Does that make me look weak?"

"Boss, I swear, I want to make this right. I'm begging you."

Lopez sat back down. "I want this dealt with."

"How do you want me to deal with it?"

"I want you to find this fucker."

"Do you want us to kill him?"

Lopez sighed and began to smile. "Oh no, the gringo? You bring him to me. I will tell you where I want you to bring him.

And we're going to go to town on him. He's going to get the special treatment."

Rico nodded nervously. "I understand."

"You bring him to me. He is going to suffer like he's never suffered before."

Forty

Reznick was on his third single malt, surreptitiously watching the old man and the girl on the balcony. They were still drinking glasses of champagne, laughing, joking.

His cell phone vibrated in his pocket.

Reznick took out his phone. "I'm listening."

"Jon, we've got a match. The girl is Camila Ramos. She's still calling herself Gigi Cortez. She was signed in under that name. But that's her. The health records I have show that she's only sixteen."

Reznick felt his blood turn cold. "Sick bastard. And the old man? It's definitely him?"

"One thousand percent Brett fucking Miller, Hollywood director."

Reznick ended the call and slipped the phone into his jacket pocket. He sipped his single malt as he wondered how he should deal with this. A germ of an idea was beginning to form in his mind. He could see how it might unfold.

The girl stood up and headed toward the bathroom, carrying her bag. Miller was alone on the terrace, cigar in hand. Reznick waited until the girl had disappeared. Then he picked up his glass and walked out to the terrace, sitting down opposite the mahogany-skinned old man.

Miller was smoking his cigar, drinking a brandy.

"Big fan of your work, Brett."

Miller looked bemused and shrugged. "Do I know you, man?"

Reznick put his glass down on the table and leaned closer. "So, here's the thing, Brett. A friend of mine—"

"I'm sorry, who the fuck are you?"

Reznick smiled, his gaze fixed on Miller. "I should have made it clearer. I want to tell you about a friend of mine. He was a veteran. And he was found tortured and killed. He had been looking for his daughter."

"What are you talking about? You've got the wrong person, pal."

Reznick shook his head. "I don't think so. You see, the girl you're drinking with, she goes by the name Gigi Cortez. But her real name is Camila Ramos. That's my dead friend's daughter."

"What the fuck are you bothering me for?"

"I'm assuming you've promised her the earth and a part in your films. Is that the deal?"

Miller puffed on his cigar and laughed, exposing his pearly white veneers. "I don't know who you are. I'm assuming you're high. Is this a prank or something? Do you want me to call security?"

"By all means, be my guest. Just so we're clear, a friend of mine, a cybersecurity expert, is watching everything in this club in real time. He's watching us as we speak. He has the footage of you with the girl. And just so you know, she's sixteen. I checked."

Miller's tanned skin seemed to flush a dark crimson as he sipped his drink, his eyes now darting around the terrace. "I don't know what the hell you're talking about. I talk to a lot of people. That's my line of work."

"I have no doubt that you did not kill my friend. The friend that was tortured and killed down in Venice Beach. You been down there recently?"

"Man, I have not one fucking clue what you're talking about. Are you strung-out or something?"

Reznick laughed softly. "Do I look strung-out to you, Brett?"

"What do you want? Do you want money? Is this what this is about? Is this a shakedown?"

"Brett, here's what is going to happen. Right here and right now. The girl is a child. I'll reiterate, in case you're not following. She is my friend's daughter. I will be escorting her to safety when she returns from the washroom."

"She is not a child. She told me she was twenty-two. Who the hell do you think I am?"

"Do you want my friend to send the media the still photos or a video of your little dalliance with a child this evening? TMZ would have a field day. Dining with a sixteen-year-old hooker who works at strip clubs? Do you really want to go there? Do you see the optics?"

"Are you blackmailing me?"

"You don't seem to understand the situation, Brett. You have a choice. It's time to make the choice. You can call security and make things difficult for yourself. But I can guarantee that will end badly for you."

Brett stared into his drink, not looking so cocky now.

"Second option, you walk away, and we're good."

"Who are you?"

"My name is Jon Reznick."

The color appeared to completely drain from Miller's dark tan.

"I suspect you know my name. You been getting your heavies to do your dirty work, Brett?"

Miller finished his brandy, knocking it back in one. "You don't know who you're dealing with, pal. This is my town."

Reznick leaned forward, through the fug of cigar smoke from Miller's breath and his expensive cologne. "I don't give a fuck about your town. And I sure as hell don't give a fuck about you. You need to leave. Now. Get the fuck out of my sight!"

Miller slowly got to his feet, stubbed out his cigar, and ambled away. "You haven't heard the last of this."

"Fuck off."

Miller huffed off and headed toward the elevators. He stepped inside the elevator and the doors closed.

Reznick finished his Scotch and checked his watch. It was 11:11 p.m. He waited for the girl to return. She had been gone for nearly six minutes. He wondered if she had slipped out and disappeared. But eventually, he caught a glimpse of her inside the bar, checking her phone as she walked out onto the terrace.

He looked up at her and smiled. "Take a seat."

The girl's eyes were glazed, as if she had been doing coke in the bathroom. She shrugged. "Where's Brett?"

"Sit down. I'll explain."

"Are you a friend of Brett's?"

"No. I was a friend of your father's. Camila, isn't it?"

The girl sat down, sniffed, fidgeting with her fingers. "I don't use that name. Everybody knows me as Gigi."

"I know." Reznick studied her closely. Her brown eyes were bloodshot, with dark shadows underneath despite the heavy makeup. She wore bright red lipstick like a costume. "I'm here to help."

"Help? Who the fuck are you?"

"I knew your father."

The girl's eyes began to well with tears.

"Your father was Angel Ramos. I was a colleague of his."

"So where is he?"

"I'm sorry . . . but your father is dead."

The girl stared at him. Then she took a cigarette from her purse and lit up, blowing smoke out toward the city. "Bullshit."

Reznick shook his head. "I made sure he had a proper funeral. I served alongside your father."

"How do I know you're telling the truth?"

"You can call the LAPD if you want. I've spoken to them and the Feds."

"You say you served with my father. You were in Delta Force?"

"I was. Your father, God rest his soul, was one of the bravest men I ever knew."

The girl just stared at him. "Why didn't I know my father was dead?"

"I can't answer that. I guess you lost touch. You drifted away, right? It happens."

The girl dragged hard on her cigarette. "Shit, I had no idea."

"I'm sorry to be the bearer of bad news."

The girl looked around. "I can't see Brett."

"He's gone. Forget him."

"What?"

"I said he's out of here. Tell me about your father. I heard he'd fallen on hard times. Real hard times."

"He was a complete mess. And that was more than a year ago. That was the last time I saw him. I tried to help him. But I knew I couldn't. So I tried to save myself, if that makes sense."

"I understand."

"Where's Brett?" she asked again.

Reznick spoke slowly and forcefully. "Like I said, he won't be coming back. Trust me."

"Why?"

"I explained that you were underage. He seemed to get cold feet."

The girl flushed. "You've got no right to interfere in my affairs."

"I've got every right."

"Who are you, a cop?"

Reznick shook his head. "I know all about you, Camila. How you came to Los Angeles from Miami to try and find your father, and he was on a downward spiral. I know all that. And I know that you cared for him. Deeply. I know you tried to save him. But you got lost, being here in the city. To survive, you had to sell yourself. I'm not judging. I'm just telling you what I know."

The girl closed her eyes, tears spilling down her face.

Reznick took out a photo from his wallet. The photograph of the pair of them together. Reznick alongside the fearsome Angel Ramos in Fallujah. He handed it to her. "That's your dad in Iraq. With me. He was a brave man."

Camila took the photo, taking in the image. "Oh, Dad . . . I'm sorry, Dad!"

Reznick sat in silence.

"This is him," she said. "It's in the eyes. Look at him. I can't believe it."

"Would you like to keep that photo?"

Camila nodded. "Very much."

"It's yours. Camila."

"Why did Brett leave? He promised he'd help me."

"Camila, men like Brett Miller are predators. He promises the earth. That's what he does. Meanwhile, he's having sex with you, right?"

Camila stared at him. "How do you know?"

"We can talk about this another time. I just need to get you out of here."

"What if I don't want to?"

"Camila, you're only sixteen years old."

"Fine. So you knew my dad. What do you want from me?"

"I don't want anything. I just want to take you someplace safe. I want to get you away from this world. Nightlife, nightclubs, bars, escorting, drugs."

Camila looked at him, blinking away tears. "You're not going to hurt me, are you?"

"Hurt you? Quite the opposite. I'm here to help. But you need to trust me."

She looked again at the photo. "You heard that my father had died and that's why you're here in LA, right?"

"Correct. When I heard he had a daughter, I couldn't walk away. Your father never walked away. I believe he was searching for you before he was killed."

"Really?"

"Really. He was looking all over town, people have told me. And he was cleaned up. Getting his shit together."

"My dad was looking for me?"

"Until the very end." Reznick leaned in close. "Let's get out of here. What do you say?"

Camila looked at him.

"I'm here to help you. But you need to help yourself by coming with me. Trusting me. Do you trust me?"

"I do."

"So let's get out of here."

Forty-One

Reznick sat opposite Camila Ramos at a table in Denny's diner in West Hollywood. Her eyes were like pinpricks, nervously darting around the room.

"I know it's a lot to take in," he said. "I understand. You hungry?"

"Why are you doing this?"

"I want to get you away from that life. You're just a kid."

"You're not going to take me to the cops, are you?"

Reznick shook his head. "Absolutely not. I just want to get you someplace safe. The fact that you're here, with me, not fighting me on this, I take it that's what you want as well."

She picked up a napkin and dabbed at the tears filling her eyes. "I'm scared. I don't have anyone. I always thought my dad was going to be around. And now you're telling me he's dead."

Reznick was reluctant at this stage to say how her dad had died. He thought it best not to terrify her. "It's tough. No getting away from that. How did things get to this point? I don't understand how you can go from caring for your father to the life you're living?"

"Bad choices since I got to LA. Crazy thinking. That guy I was with, Brett, he said he wanted to be a father figure to me. I liked that."

"He said that?"

Camila nodded. "Not smart, I know. I realize now what he was. But he said he might be able to get me into one of his films. If I just stuck around for a while."

"That guy is a predator. He will abuse you, he will use you, and he will dump you. That's the deal with guys like him."

Camila nodded, eyes downcast. "He filmed me."

"He filmed you?"

"He got off on that. I knew he did it. He told me last night. He supplied me with whatever I wanted or needed. Coke, pills, heroin, Xanax, uppers, downers, whatever."

"You need to make a promise to yourself. A promise to your father. From this day on, that life is over. You have to promise that you're going to start over. It's a new life. Do you think you'll be able to do that?"

"I don't know. I'll try."

Reznick smiled at her. "You can do it. If you're as determined and single-minded as your dad, you'll turn your life around."

"I'll try my best, I promise."

"Good for you. So, tell me, you hungry?"

"Starving."

"Well, you're in the right place. Order whatever you want."

Camila perused the menu before staring long and hard at Reznick. "I've got nobody."

"I'm here for you. And I'm going to make sure you're safe. What else did that creep Miller promise you?"

"He promised me he'd buy me an apartment and get me a starring role in his next film. Empty promises."

"That's what sleazeballs like him do. They exploit people. You're a child."

Camila called over a waitress. She ordered blueberry pancakes with maple syrup and a glass of Coke.

Reznick ordered a black coffee and a slice of apple pie and whipped cream. He followed her eyes around the diner. A smattering of construction workers, a couple of cops, and a group of stoned slackers slumped in a corner booth. "You need to get yourself a proper job and a proper life. Work regular hours."

"What the hell does that mean? Scraping by like the poor bastards working nights for tips?"

"Everyone has to start somewhere. Low wages, tips, whatever it takes to get by."

"I was getting by."

"You took the fast route. You sold your body. Your soul. Your self-respect."

"What route would you suggest?"

Reznick said nothing. He waited until the waitress returned with the food and drinks.

"Enjoy your meal, folks," she said. "My name is Linda."

Reznick thanked her. Then faced the haunted girl opposite him in the booth, who looked miles away with her skeletal figure and ghostly, vacant eyes. "You think Linda's not getting by? Linda is working hard for herself and maybe her family. And good for her. You need to work hard to get anything out of life."

"I want to have it now. I want to live my best life."

"You think you're living your best life, do you? And what exactly have you got to show for it, huh? I'll tell you what you've got. A sleazy seventy-something guy supplying you with drugs."

Camila's eyes filled with tears. "Why are you judging me?"

"I'm not judging you. I'm just trying to explain a few hard truths."

"I know what I am. I know exactly what I am. You don't have to tell me. I'm a prostitute. I'm a drug addict."

Reznick leaned toward her. "Keep your voice down. And eat your pancakes before they get cold."

Camila poured maple syrup over the thick pancakes before she greedily wolfed them down. She closed her eyes and chewed luxuriously.

"You *are* hungry."

"Starving."

Reznick ate his pie, and washed it down with hot black coffee. "Eat it all up."

"Can I order a beer?"

"No."

Camila rolled her eyes. "Seriously?"

"Let me ask you something. You moved to LA to find your dad, right?"

"That's right. My mom kicked me out for smoking weed. She told me all about him when I was fourteen. I wanted to find him. And care for him."

"I admire that. That was very brave. Noble. The right thing to do."

Camila blushed. "Well, he was my dad. I never had him in my life until that point. My mom was a mess. I didn't want to lose him again. I wanted to help him. Get him back on his feet. I wanted him to be proud of me."

"It was the right thing to do. So how did your life change so much since then that you ended up with a creep like Brett Miller?"

"I began to drink to forget. I began to hang around the stoner crowd down on Venice Beach. And I got into heroin too for a while. Smoking it."

"You stopped that?"

"I replaced heroin with cocaine. But coke costs a lot of money."

"I'll pay for you to get clean. I promise you."

"So, what's in it for you?"

"Nothing. I'm doing this because it's the right thing to do. And because I want to get you better. It's what your dad would've wanted."

Tears spilled down her face.

"What is it?"

"I miss my dad."

"I know you do."

"I wish he was here now. I wish I could've helped him."

"Sometimes you need to help yourself. I think he gave up on life. But I heard he got clean in the weeks before he was killed. He was trying to find you. He wanted you in his life. That's why he got himself clean."

"Oh my God, I wish I knew!"

"You still have a chance," said Reznick. "You need to take it."

"I want to change my life. I want to do it for my dad."

"You need to want to do it for yourself. You've got your whole life in front of you. The way you're going now? You'll be lucky to see eighteen. And that's the goddamn truth."

Camila sipped her Coke, wiping her mascara streaked face with a napkin. "Look at me. I'm a mess."

"I want to ask you something. And you need to give me an honest answer."

"I'll try."

"If I find a place for you to stay, I need you to promise to stay clean, stay sober, and turn things around. Not only in memory of your father, but for yourself more than anyone."

Camila closed her eyes and said a whispered prayer.

"Look at me."

She stared at him.

"Your father, God rest his soul, would have wanted you to get clean."

"Yes, he would have."

"And he would have wanted you to get a good job. Go to college."

"I have dreams. Dreams of being famous."

"Those aren't dreams. Those are illusions. I'm talking working hard. Very, very hard, to pursue a career of your choosing. What do you want to do?"

"I want to earn money."

"Okay, good. You want to earn money. But you need to work, and get an education."

"I can do that."

"You need to not just talk the talk, but walk the walk. So, if I find you a place to get your life back on track, you'd be fine with that?"

Camila smiled, tears spilling down her face. "I need to do something. So I'd be more than fine with that. I want to change."

"You still hungry?"

"I want a burger and fries."

"Another Coke too?"

She smiled. "Thank you."

Reznick ordered more food for Camila and a strong black coffee for himself.

"So, you fought alongside my dad?"

Reznick nodded.

"He didn't talk about it."

"When you've been in the heat of battle, you don't want to talk about it. You really don't want to talk about what you've witnessed. The friends you've lost. It brings the battle back."

"I understand."

"Your father showed unimaginable courage. You've got a tough road ahead of you. Just think of what he faced. You've got to have backbone, courage."

Camila reached for his hand. "I'm scared."

"I understand."

The waitress returned with their second order.

Camila picked up a couple of fries and wolfed them down.

Reznick got to his feet, taking out his cell phone. "I've got to make a quick call. I'll be back in a few."

She nodded, focused on her food.

Reznick stepped outside the diner to the parking lot. He pulled up the number for the Catholic church in Venice Beach, run by Father Patrick O'Donnell. It rang five times before it was answered.

"Father O'Donnell. Who's calling at this time of night?"

"Father . . . it's Jon Reznick. We spoke the other week about my late friend Angel Ramos."

"I remember, Jon. How are you?"

"I'm okay. I'm sorry it's late. Father, I need a favor. A big favor. Can you help?"

"It depends."

"Do you have accommodation in the diocese for alcoholics or drug addicts—women—to try and help them get straight?"

"One of our community, she runs a center. That's exactly what she does. The church supports the center."

"I found Camila Ramos, Angel's daughter."

"Jesus wept."

"Can I bring her to the center?"

"Now?"

"Within the hour."

Father O'Donnell gave an address two blocks from the church. "Mary Perez. She's an angel. I'll tell her to expect the girl."

"You're a lifesaver, Father. Thank you."

"It's God's way, my son."

"Not a word to anyone. Just you and Mary Perez. Guard her with your life."

"You don't need to tell me. We'll keep her safe. And we'll get her well."

Reznick ended the call and headed back inside the diner. "I've found you a place. A place for you to get better. A place that specializes in young women like yourself."

"You're kidding me?"

Reznick smiled. "It's going to be okay. I'll make sure of it."

Forty-Two

Jerry Levinson was reading a John Grisham novel on his iPad at his palatial home in Pacific Palisades. It was 2:41 a.m. and he was wide awake. He had been sleeping less and less these days. His wife had suggested sleeping pills or therapy. Neither appealed to him. The last thing he needed for himself or his clients was to be sleeping in, not turning up at the office or answering calls. A top-tier producer might be calling from the French Riviera. An A-list actress from Bali. The next big screenwriter from a film shoot In Tangiers. This was the sort of shit he dealt with each and every day. But the stress was killing him. Peptic ulcers, his doctor had said. He took pills to treat the condition.

When his cell phone vibrated on his bedside table, his wife woke up. "Jerry, turn it off!"

He put down his iPad. "I can't, honey. These fucking clients."

"That better not be Brett fucking Miller again."

"Honey, relax. Take an Ambien."

His wife turned away from him, grumbling, as he reached over and picked up his phone from the nightstand. Brett Miller's name was on the screen. His heart sank. He was tempted not to answer. But he knew if he didn't he would no longer have a lucrative client in the morning. "I need to take this," he muttered. He got out of bed and padded through the house to his office, shutting the door behind him. He switched on his desk lamp and slumped down, picking up the phone. "Yeah, Jerry speaking. What's going on, Brett?"

"I'll tell you what's going on. I'm freaking the fuck out, Jerry."

"Slow down, Brett, what's the matter?"

"A few hours ago, I was enjoying a pleasant night with a girl at my club. Sloane's. Nice discreet crowd."

"Okay."

"And who turns up?"

Jerry closed his eyes, not wanting to hear the latest episode in Brett's chaotic social life. "I don't know."

"Jon fucking Reznick, that's who."

Jerry thought his heart was going to stop. "What?"

"I swear to God, the dude everyone is talking about, he's in my life. In my life. And in my face. Who the hell is this guy? What does he want? It's fucking terrifying."

Jerry thought Brett was slurring some of his words. He wondered if he was loaded. It was how Brett got through a typical day—a dizzying combination of pills, booze, and coke. "I understand."

"What the fuck does that mean, Jerry? How can you understand?"

Jerry was concerned that Brett was going to say something incriminating on the line. If he'd been bugged by the cops or the Feds, if they were building a case based on Brett's reputation in the film industry for hanging around underage girls in Hollywood, the wrong phrase could land them both in trouble. Maybe he should get a secure line set up. "Let's figure this out, okay?"

"Good."

"Where are you?"

"What do I do, Jerry? Tell me."

"Where are you?"

"I'm at my place in Malibu."

Jerry figured it would take around twenty minutes to drive along the Pacific Coast Highway. "Stay where you are. I'll be there soon."

◆　◆　◆

When Jerry arrived, carrying his briefcase, he found Brett sitting on his deck, overlooking the ocean, two bottles of chilled Chablis in an ice bucket, a glass of wine in one hand, a cigarette in the other. He sat down beside the director. Brett was wearing chinos, scuffed boat shoes, and a Hawaiian print shirt open to his navel, exposing his dark brown skin. The sound of the waves crashing provided the only soundtrack.

"You fucking believe this shit, Jerry? I was just chilling with this girl, relaxing, and boom, my world exploded. In my club!"

Jerry took out his legal pad. "Time?"

"Eleven . . . midnight . . . a few hours ago. I don't know."

"And what exactly happened?"

"What happened? The girl—"

"Who was she?"

"Chick I've been seeing recently. Gigi Cortez. Gorgeous girl."

"Wasn't she the girl in your pool the other night?"

"Yeah, beautiful girl."

"Tell me your recollection of the events of last night. You and this Gigi were chatting?"

"We went to Sloane's. Shooting the breeze. And I think she's exactly right for a role in a new sci-film I'm developing. She's perfect."

Jerry pursed his lips, knowing this was bullshit. Brett was fucking her, pure and simple.

"Anyway, she goes to the bathroom, powdering her nose or some shit. Next thing I know, this fucking maniac Reznick, cold as ice, sits down across from me."

"And Gigi is still in the bathroom at this point?"

"Correct."

"What did this Jon Reznick say? Did he threaten you? Point a gun at you?"

"Hell no. First, Reznick introduces himself. Then he tells me to leave the club, says his friend is watching surveillance footage from inside the club in real time, and he would leak the film of me with Gigi to TMZ or some outlet like the *National Enquirer*. Said Gigi's real name was Camila Ramos, daughter of Angel Ramos."

Jerry felt sick. He wondered if Brett had forgotten that he'd told him her name previously. Or if he'd had a blackout. His client had no idea of the extent of the illegal stuff Jerry did for him. He would be locked up for a hundred years if it got out. His life would be ruined.

Levinson had ordered the English photographer to be "disappeared." He'd known that meant she'd be killed and dumped. And all to keep his breathtakingly ungrateful client, Brett Miller, safe.

"Said his pal was a guy that was in Delta with Reznick. But he was homeless, wound up dead in Venice. Swear to God, Jerry. I was spooked."

"Of course. It's upsetting. What did he want?"

"That's the weird thing. He didn't want money. I would understand that, right? A shakedown for some money. It happens."

"All the time."

"Right, but this guy, this fucking . . . psycho, he just wants me to leave. He said he's taking the girl someplace safe."

Jerry put his pad and pen on the table. He felt as if he was drowning in quicksand. "I can see why you were unsettled by that."

"So, what do you think?"

Jerry mulled over the scenario that Brett had described. "Well, there are various strands to this. Harassment, blackmail, threats, intimidation, these are all things we can take to the cops. And we've got to figure he's not a member, so how did he get into the club? Did he break in? Ordinarily, the LAPD would be our first call. But I can see why that's not an option here."

Brett sipped his wine and dragged hard on his cigarette, blowing the smoke away from Jerry's face. "I don't want that. I can't have that intrusion into my life. I like my life, Jerry. And I want it to stay the way it is. That's why I called you."

"That's what I'm here for. Thing is, if this Gigi Cortez is underage, you would get some heat for that."

"I know that."

"So let me ask *you* something. What do you want me to do?"

"I suppose you could have him killed?"

Jerry stared back at Brett, fixing his gaze. "I'm assuming you're joking."

Brett's face scrunched up, almost confused. Jerry saw it dawn on his client as he realized that the mood had changed. "Of course I'm kidding. So what can we do about it? What's your advice?"

"My advice, Brett? Suck it up. The guy is out of your life. He wanted that girl, Gigi—"

"What does he want her for?"

"Let's assume, out of the kindness of his heart, he just wants to help her."

Brett rolled his eyes. "I could have made her a huge, huge star."

"Just let it go. You don't want any heat. Let's just let it go. And you get on with your life. Jon Reznick is out of your life. It's a win-win. That's what you want, right?"

"Right."

"He has no reason to go after you now, does he?"

"Don't think so. What about the footage in Sloane's?"

"Leave that to me. I'll secure that, and we can get rid of any trace of Reznick and that girl."

Brett finished his wine and smiled. "I love you, man. What sort of lawyer turns up in the middle of the night for a client?"

"One that charges more than two thousand bucks an hour."

Brett laughed, throwing back his head.

"And Brett, one more thing."

"What?"

"Be careful what girls you date in the future. Legal is best."

Forty-Three

A foggy dawn rolled in over Venice Beach.

Reznick headed along the boardwalk, past graffitied shutters, relieved that he had tracked down Camila Ramos. She was safe. At least for now. He zipped up his jacket against the chilly early-morning air. Mist shrouded the town in an overcast gloom.

He sat down on a bench and stared out at the gray ocean. He wondered where he should go from here. He had achieved his mission.

When he'd dropped Camila off, he had filled in some paperwork before leaving quietly and making his way down the beach. He felt good that he had found her and she was alive. She was pretty strung-out and probably needed months of therapy and love to begin the long road to recovery. And there would be setbacks, no doubt. It was almost inevitable. But he felt a sense of pride that he had gotten Angel's girl someplace safe. It wasn't a long-term solution. But it was a place where she would be cared for. She would be fed. She would learn skills. It was in the fabric of the center. She would have to work, cleaning her accommodation, cooking for others, and this would instill in her the work ethic and the humdrum nature of most people's day-to-day existence. It would be a cold splash of reality after her existence in the twilight world of nightclubs, bars, prostitution, and getting wasted.

It wasn't the end for Camila. But it would be a long road back to sobriety.

Reznick felt famished all of a sudden. He headed over to Great White, a café on Pacific Avenue. He walked in, their first customer of the day.

"Someone's up early," the cheery guy behind the counter said.

"Good morning."

"What can I get you?"

Reznick looked over the menu. "Scrambled eggs, rye toast, strong black coffee, and—what the heck—pancakes and maple syrup."

"Going all in. I love it. Take a seat."

Reznick sat down. A few early-morning customers drifted in slowly. A construction worker, a surfer dude, a jogger in sweatpants and a Nike T-shirt, breathing hard, face flushed.

He took out his cell phone, checking for any messages. He had missed a call from his daughter only a few minutes ago. It would be just after nine at night in Indonesia. He called her back.

"Hey, Dad, I hope I'm not disturbing you," Lauren said.

Reznick felt his throat tighten, overwhelmed to hear her voice again, thousands of miles from home. "Hey, Lauren, great to hear from you. Just about to have breakfast in LA."

"You still hanging around there?"

"Long story. But it's all good. Tell me, more importantly, how are you? I missed your call."

"Just wanted a little chat."

Reznick detected a sadness in her voice. "Sure . . . Everything all right, honey?"

"Yeah . . . well, you know, homesick. But, hey, I guess that's to be expected."

"It happens. I get it, seems like you'll never see home again. But you will. It'll be over before you know it."

"Time is really dragging here, Dad."

Reznick wondered if there was more to this than homesickness. "How's work? What about your colleagues?"

"Work is busy. All the time. The people . . . they can be challenging."

Reznick wished he could be with her to give her a hug, reassure her that everything was going to be alright. He knew what CIA operators could be like. Prickly. Less collegial than the Feds. But invariably they were highly focused and driven individuals, whatever their role.

"I guess I'm just missing my old life. My friends in New York."

"The Feds?"

"Especially the FBI and my colleagues there. They were friends too, some of them. I guess I miss the camaraderie. You don't really think about it, the things you enjoy—like the park, or hanging out in bars in the East Village. But you do when you're far away."

Reznick pined for his daughter. He still worried about her. It wasn't like Lauren to complain about things. She was resilient. "Have you talked to anyone out there about it? At the station? Your boss, for example."

He could practically hear Lauren rolling her eyes from thousands of miles away. "Yes."

"And what did they say?"

"To get over it."

The server brought over his coffee. "Breakfast will be about two minutes."

Reznick thanked him, and sipped his coffee.

"What would you do, Dad, in my shoes?"

"But I'm not in your shoes. Everyone is different. I didn't mind being deployed to any country."

"You were trained to deal with just about anything thrown at you. The mental component, I mean."

"Honey, what do you want me to say?"

"What should I do, Dad?"

"How is your situation making you feel? Is it making you doubt yourself? Is the posting making you wonder what the hell you're doing?"

"That's exactly it. I don't want to be here anymore. That's the problem, Dad."

"Well, I guess you already know what you've got to do."

"I want you to be proud of me."

Reznick pressed the cell phone tight to his ear. "I couldn't be prouder. A father could not wish for a better daughter. I love you. I want you to be happy, content in your work. Fulfilled."

The sound of sniffing came over the line as Lauren cried.

"Lauren, get yourself home. I don't know if it's the work, the location, or if it's just not the right thing for you. It doesn't matter. None of that matters. Get yourself home."

"My supervisor said the same thing. He said to take a month back home. I have vacation time. And see how I feel at the end of it."

"Smart advice. So do it. Recharge your batteries. Meet up with your old friends and buddies in New York. I'll visit you too. And you can head up for some peace and quiet in Rockland."

"That sounds nice."

"If you still feel the same about returning, it's obvious that you need a change of scenery. That's perfectly fine."

There was a long sigh in Reznick's ear. "You're the best, Dad. I love you. That's all I needed to hear."

Reznick sat in quiet contemplation.

"Are you still there?"

"I'm still here, honey."

"You seem distracted. Is everything okay, Dad?"

"Don't worry about me, honey."

"But I do worry about you. A lot."

"It's lovely to hear your voice. Get yourself home. And you can take some time to reflect on where you want to go. Know this. I love you."

"Ditto. Oh, and Dad, the next time we're in New York, it's my treat."

"I'll hold you to that."

"I've got to go, Dad. Take care."

"You too, honey."

Reznick ended the call. He felt helpless being unable to reach out and hug her tight. But she wasn't his little girl anymore. She was a grown woman, working for the CIA, and she would work it out, one way or another.

The server approached, carrying his breakfast along with a fresh cup of coffee. "Enjoy your meal. And enjoy your coffee. My name is Tom, if you need anything else."

"Thanks, Tom."

Reznick ate his scrambled eggs and toast in peace. He picked at the pancakes and maple syrup, enjoying the sugar rush. He drank his strong black coffee. He glanced out the window as a kid on rollerblades glided past, headphones on. The more he thought about Lauren, the more he was relieved she would be heading home. He thought of them walking together in New York. Visiting a museum. Going to Central Park. Having lunch in Bryant Park. A jazz concert at the Blue Note jazz club in the Village. A fancy meal at Minetta Tavern. But more than anything, just time to enjoy hanging out with each other.

Reznick finished his second coffee of the morning. The waiter offered a refill which he gladly took. He nursed his third coffee, taking a couple of Dexedrine to pep himself up. He was practically running on empty.

His cell phone rang.

"Morning, Jon." Trevelle. "Back at the beach, I see?"

"You know it."

"Quite an eventful twenty-four hours."

"While you're on the line and while I remember, could you do me a favor?"

"Name it."

"Is it possible for you to remotely access that footage from last night. I'm interested to see Miller with Camila."

"Sure thing."

"One other thing. And this might be trickier. Camila told me that Brett Miller filmed them having sex."

"What?"

"I know, total sleazeball. I imagine he saved that to his computers or something, backed it up to the cloud, I don't know."

"You want me to get the sex tapes made by Brett Miller?"

"Yes, I do. And when you do, send them, securely, to the FBI's Crimes against Children task force in LA. He needs to be stopped. Is there any way of keeping Camila's identity anonymous on these sex tapes?"

"Identity shielding is what you want. I'm assuming this is to get Brett Miller arrested once and for all."

"I want the bastard in jail. I want him to be hauled off the streets. He's a predator."

"I can't promise anything, Jon. But let me see what I can do. Meanwhile, I've got some bad news for you."

Reznick sipped his coffee.

"Remember the girl you visited up in the hills. Friend of Camila's?"

"Oh yeah, Flo Jackson."

"She was found dead an hour ago by her boyfriend."

Reznick's mind flashed back to his visit. "What happened?"

"Home invasion apparently. And it escalated horribly. It was savage."

Reznick set down his mug.

"It's believed to have happened a couple nights ago. Not long after you spoke to her. She was stabbed repeatedly. And raped."

Reznick felt sick to his stomach. He knew in his heart it was no coincidence. "Does the LAPD know about this?"

"They're on the scene."

"Does Lopez have anything to do with this?"

"Surveillance footage not working at Flo's property, apparently. But I've accessed nearby footage backing onto the property. And a vehicle was seen cruising the area several times before the alleged time of death."

"What kind of vehicle?"

"A van. A van registered to a pool-cleaning company. Hollywood Pool Cleaning. Owner?"

"Carlos Lopez?"

"Got it in one. You believe in coincidences?"

"No, I don't."

"Me neither."

"Son of a bitch!"

Trevelle exhaled. "We've known Lopez is a maniac. He owns the cleaning firm, a removals firm, a security company, and a handful of sleazy bars and clubs. He's a wealthy businessman."

Reznick took out his wallet. "He's a wealthy psychopath."

"No question."

He got up from his seat and walked over to the counter. He paid his bill, leaving a fifty-dollar tip in the jar. "Where is he now?"

"Lopez?"

"Yeah. Where the fuck is he? Right now."

Trevelle gave an address. "A boxing gym in West Hollywood."

"He's there as we speak?"

"Right this minute. Arrived twenty minutes ago. Jon, you can't go there."

"Why not?"

"The gym, it's frequented by steroid-popping bodyguards, doormen, and security guys, all working for him. You won't get near him."

Forty-Four

Reznick knew his work wasn't done. He needed to finish this business once and for all. His motivation was pure and simple. He felt a cold, blind, incendiary fury inside of him. Flo Jackson's rape and murder had been no coincidence. She would still be alive if he hadn't turned up on her doorstep. The latest revelation was the final straw. Lopez needed to be taught a lesson he would never forget. His reign of terror against vulnerable girls in the seedy underbelly of Los Angeles had to end. Enough was enough.

Reznick walked a couple of blocks to a parking garage and headed up the stairwell to the third level and saw a powerful motorcycle. He took out a military-grade vehicle fob, gifted to him by Trevelle, and remotely disabled the alarm of the BMW bike. A helmet hung from a chain. He took out his gun, shot off the chain and pulled on the helmet, putting the visor down. The fob switched on the bike. He revved it hard and rode off, down the ramp, and back on to the street.

He rode along Venice Boulevard, headed toward West Hollywood. He wondered if Lopez would still be at the gym. He hoped so. The notorious LA traffic was getting heavier as he drove along West Sunset.

Reznick rode past a low-rise condo building and took a right after a luxury apartment block. He turned into a parking garage, heading down two levels before finding a spot. No one around. He left the bike there and walked up the stairwell.

Reznick took off his helmet and walked out of a back entrance as he got his bearings. He headed down an alley. Up ahead, he saw a sign for the boxing gym.

A black limo was parked outside.

Reznick caught sight of bodyguards. A couple of chiseled, pumped-up, tattooed goons watching him as he approached. He smiled as he walked up to the guy closest to him.

"Can I help you, güero?"

Reznick knew the Spanish slang word for a white person. He smashed the guy square in the jaw with the crash helmet. There was a crack. Blood poured from the guy's mouth and nose. He crumpled to the ground and Reznick kicked him hard between the legs. The guy writhed in a bloody heap.

The other man pulled a knife and lunged wildly at Reznick, who parried it away with a blow to the arm. Then he punched the guy hard in the neck. He went down, dazed, semiconscious.

Reznick stepped forward and kicked him hard on the side of the head. The guy was out cold. The first guy looked woozily up at Reznick, blood still pouring from his mouth. Reznick kicked him on the side of the head. The guy's eyes rolled back. Motionless.

Two down. The pair of thugs lay in pools of their own blood, unconscious. Rule number one. *There are no rules.* Rule number two. *Get them before they get you.*

Reznick walked into the gym. It was empty, except for another tattooed, beefed-up monster, muscles rippling with the exertion, who was bench-pressing in the corner. The pungent smell of stale sweat hung in the air. The guy in the corner wore metallic blue headphones. He sat up. It was Carlos Lopez. Reznick recognized the scars across his mouth.

Reznick dropped the helmet on the ground as he strode up to Lopez.

Lopez must have sensed there was someone who didn't belong here, because he spun around as Reznick approached. He took off his headphones. "Sorry, we're closed, white boy."

Reznick grinned as he reached Lopez. He stared down at the weathered features of the killer, then pulled out his trusty 9 mm Beretta.

"Hey, what the fuck you playing at!" Lopez said.

Reznick lowered the gun and fired one shot at Lopez's right knee. The blast echoed around the concrete walls of the gym.

The man screamed in pain, blood pouring from his knee. He clenched his teeth and screwed up his face in agony. "What the fuck?"

"Have I got your attention, you dumb fuck?" spat Reznick.

Lopez's eyes became hooded, black. The psychopath shivered, as if going into shock. "Do you know who I am? Do you fucking understand that you've signed your death warrant?"

Reznick saw a cell phone lying on a bench. He reached over and shoved the phone in Lopez's face. The face recognition opened up the phone. He quickly changed the six-digit passcode to 010101. While he trained the gun on Lopez, he scanned the recent messages, emails. He checked the photos—hundreds of photos of Carlos in the gym, boxing. He flicked through more. He saw a video showing the beating of a woman. Then it showed her being hanged. He was sickened. He showed Lopez the video. "This your handiwork?"

Lopez laughed. "Let me tell you something. That bitch won't be annoying any more important people in the city. You should thank me."

Reznick felt his stomach tighten. He scrolled through other videos on the phone. There was one taken only a couple of days earlier. It showed a young black woman, Flo Jackson. He watched, horrified. The girl was screaming, begging for her life, surrounded by Carlos and his psychotic gang. He ended the video. He felt a wave of rage and revulsion wash over him. It spread within him, consuming him like a cancer. "You a tough guy, hanging a woman? And raping and killing that girl up in the hills? Flo Jackson was her name, you piece of shit."

Lopez winced, blood still seeping from his knee.

"You filmed them?"

"What you gonna do about it?"

"You filmed their deaths? Like a snuff movie? You get off on that filth? You wretched piece of scum. I know where you're going. You're going straight to hell."

Lopez averted his gaze. "Hell doesn't scare me. I've been there. And you think American jails scare me? Hell no. I've been in jails in Mexico. Nothing scares me after that."

Reznick aimed his gun at the other knee. "Who said anything about jail."

"Go fuck yourself."

Reznick fired off another shot, blasting the other kneecap. Blood splattered across Lopez's legs and face. He screamed.

"Motherfucker, you're going to die!" Lopez clenched his teeth tight, his eyes shut. "You're so fucked, white boy. What do you want?"

"I'll tell you what I want. I'm not leaving here until I get answers."

Lopez was doubled over in pain, his elbows to the floor. "What do you want to know?"

Reznick pressed the gun near Lopez's sweating brow. "You're bleeding out, you dumb fuck. You'll be unconscious soon. I can put you out of your misery once and for all."

Lopez was shaking bad. "Who are you?"

"My name's Reznick."

Lopez stared up at him, breathing hard, sweat beading his brow. "So you're the one. Reznick, huh?"

"You killed my friend. Angel Ramos."

Lopez curled and uncurled his fist, fighting back the pain. "Man, you must be out of your mind. You're going to all this trouble for that homeless piece of shit."

"Why did you kill him? On whose orders?"

Lopez winced, grasping his bleeding knees. "Man, I don't know. I was told that this guy was making trouble. I was told that the trouble had to end."

"You killed him?"

Lopez shook his head.

Reznick nudged Lopez with his foot, flipping the man onto his back. He lifted a dumbbell from the floor and dropped it down onto Lopez's chest. "You like that?"

Lopez gasped and pushed the weight off him. "I killed him! What the fuck is it to you?"

Reznick stared down at Lopez, who was lying prone on the ground, bleeding out. He pressed his heel down onto the man's bleeding left knee. "You've got a choice."

Lopez screamed.

"You can either live . . . or you can die. No big deal to me, either way."

"You think I'm scared of dying? Me? Fuck no. And that's what guys like you will never understand. I don't get scared. I don't fear anything or anyone."

Reznick leaned over and pressed the gun to Lopez's head. "Last chance, dipshit. Who ordered the killing of Angel Ramos? Who was it?"

Lopez stared up at Reznick, tears in his eyes. He began to laugh, hysterically. "You think you scare me?"

Reznick pressed the gun tighter to his head. "Why did you kill him? On whose orders?"

"I killed him because I was told to kill him."

"Who ordered the hit? Gimme a name."

"I don't remember."

"You tell me and I walk out of here. You don't tell me, you die."

Lopez shook his head.

"You tortured him, didn't you? You drilled holes into his head. Through his eyes. Didn't you?"

"I didn't do that."

"Who did?"

"My guys. Some of them are pretty crazy."

"Bullshit. It's on you. You carried out his killing. You tortured and killed him. And you did the same to Flo Jackson. An innocent kid. So who sent you?"

"I can't answer that."

"Can't, or won't?"

Lopez spat up at Reznick. "We deal with things the way we deal with things."

Reznick pressed the gun into Lopez's mouth. He rammed it into the back of his throat. "Tell me what you know. Who ordered the kill?"

Lopez was gagging on the Beretta. "Okay!"

Reznick kept the gun in his mouth but gave him room enough to speak.

"The art dealer. He's the one."

"Name?"

"Robert Kassan."

"Why?"

"I don't know why. I think your friend Angel was threatening him. He found out his daughter had fucked Kassan at some party at Brett Miller's house. I swear."

"I don't believe you."

"It's true, man. He's a bad dude."

"How did you get hooked up with him?"

"He's a powerful guy. He moves money around. That's all I know."

"Moves money around for who?"

"The cartels. Mexicans. He's a smart guy. He's connected."

"To who?"

"Paramilitaries. Crazy people. Lebanon. Beirut."

"What?"

"I swear, the guy has connections across Lebanon. Europe. I swear, man."

Reznick pressed the gun to the back of Lopez's throat again. "If you're lying . . ."

"I swear."

Reznick was sorely tempted to pull the trigger. But he didn't. He slowly pulled the gun from Lopez's mouth. He stared down at him. The fucker had peed himself. Lopez's eyes were rolling back in his head. He was drooling, still bleeding out.

"What else do you want, man? I told you what I know."

Reznick checked his watch. He waited a couple of minutes until Lopez had blacked out. Then he turned around, picked up the crash helmet, and headed out the gym's exit, down a side street, circling back to the parking garage.

He took out the cell phone he had taken from Lopez. He tapped in the new six-digit code and scrolled through thousands of Lopez's messages and emails. He pulled out his own phone and called Trevelle. "I've got a cell phone I want you to examine." He told him the number. "You got it?"

"Copy that."

"This is Carlos Lopez's phone. I want to know if it contains anything about who ordered the killing of Angel Ramos. Person of interest? Robert Kassan."

"It'll take time."

"Do whatever it takes. Get to it."

"I take it you've dealt with Carlos Lopez?"

"Affirmative."

"Jon, you've got to be careful, man."

"Find out if there's anything else on the cell phone. And get back to me soon."

Forty-Five

Jerry Levinson was pacing his downtown office, trying to enjoy his second cup of coffee of the morning and preparing to head to a face-to-face with a new client, when his cell phone rang. He picked up.

"Jerry, are you watching the news?" It was Brett Miller.

Levinson dreaded what was about to come. "What's on your mind now?"

"Are you watching TV?"

"Brett, I'm a lawyer. I don't watch TV in the mornings."

"Turn on Fox 11. Right now!"

Jerry picked up the remote and turned on the TV hanging on his office wall. He flicked through the channels until he got to the correct station.

A young reporter was standing in front of a police cordon, lights flashing, in downtown LA. "We're hearing from multiple sources that the talented British photographer Heidi Stratton has been found dead this morning at her studio in LA. Police were tipped off by her boyfriend."

Levinson stood, transfixed, as they showed an archive photo of Stratton, a long-lens camera around her neck. He realized what had happened.

"Jerry, talk to me. What the fuck, man? I wanted this to go away. But I didn't want this."

"Shut up!"

"What?"

Levinson was terrified that Miller's phone was bugged. "Just shut up. I need to think. Don't say anything else. I'm on my way."

◆ ◆ ◆

Forty minutes later, after enduring gridlocked traffic, Jerry Levinson drove through the electronic gates to Miller's Bel Air mansion. He strode through the house to the pool area.

Brett stood by the pool, drinking directly from a bottle of Scotch. He stood up straighter, snarling, "Where the fuck have you been?"

"Shut up and listen to me."

"We've got a fucking problem, Jerry. I don't like problems."

Jerry pointed to his client. "Sit the fuck down."

Brett meekly put down the bottle and pulled up a seat by the pool. "I had no idea this would be the end result, Jerry. I assumed this was going to be taken care of, like, here's a hundred thousand bucks, now fuck off! That kind of thing."

Levinson sat down beside Brett. "This is not exactly what I had in mind either."

"So what the fuck happened?"

"I made a call. The deal was in place to buy the photos from Heidi Stratton and she would leave town."

"What the fuck happened?"

"She changed her mind. She said the deal was off. She got offered a million bucks for the photos."

"Shit. So they killed her?"

Jerry shrugged. "It all got fucked up."

"Are you kidding me?"

"I don't know how it turned out like this. It's like it got lost in translation. Usually when I say I want a problem to go away, it just goes away. The people I work with know what I mean. The deal is done. Everyone's happy."

"Everyone's happy? A woman has been murdered, Jerry."

"We didn't kill her."

"Oh, for fuck's sake, man. Is it someone you've used before?"

"The person I usually use is in hospital. Cancer."

"And?"

"So I was introduced to a new intermediary about a year ago," said Levinson. "A private investigator. Smart, I was told. He's a former cop. Gets things done. Very discreet. And it seemed to be working, on a few cases I sent his way."

"*Seemed to be working?* Jerry, it's one thing to squash photographs of me doing blow in a club with a stripper. It's quite another for me to be linked, no matter how tenuous, to the death of a photographer. This is insanity. They killed her?"

Levinson leaned in close. "Listen to me very carefully. Our fingerprints are not on this. Your fingerprints. No digital fingerprints either."

"Did you meet the guy in person?"

"I did. But there's no trail."

"So what do we do?"

"We do nothing."

"Nothing?"

"Correct."

"What if this gets out?"

"It's already out. You are in no way linked."

Brett ran his hands through his hair. "And life goes on?"

"Life goes on. Shit happens. You make deals, you make films, you go for lunch, you do what you have to do. Take your wife on

290

a long vacation. Get the hell out of town. We'll get the PR people to describe it as a second honeymoon."

"Yeah, I like the sound of that."

"Take my advice. Get out of town. With your wife, not a stripper. And you'll see. It'll all die down. By the time you get back, everything will be good again. Like it never happened."

Forty-Six

Reznick turned into a narrow side street of townhouses in Marina Del Rey. He dumped the BMW bike and walked half a dozen blocks. He saw a beautiful, classic Harley, chrome gleaming, unchained.

He took out the fob and started up the bike. He climbed on and sped away, back into town, stopping off at Denny's in West Hollywood. He was on borrowed time. He knew that either the LAPD or the remaining members of Lopez's crew would be after him. That was a given.

Reznick started on a burger, fries, and a black coffee. He needed to keep on the move. He knew it wouldn't take long for the cops to find him. If not the cops, then maybe one of Lopez's henchmen who would try and take him out. Part of him regretted not killing Lopez. It would have been justified. But Reznick did have the satisfaction of having left him unconscious, his kneecaps blown to pieces. The bastard would be in pain for a long while. He would have lost a lot of blood. And he would never walk right again. It was a small price.

Reznick wondered how Camila's first day and night had gone under the guidance and care of Mary Perez. His experiences with ex-Delta comrades succumbing to drug addiction told him how difficult it was to wean anyone off highly addictive drugs. It was going to be a hard road ahead for Camila. Realistically, her recovery was only just beginning. It wouldn't happen overnight.

What Reznick had done was help her take the first step on the long road to recovery. She would get wholesome food, sleep, and most importantly, she would get away from the crazy life she had lived. There would be no worries about where she was going to sleep. It was a safe refuge in the heart of Venice Beach. She might be tempted to try to go back to her old ways. But her future was now in her own hands and the lap of God.

Reznick felt a sense of closure. Angel's daughter, who had tried to care for her father before going off the rails, had been guided to a safe harbor, at least for now. She would, at some time in the future, have to stand on her own two feet. But that would only happen when she was able and willing to start fresh.

His cell phone rang. It was Trevelle.

Reznick stepped outside the diner to take the call. "Yeah, Trevelle, talk to me. Got any updates?"

"You'll be pleased to know that I've downloaded the full contents of Carlos Lopez's cell phone."

"And?"

"It's horrific. Truly beyond anything I've ever seen before."

"I only saw a couple videos."

"Jon, this is X-rated shit. Snuff-movie-level horrific."

"I know. What did you find out about the art dealer?"

"I finally managed to get a fix on Lopez's cell phone. And I accessed his messages. That seems to be how the art dealer communicated with Lopez. Robert Kassan."

"Why did this guy order Angel's killing?"

"What I'm seeing from CIA reports is that Kassan is a high-end art dealer, but the dude also deals in exports and imports of priceless ancient artworks. Then there's the other stuff."

"What else?"

"This is where it gets interesting. Two nights before Angel was killed, there's video footage of Angel outside Kassan's gallery in Beverly Hills. He's arguing with Brett Miller and Kassan on the sidewalk outside the art gallery. Brett Miller is a big client of Kassan's. Last year he bought art worth just shy of nine million dollars."

"You're kidding me."

"No, the security footage is on the phone in a message to Carlos Lopez. This was sent only seven minutes after the altercation."

"So the message was sent from whom?"

"Robert Kassan sent an encrypted message to Carlos Lopez."

Reznick hadn't seen that coming. He'd had assumed it was Brett Miller or one of his associates who had ordered Lopez to kill Angel. But this changed everything. "Let me guess. It was Robert Kassan who asked Lopez to deal with Angel?"

"Not so much asked as *ordered*. He's the one. The encrypted message was concealed in a photo sent from Kassan."

Reznick's mind was racing. "What was the photo of?"

"An innocuous photo of the Hollywood sign. But each pixel represented a particular color, and when I dug into the code for the color, I saw it had been subtly manipulated. Steganography. The naked eye couldn't detect the message. But it was there."

"So Lopez is using these techniques? Pretty advanced."

"Absolutely."

"That must've taken you hours to decipher."

"Not at all. I was a cryptologist with the NSA once upon a time."

"Of course you were."

"I know how to detect and decrypt messages."

"What exactly does the message say?"

"The message says, and this is verbatim, *Find this guy and get rid of him. Fuck him up bad. Then kill him.* And it also contained the still photo of Angel Ramos outside the gallery, brandishing a wine bottle."

"Lopez told me Angel threatened Kassam after finding out that Kassan had fucked his daughter at a party at Brett Miller's home."

"So how the hell does a gallery owner get caught up in this?" said Trevelle.

"Kassan, like Lopez, is pure evil."

"I would guess that the art dealing is a smart cover for laundering dirty money, bitcoin transactions, et cetera."

Reznick pondered all of that. "Who the hell is this Robert Kassan? What do we really know about him?"

"Glad you asked. I've also been doing a lot more digging into this guy. Remember how Carlos Lopez's car was outside Kassan's property?"

"That's a connection, right?"

"Most certainly. Lopez is the main guy for the Mexican cartels, funneling drugs into California. And Robert Kassan was on the FBI's radar many years back, for money laundering."

Reznick paced the parking lot, cell phone pressed tight to his ear. "So why hasn't Kassan been investigated and put on trial?"

"Your guess is as good as mine. Is he a cutout, passing intel to the CIA about drug shipments, Hezbollah money getting shifted?"

"And that's why he's allowed to get away with this shit?"

"I'm guessing."

"But it makes sense. The involvement of Daniel Black, who admitted he works for the Agency."

"It's all very shady shit," said Trevelle. "So all this began when Angel Ramos confronted Brett Miller outside the art gallery owned by Robert Kassan. Then he was screaming abuse at Kassan. Angel was also spotted prowling about outside Brett's property by private security a few months back. But it was the altercation outside the gallery that sparked it all. We now know it was not Brett who gave the go-ahead to kill Angel. But Brett is clearly linked to this whole shady business. Maybe through girls exploited and trafficked by Carlos Lopez, fed to predators like Brett Miller, Kassan, and their ilk."

Reznick's mind raced in all directions, trying to make the connections.

"You've ridden your luck so far, Jon. But luck eventually runs out."

"True."

"What are you going to do?"

"I want to find out what's on Kassan's cell phone. Where is this so-called art dealer right now?"

The sound of the tapping of a keyboard. "The last cell phone data shows him at his home in North Kenter Avenue earlier today. But you'll want to find out where he is right now."

"Get on it. Get a fix on his location. Then call me. In the meantime, take a more extensive look at Carlos Lopez's cell phone. I wonder if there are any other video nasties the cops need to know about."

Forty-Seven

A blood-red sunset blanketed Los Angeles. Brett Miller sat alone, staring into his pool.

The earlier conversation with Jerry Levinson had been a sobering experience. He had never felt so shaken up. The booze, pills, and cocaine were beginning to wear off, but he still couldn't think straight. He wanted to take calls and set up meetings about his upcoming film. But he worried he'd come off freaked out, paranoid, wired.

The hours he had spent alone had whipped him into a frenzy. He had taken repeated calls from his irate wife, who was in the Maldives. She was reading gossip magazine articles about Brett's "flamboyant" lifestyle. She was pissed. But that was nothing compared to learning that the English photographer and Flo Jackson had both been brutally murdered by Lopez and his crew. He hadn't asked for that. He hadn't wanted that. Or at least, he didn't remember wanting that.

Then his phone rang again. He checked the caller ID. It was his daughter.

Brett's heart sank. A head-to-head with his daughter was the last thing he wanted. He sniffed hard—residues of cocaine still in his nostrils.

"Hi, honey, enjoying the vacation?"

"Am I enjoying the vacation? Are you serious?"

"What's wrong, honey?"

"Dad, is it true?"

"Is what true?"

"That you're divorcing Mom?"

"Nothing could be further from the truth. I don't want to divorce your mom. I love her. Your mom has been filling her head with all that entertainment news bullshit and gossip again. Insiders say this, insider sources say that. It's bullshit. I'll be suing those bastards. And that's just the beginning."

"Dad, please don't do this. Mom couldn't take it. After all you guys have been through."

Miller felt his heart skipping a beat. "Honey, relax, it isn't going to happen. Put your mom on again. I'll tell her the truth."

There was a muffled conversation as the phone was handed over. Then his crazy wife was on the line. "What the fuck do you want, Brett? What do you want from us?"

"I don't want anything. I've just been crazy busy, you know how it is. What's all this about divorce?"

"I heard that you're cavorting around town. Girls as young as your daughter? Have you no shame?"

"Slow down. This is bullshit. I was just explaining. It's gossip."

"I also heard, Brett, that you consulted with a divorce attorney. Is that true?"

"That's bullshit too, my love. Magazines, gossipmongers, it's Hollywood. And I'm going to sue their asses. That's outrageous."

"It says you're lining up to divorce me by enforcing the prenup."

"Categorically, it's not true. Besides, I've been too busy. I'm prepping for my next film. Remember the action comedy I was telling you about."

"Well, Brett, just so you know, I've got an attorney of my own. And he'll pick holes in the prenup. You're going to have to hand over the house and three hundred million, minimum."

"Honey, I love you. What are you talking like that for? I'll talk to Jerry. He'll be furious when he hears this shit."

"You're the one that's full of shit. We're done." His wife hung up, leaving Brett more enraged than he had felt in weeks.

He always felt frazzled after having to speak to or interact with his wife. The nausea was nothing, though, compared to how he felt about the deaths of Heidi Stratton and Flo Jackson.

His cell phone rang again, snapping him back to the present. He checked the caller ID expecting it to be his wife, back to scream at him some more. But it was Jerry Levinson.

"Jerry, what the hell? I thought we were done."

"Brett—"

"Jerry, relax, I heard what you said earlier. I get it. I'm going to listen to everything you said. I'll lay low. No more clubs. No more girls. Satisfied?"

"Turn on the TV."

"What?"

"Brett, turn on the goddamn TV. *60 Minutes*. I'll stay on the line."

Brett detected a trace of tension and apprehension in Jerry's voice, which was normally calm and exuding control. He went inside, holding his cell phone, and switched on the huge TV. He flicked through the channels until he got to *60 Minutes*. He stared at the screen. A reporter in Haiti was standing outside a ramshackle house, interviewing a forty-something black woman with sad eyes. The woman was showing photos to the camera of her daughter who had died in Los Angeles.

He recognized Mirlande, the stunning Haitian escort he had been hanging out with a few weeks back.

"You seeing this?" Jerry said.

Photos of Brett with his arm draped around the scantily clad girl. He felt sick to the bottom of his stomach. "Jerry, talk to me, what the fuck is this?" He muted the sound on the TV.

"I got no heads-up about this. My wife just told me to turn it on."

"Holy shit. I'm ruined, Jerry. I'm going to be destroyed."

"I'll reach out to some PR crisis management experts."

Brett no longer felt sick. He felt numb. He could only imagine what his wife would say. He wondered if she would be next to be interviewed by *60 Minutes*. "Jerry, what do I do? What do I say?"

"Nothing. We wait until the crisis management team gets together. I'll line up a meeting."

"I'm going to be ruined."

"How does anyone know they're even real?" said Jerry. "The photos?"

Brett went quiet as a stone, suddenly resolute in contemplation. "Will that line work?"

"I don't know. But what you don't do is answer the phone to anyone apart from me. You don't speak to your wife. You don't speak to anyone."

"Why?"

"I figure the rest of LA's news teams and TV reporters will be heading up to your place. Get inside. Away from prying eyes."

"So I'm a prisoner?"

"Don't be so dramatic. You live in Bel Air. You're not confined to San Quentin. However, you do need to hunker down. This is a media firestorm. They'll send drones up over your property. You need to be prepared. Get inside. No bottles or drug paraphernalia around the pool. No girls."

"This is going to destroy me, man."

"Not if I can help it. Just do what I say!"

"I'll get the housekeeper to deal with tidying up the pool area. Pull down the blinds too."

"We'll get through this, Brett. We always have. Hunker down. We'll ride this out. We're going to deny everything. Say nothing. And we will sue any fucker anywhere."

Forty-Eight

Robert Kassan slowed down as his car's headlights picked out the north gate of the isolated Hollywood Reservoir. He felt an overwhelming sense of foreboding as he pulled up. He was due to meet a man at a precise location, beside the water, high up in the Hollywood Hills. A man he had only ever spoken to on the phone. He wondered what the guy wanted.

He switched off his engine and checked his mirrors. He was alone, not a soul in sight. He picked up the backpack and exited his vehicle, shutting the door quietly. He locked his car, his mind and heart racing.

Kassan's life was ordered. He liked routine. And he hated being snapped out of that routine. He wondered why he had to have a face-to-face meeting. He wondered if he should have brought his brother. His brother was tougher. Braver. But the instructions had been very specific: *Come alone, Robert.*

Kassan walked up toward the north gate. He tried it. But he could see it was clearly padlocked and the lock was intact. He had been told it would be locked. He took out the key he had been sent and inserted it. The lock opened. He pushed the gate, carefully shutting and relocking it behind him.

He walked up the road until he reached a chain-link fence encircling the water. The lake was a man-made reservoir, located west of Griffith Park—a favorite during the day for hikers and cyclists.

He enjoyed the outdoors. He would have loved nothing better than hiking the three-mile trail around the lake. It would be great exercise, invariably under a warm Californian sun. But this midnight expedition was altogether different. There was no one around, except the man who would already be waiting for him.

A full moon in the inky black sky illuminated his route.

Kassan walked alongside the chain-link fence and peered beyond the pine trees. Pale moonlight shimmered on the water. A rustle in the bushes behind him startled him. He turned around as a bird flew into the sky.

In the far distance, the silhouetted Hollywood sign glowed like a beacon.

Kassan felt more anxious as he walked on. He reached a tree, marked by luminous lime-green pen. He knew it was a sign the man was already here and giving him precise directions.

He headed up an incline. Then he walked along the paved trail until he got to a second gate. He unlocked that too, careful to padlock it shut behind him.

He walked on until he reached his favorite bit of the trail. The thousand-foot section of the Mulholland Dam.

Kassan spotted a silhouetted figure in the distance, standing and staring over the silvery lake. His stomach tightened as he walked toward him, his eyes adjusting to the darkness. He had never met the man before.

Kassan knew him only by his code name, *Zeiter*. He'd had no direct dealings with him until he'd gotten the handwritten message delivered by a courier to his door saying, *Dam. Lake. Midnight.* He wondered what was so urgent. What could be the emergency?

He approached, and the silhouetted man turned around and faced him. The man smoked a cigarette, and the vague smell of mint blending with tobacco indicated it was a menthol.

"You're late. You're not carrying your phone, are you?"

"Of course not."

The man finished his cigarette and threw it in the lake before frisking Kassan.

"I told you, I'm not carrying my cell phone."

"Just a precaution. You're fine."

"I know."

The man pulled out a packet of cigarettes and offered one to Kassan. "You smoke?"

Kassan shook his head.

"Good for you," he said, lighting up. "Filthy habit."

"So . . . here we are," Kassan said, unsure what else to say. "What seems to be the problem? I'm assuming there's a problem."

"I'm here to warn you. We have assessed that you might be compromised. Your cover. Your security."

"How?"

"We don't know. But we think it wise that you get ready to leave."

"Leave for where?"

"Somewhere abroad."

"Leave the country? I don't want to leave."

The man dragged hard on his cigarette, blowing the smoke toward the water. "The decision has been made. You need to head to Van Nuys Airport and leave LA and America. A plane is en route."

"It is?"

The man nodded.

"Who decided this?"

"The Executive Council."

Kassan's blood ran cold. There was no point in arguing with the Executive Council of Hezbollah. "My work is here."

"Your work is over. At least in America."

"You must know where I'm going?"

The man was silent.

"You must have an inkling."

"Think Europe. Possibly Switzerland."

Kassan nodded. "I can live with that. What about my brother?"

"He will go with you. But time is of the essence. You are too useful to be compromised. That's the only reason for this move."

"Europe is fine."

The man stepped forward and hugged Kassan tight, whispering in his ear, "I wish you a safe and peaceful journey. May God protect you."

Kassan watched as the man turned and headed back across the dam, disappearing from sight, presumably to head back down the trail.

He took in a deep breath, his heart pounding. His time in LA was coming to an end.

Forty-Nine

Reznick's cell phone rang. He knew it was Trevelle before he checked the caller ID.

"Where the hell have you been?" he said.

"Doing what you asked me to do. I did a technical full-spectrum analysis of Lopez's phone. It's unbelievable. Worse than you could ever imagine. But it's also provided interesting links between him and a certain art dealer in the city. Definite links."

"Some dark shit?"

"Lopez has sent terabytes of clips to Kassan. Videos of the killings carried out by Lopez and his crew. And Kassan is uploading this to sites on the dark web; people pay money for this sort of stuff. He's raking in serious money from this."

"Are you fucking kidding me?"

"The money he makes is getting funneled to medical charities across the Middle East. Gaza, Lebanon, Yemen. All controlled by people with links to Hezbollah."

"He's monetizing torture killings?"

"That's just the tip of the iceberg. Everything Kassan is doing is laser-focused toward raising money, either through selling artwork, laundering money, bitcoin fraud, a ton of stuff. Selling and buying high-end art for tax evasion purposes and money laundering are the main ones. And a percentage always gets funneled to the same so-called humanitarian charities."

Reznick took a few moments to wrap his head around the horror of it all. "Is Angel's killing right now on the dark web?"

"It's all there. It's terrible. I saw the beginning of it. I had to turn it off. Drills, electric shocks. Screaming. Terrible screaming. And blood. That clip lasted a full fourteen minutes."

"So we've got proof linking Lopez and his crew to the killings. But we also now have Robert Kassan and his nefarious activities."

"I'm starting the process of peeling back Kassan's world," said Trevelle.

Reznick went quiet in grief. He thought of Angel's horrifying final minutes. He felt an unbearable sadness. A man who had served his country with such courage. A man who had feared no one as a soldier. Angel's final hour had been the stuff of nightmares. He couldn't watch the video even if he had the stomach for it.

"I think the Feds can really nail this Robert Kassan son of a bitch. And Lopez."

"I've heard enough. Trevelle, this is what I want you to do. Send an encrypted message to the FBI Director, Bill O'Donoghue. Send what you have, all that stuff on the phones of Lopez and Kassan, but send it securely."

"Affirmative. What about you?"

"What about me?"

"What are you going to do?"

"I don't know. Tell me, where is Carlos Lopez?"

"Hospital, where do you think?" said Trevelle.

"I also want you to send what we've uncovered about Lopez and Kassan to a Detective Andy Chow of the LAPD. And send what we have to Samantha Isaac, my attorney. And fuck it, let's send it all to Daniel Black at the CIA too."

"You're really ruffling a few feathers. What now? You going after Robert?"

"One down, one to go. Where's that fucker now?"

"He's at his house. Signal is now active again. Cell phone GPS shows it clearly."

"I think it's time I pay him a visit, don't you?"

"One final thing, Jon."

"What?"

"Some interesting intel on exactly how Lopez and Kassan operate. And it's pretty devastating."

Fifty

Reznick wondered where Trevelle was going with this.

"I think it's important, Jon, that you understand what we're really dealing with. And why it's taken so long to decrypt all this stuff. The level of sophistication in how they operate, apart from the savagery of Lopez, is striking."

"In what way?"

"What I encountered was the most highly advanced encryption I've seen for a while. These are no amateurs. Someone is getting state-level help or assistance."

"What does that mean?" said Reznick.

"I'm guessing they're buying the services of former cybersecurity pros."

"That makes sense."

"They use a multi-layered process to encrypt messages. Ordinarily it would take a lifetime to decipher this. But I can see what they're doing, thank God."

"Give me an idea of this process. How did they encrypt it?"

"Here's the thing," said Trevelle. "The first text message I unearthed was pasted into an Excel document. So, in effect, the sender is using their own macros to encrypt the message. Then, the message is copied and pasted into a Word document, then saved with a professional password—random sixty-five characters, impossible to decrypt without access to military software. And if that's not enough, the Word document is compressed and encrypted using another program, with more long and complex passwords."

"That's insane."

"It's done automatically by this advanced encryption. What I've explained to you is what's going on under the hood of their messaging system. But it doesn't end there. The final stage of this convoluted process is the document being uploaded to web-hosting sites through a URL shortener."

"Why?"

"It anonymizes the metadata. I believe this is how messages are communicated by Mexican cartels."

"Gather all that intel, copy it, do whatever you have to do, make backups. And forward it to your contact at the NSA. I want the American government to know what's going on. This is a national security risk."

"Doing that now, Jon. I also want to bring your attention to other decrypted messages I've accessed remotely with spyware on Robert's cell phone."

"What?"

"So I ran a program on Kassan's cell. The guy who ordered the kill. And this is where it gets pretty fucking crazy. He initiated multiple bank transfers between a Mexican company in the Caymans to a business in Qatar. You see where I'm going with this?"

"Qatar? That's interesting."

"The company in Qatar has a significant shareholder boasting the same name as Robert Kassan. Different date of birth. This shareholder is seventy-five years old."

"What?"

"And get this. The shareholder known as Robert Kassan, he was born in Beirut. But it's not the same guy."

Reznick's mind was racing to keep up.

"It's his father," Trevelle said.

"Wow."

"He's cloaking transactions and companies. The only glimpse into his real identity is this reference to the father. And before you ask, I checked and cross-checked birth certificates of both father and son."

"So the art dealer here in the city, he's the point man for this operation?" said Reznick. "Born in Beirut, moved to Greece as a baby, but father from Lebanon. Presumably they're both Hezbollah supporters or financiers, right?"

"You got it. The State Department has records of the father . . . but it's mostly secondhand reports by informers who were working for Mossad."

Reznick's heart began to beat just a bit faster. "Kassan is still at home?"

Trevelle clicked a few keys. "No, scratch that. He's showing up at the Hollywood Reservoir. Checking cameras in the area . . . yeah, he's at the reservoir. Car parked there."

"How far away is that?"

"Just over four miles away. Twenty minutes normally."

"License plate?"

Trevelle gave him the number. "It's a jet-black Audi SUV."

"What's he hanging out at the reservoir for?"

"Not a clue. It's a popular area for hiking and jogging."

Reznick climbed back on the Harley. "I'll be in touch." He ended the call and put the phone in his pocket. Then he took out the fob and started up the bike. He quickly turned it around and sped away, heading north along Gower Street, then up and along winding Scenic Avenue, along El Contento Drive, and then along Weidlake Drive.

He pulled up beside the Audi and looked inside. There was no one there.

Reznick climbed over a locked gate. He walked up an asphalt road until he could see the huge reservoir. The moonlight bathed the inky black waters in a pale glow. His cell phone buzzed in his jacket. "I'm up at the reservoir. There's no sign of life."

"Jon, I'm sorry . . ." It was Trevelle. "It's a wild-goose chase. He's not there."

"His car's here."

"The cell phone signal is there too, at that exact spot. Check if his phone is under his seat. If not there, check the glove compartment."

"So where is he?"

Trevelle took a minute to see if he could come up with an answer. Finally, he said, "Jon, this guy is smart. I began looking through the messages on Robert's cell phone. Thirty-two minutes ago. To his brother. *Pick me up at the reservoir.* You just missed him."

Reznick's mind began to race as he pieced it together. "They're laying a false trail, right? And that's why Robert dropped off the car and cell phone here."

"Affirmative. They'll have heard what happened to Carlos Lopez. I think they got spooked. It was only a matter of time. They're one step ahead."

Reznick ran back down the road and climbed over the gate and started up the motorcycle. "For now. He's with his brother, right?"

"Yes, and . . . hang on." More clicking from Trevelle. "Got them both! He's on the 405. The San Diego Freeway. Driving a yellow Porsche. Got a fix on the car in real time."

"Where are they headed?"

"Gimme some time, Jon . . . I've gained access to the brother's cell phone."

Reznick revved the bike.

"I've activated the microphone. Hang on. There's a guy talking in the vehicle."

"Who?"

"Gimme a few—"

"Hurry!"

"Yes, the voice of Robert Kassan is a match. He's in the car with his brother. Right now."

"You're my eyes and ears. Which is the best way?"

"Get on the Hollywood Freeway. And stick on that till you get to the 405. You're about eight miles behind them. You need to go!"

Reznick ended the call, putting his cell phone back in his pocket. He pulled on the helmet and accelerated away hard in a cloud of dust. A couple of minutes later, he was speeding along the freeway, head down, cranking through the gears.

Headlights flashed past as he accelerated, squeezing every bit of juice out of the machine. He hit ninety. Then one hundred. In and out of traffic. Then he saw a sign for the 405. He veered off to the right and then headed north, wondering if he was going to make it in time.

Fifty-One

Robert Kassan checked his watch from the passenger seat of his brother's Porsche as they sped through Van Nuys. He felt nervous. They had a private plane to catch. "Not long now," he muttered, as much to himself as to his brother.

"This is all very sudden," his brother reminded him again.

"I was told to leave. That was the end of it."

"So we just start a new life at the drop of a hat?"

Robert turned and stared at his brother. "Precisely."

"I like LA. I like my life."

"So do I. But we have no choice. We've been advised to leave. That means get moving."

His brother's cell phone rang and Robert reached over to pick up. "Who is this?" The voice of Zeiter.

Robert's stomach tightened "It's me, Robert."

"Why are you still in America? Why haven't you left?"

"Just tying up a few loose ends. I had to pick up a bag."

"Enough! You must leave. Your plane is waiting. You should be on it right now."

"We're on our way."

"The plane has been refueled and it is sitting on the asphalt. Waiting. A crew is waiting for you and your brother. And so am I."

"You're on the plane?"

"Correct."

"We won't be long."

"We have been monitoring LAPD radio channels. You need to get a move on. Police radio has put out an APB."

"Saying what?"

"Saying that Jon Reznick was seen on a motorcycle near the reservoir, speeding along the freeway headed north to Van Nuys."

"That's impossible."

"The police radio has identified him."

Robert relayed the information to his brother. "Speed up! Reznick is closing in."

"Seriously?"

"Get a move on!"

"Robert, I don't want to get pulled over by the cops."

"Fuck the cops. It's only five miles."

Zeiter said, "Do not miss this flight. It leaves in fifteen minutes, with or without you."

The line went dead.

Fifty-Two

Reznick accelerated hard along the dark freeway.

Weaving in and out of traffic, he glanced in the bike's mirrors. Blue lights flashing, two cop cars now on his tail. *Fuck*. Up in the sky, chopper lights illuminated the road ahead. He revved hard. He caught sight of a sign for Van Nuys Airport. He turned off onto a ramp and toward the target's getaway destination. Mile after mile. The sound of more sirens in the distance, flashing lights behind, the chopper still overhead.

He sped toward the FlyAway parking garage and rode up to level two, scouring for the Porsche. He figured that Kassan would park the car and catch his flight. So it had to be here.

The sound of screeching tires behind him; the smell of burning rubber.

Reznick spun around on the bike. A Porsche charged toward him. He jumped off the bike a split second before it was crushed by the sports car. He took cover behind a Buick SUV. Reznick took out his Beretta. The Porsche had the bike jammed underneath it. Revving hard, it began to reverse. The bike got stuck underneath the front grill, shooting sparks across the garage.

Reznick crouched low. He took aim at the rear window and fired off three quick shots. The glass shattered as the car spun out of control, smashing into a concrete wall. He sprinted toward the vehicle.

The driver emerged from the car, bleeding from the shoulder, gun drawn.

Reznick shot him twice in the head. The man dropped to his knees before falling face first onto the asphalt. Reznick crouched down and crept around the vehicle. He found a figure dazed in the passenger seat. It was Robert Kassan. He fired off one shot to the side of the head. The figure slumped forward. Peering inside, Reznick could see the man was miraculously still moving. He slowly lifted his head to face Reznick, a gun in his bloodied hand.

Reznick fired off two shots into the man's forehead. Blood and gray matter spattered over the inside of the windshield. He stepped over the dead man on the ground and looked inside the Porsche. The passenger was covered in blood. Reznick took out his cell phone and took a photo of the man's blood-smeared face. He sent the photo to Trevelle.

His cell phone rang almost immediately, as the police sirens got closer.

"You got him, Jon. Facial recognition identifies this man as Robert Kassan."

Reznick ended the call and put his phone in his back pocket. He had taken his revenge on the man who had ordered the killing of Angel Ramos.

A police cruiser screeched to a halt next to him. A couple of fresh-faced officers got out, guns drawn, taking cover behind their open car doors.

"Drop the weapon now!" one shouted.

Reznick complied.

"Hands in the air!"

He slowly lifted his hands and placed them on his head. An additional three police cars and an ambulance pulled up, lights on, sirens blaring. Officers got out and held their ground.

Two officers tentatively approached, guns fixed on Reznick.

"On your knees!" one shouted.

Reznick complied.

Two officers took an arm each and handcuffed his hands behind his back.

"You're under arrest."

Fifty-Three

The cops took Reznick to the nearby Van Nuys station in the Valley. He was once again booked, photographed for his second mug shot since arriving in LA, and taken to an airless interview room on the third floor before being handcuffed again. There, he was given a black coffee and a bagel.

Twenty minutes later, a burly detective walked in. "Quite a few days you're having, Jon."

Reznick looked up from eating his sandwich. "I want to speak to a lawyer."

"There's one already on her way. You must have friends in high places."

"What are you talking about?"

"A guy by the name of Daniel Black, works for the CIA, called one for you. He seemed to know what was going on."

Reznick nodded. He wondered if it was the same attorney he'd had previously.

"How are you enjoying LA?"

"I'm starting to like it."

The cop smiled. "Out of sight, man."

Reznick sipped his coffee. He knew Black had been watching proceedings unfold since Reznick's plane had landed in LA. What was also clear was that the LAPD had stood down, probably on Black's orders. "You got a name for this attorney of mine?"

"Samantha Isaac, big-shot lawyer." The cop scrunched up his empty coffee cup and tossed it in a trashcan.

A few minutes later, Samantha walked into the room. She advised him on this occasion to take the Fifth.

Another detective came and sat down beside his colleague. They went back and forth with rapid-fire questions.

Isaac diligently noted down the questions. And all the while, Reznick answered that he was taking the Fifth.

When it was clear that no progress was being made, he was transferred to the jurisdiction of the FBI field office in Westwood. It was just after 6:30 a.m. It was the second time he had been taken there. The whole time, Samantha Isaac was by his side.

"What's the deal?" Reznick asked her.

"You can talk to the Feds. Daniel Black worked out a deal. Trust me, it's a good one."

"He worked out a deal?"

"Yes, everything is fine."

Reznick was taken to an interview room on the seventeenth floor, just as he had been the last time. And like the last time, Special Agent Rodriguez sat across from him, behind the desk.

"You never heeded our advice, our Duty to Warn," she said.

"I guess not."

She sighed as she took some notes, a thickset, well-dressed colleague sitting beside her. "Your lawyer has instructed you not to talk to the police. But we have come to an arrangement that you are free to talk at will. It's your choice where we go from here."

Reznick nodded.

"You sent over, or rather an associate of yours sent over, gigabytes of intel related to a man known as Carlos Lopez, correct? These included videos, photos, and text messages."

"That is correct."

"Jon, do you understand what you've gotten yourself involved with?"

"I'm scratching the surface. That's all I know."

"Carlos Lopez and two of his associates are in the hospital. Lopez is permanently disabled from a kneecapping at close range."

"That's too bad."

"You're not the judge and jury in these matters, Jon."

"I guess not."

"You don't seem too perturbed."

"Spare me, will you?"

Rodriguez bristled. "Excuse me?"

"Carlos Lopez got what was coming to him. He deserved to die. He was lucky he caught me on a good day."

"It's not your job to go around dishing out summary justice."

"How did we let him into the country? He's a disgusting, psychopathic killer. Why the fuck is he allowed to be on our streets?"

Rodriguez leaned back in her seat, chewing the end of a pen.

"The FBI must've known about him," he said. "You must know that's not his real name. His real name is Diego Hernandez. Former Mexican special forces. Enforcer for a feared drug cartel. Trust me, he got off lightly."

Rodriguez and her colleague exchanged a knowing glance.

Isaac was impassive, taking notes.

"Which brings us," Rodriguez continued, "to your latest encounter, if we can call it that. The two gentlemen you killed in Van Nuys."

"Check out the intel my friend sent you. It's got a whole lot of stuff. Money laundering, an association with Hezbollah, tax evasion. Robert Kassan. Check him out."

Rodriguez stared at him. "Are you finished?"

"I nearly forgot," Reznick said. "It was Robert Kassan who ordered the killing of Angel Ramos. Highly encrypted messages, contained within images. It'll take you guys months, even years, to get to the bottom of it. But I can tell you, Robert Kassan was part of a network between the Mexican cartels and Hezbollah. And he was a regular at Brett Miller's sex parties."

Isaac glared at Rodriguez, eyes like ice. "Jon has shared everything he knows. And then some."

"And let's not forget," Reznick said, "Carlos Lopez and his crew trafficked girls. Angel Ramos's daughter was one of them. When I found her, do you know who she was hanging out with at a swanky private members' club? Film director Brett Miller. That name ring a bell? You might want to pay him a visit. He's got a thing for underage girls, as has Kassan."

Rodriguez stared at him. She was unmoved. And so began a long interview.

Reznick was interviewed for a further eight hours. They stopped for sandwiches and coffee, and a couple of bathroom breaks. When Rodriguez was satisfied she had everything she needed from Reznick, she asked him to sign a document.

"What's this?"

Isaac handed him a pen. "It's an iron-clad agreement, Jon," she said, "that neither the Justice Department nor the district attorney will press charges."

Reznick grinned. "My lucky day, I guess."

Rodriguez and her colleague remained stone-faced.

Isaac said, "National security considerations and your associate unearthing a treasure trove of intelligence on those two individuals far outweighs, in our view, any crimes that may or may not have been committed by yourself."

Reznick took the pen and signed his name and dated the document, as did Isaac.

Then Rodriguez did the same. She passed the document to her colleague, who co-signed it. She looked over the document before she fixed a sneering look on Reznick. "A word of advice."

"What's that?"

"Stay out of LA."

"Give me twenty-four hours. I need to tie up a couple loose ends."

"There's going to be no more violence?"

Reznick shrugged. "I can't give any guarantees," he teased. "But I don't envision any problems."

Fifty-Four

"Very unorthodox, Jon," Isaac said, as she drove Reznick from the FBI's field office back to his room in the apartment block in West Hollywood. She pulled up outside. "Quite an eventful few days."

"Appreciate your help," he replied.

"You're very welcome."

"Let me ask you something," he said. "I take it the American government didn't want any of this to get out. First and foremost."

"Absolutely correct."

"How were they able to operate with impunity?"

"I couldn't possibly comment."

"You think one or both of them were being used in some capacity by American intelligence agencies? Or at least cutouts?"

Isaac nodded. "Very perceptive. Well . . . it was nice knowing you, Jon. Stay safe."

"Send my regards to Daniel Black."

"Will do. And Jon?"

"What?"

"Be good."

Reznick smiled. "I'll try." He headed into the apartment, showered, and put on a fresh set of clothes. Then he packed his things into his travel bag. His rental car had been shot up. So he called a nearby Avis, who dropped off a Chevy Suburban. He drove back down to Venice Beach and parked up on Speedway.

The sun was low in the sky, casting long shadows along the boardwalk.

Reznick walked until he came to the homeless Mexican woman he'd spoken to, sitting by herself on a bench. He smiled down at her. "You mind if I sit with you?"

She shrugged, eyes the saddest he'd ever seen. She pointed to Reznick with a bony finger. "You again? I remember you. You were down here before. Showing me photos of the Mexican dude. The bad man, right?"

"The guy from Veracruz?"

"I always remember a face. He's bad."

"You don't need to worry about him anymore."

The woman looked at Reznick. She pulled a joint out of her jacket. "You like to smoke?"

He shook his head. "Not my thing. But thanks anyway."

She lit up her joint, inhaling deeply, blowing the smoke out of the side of her mouth.

"I wanted to thank you for identifying Carlos Lopez."

"He killed your friend, right?"

"Yes, he did."

"Piece of shit. He killed a lot of people. No good. May God punish him for his deeds." The woman crossed herself. "God have mercy on my soul."

Reznick reached into his jacket, pulled out an envelope, and handed it to her.

"What's this?"

"A little token of my thanks. But also a little something to get you through the next few months, and hopefully longer."

The woman opened up the envelope and her eyes widened, seeing a wad of bills. "You steal this?"

Reznick shook his head. "Consider it a gift."

"A gift from God maybe?"

"Yes, if you like. A gift from God."

The woman's eyes filled with tears as she dragged hard on the joint. She stared into Reznick's weathered face. "Who are you?"

"I'm nobody."

"Well, you must be somebody to give me money. No one ever gave me anything."

"It's time for that to change."

"I can't take it. It's too much."

Reznick got to his feet. "What's your name?"

"My name is Maria Conchita Gonzalez. I used to be a cleaner. But my fingers are arthritic."

"Well, Maria Conchita Gonzalez, take care of yourself. And God bless you."

She stared at the envelope before tucking it into her back pocket. She pointed to the sky. "He's watching over us. He's watching over all of us."

Reznick turned away, but could still hear her as he walked down the boardwalk.

"Remember, God is always watching us," she shouted. "I won't forget you."

Fifty-Five

The following morni-ng, an orange sun peeked over the horizon as dawn broke on Venice Beach.

Reznick was sitting in a diner, enjoying breakfast, when Captain Frank Garcia walked in. He sauntered over and sat down in the booth opposite Reznick.

"You mind if I join you?" Garcia asked.

"Not at all."

Garcia shifted in his seat, leaning close. "I thought we'd seen the last of you, Jon," he said.

"I'm out of here within the hour."

"For what it's worth, I got the email from that cybersecurity guy you know. Trevelle, right?"

Reznick nodded.

"I've passed what he sent on to Captain Chow at HQ."

"I hope it's of use."

"Are you kidding me? You've started an earthquake at headquarters."

Reznick chuckled as he finished his eggs and coffee. "You having breakfast?"

"In a minute. I hope you understand how things roll out here. There's a lot of politics. Heavy hitters, wealthy donors, that kind of bullshit."

"It happens. Don't sweat it."

"That's not to say you weren't out of line. You were way out of line."

"Point taken. It was personal, that's all."

Garcia smiled. "It all got a bit crazy."

"It's LA, right? I was told once by a good friend of mine that everyone is fucking crazy out here. And if you're not crazy when you get here, you will be when you leave."

Garcia laughed. "I'll have to remember that."

"So, Frank, you got a busy day ahead of you?"

"Mountain of paperwork. But I've been thinking . . . I have a brother. His family lives in a small town in North Carolina. I was thinking about moving across the country. This city has been good for me. But I think it's time to move on."

"Slower pace of life in North Carolina, that's for sure."

"I can live with that."

"I'm from a small town. I wouldn't move for the world."

"I get it."

Reznick finished his coffee and got up, dropping fifty dollars to cover the check. "Take it easy, Frank. Nice meeting you."

"You too. And stay out of trouble!"

Reznick walked out of the diner, feeling the warm California sun on his face. He strode a few blocks to the church and spotted the priest coming toward him.

"Father Patrick O'Donnell," Reznick said. "The very man."

The priest blushed. "What have I done now?"

Reznick laughed. "I'm stopping by to say goodbye. But also to ask about the wellbeing of Camila Ramos."

"Two things. She's found it tough the last couple days and nights. But she's knuckled down and has been making herself useful."

"Pleased to hear it."

"She's going to make it, I think. She's learning to take care of herself, look after her health. She's already helping Mary Perez cook. She's got a long way to go. But we believe she's got what it takes."

"What's the second thing?"

"Next month, as long as she continues to make good progress and stay clean, I've managed to line her up with a new family. A foster family."

"Already?"

"The family you visited up in Topanga? I've reached out to them. They've said they would be delighted to give a home to Camila when their daughter moves out for college. A fresh start for both of them. They'd like to give the same support, guidance, and opportunities to Camila that their own daughter received."

Reznick felt his throat tighten. "I don't know what to say. That's very kind of them, and you."

"Jon, they're good people. They know that Camila and Catherine were friends on the streets. And they're determined to provide a beautiful, safe home for Camila, God willing."

"What about the costs?"

"Nothing. They're well-off. And they're going to be enrolling her in a community college. She'll get some qualifications. Camila has indicated to us that she wants to be an artist."

"Seriously?"

"Talented girl."

"If she needs any financial backing, don't hesitate to contact me." Reznick took out a piece of paper from his wallet and scribbled down his name and cell phone number. "You need anything, let me know."

Father O'Donnell crossed himself. "God willing."

Reznick shook hands with the priest.

"Do you want to say goodbye to her?"

"Would you mind?"

"Not at all."

Reznick followed him a couple of blocks, to a small cottage.

The priest said a few words to Mary Perez and she went inside and fetched Camila.

Camila walked toward Reznick smiling, her head held high. She was already like a new person. Eyes clear. "Hey," she said to Reznick.

"Hey, you look well."

"Putting myself back together again. Thanks to Mrs. Perez."

Reznick took her in. Her eyes were sparkling, her skin less blotchy. She looked alive. "I just wanted to see that you were alright. And to wish you all the best."

Camila opened the gate and rushed toward Reznick, hugging him tight. "Thank you."

"For what?"

"For finding me."

"Can I offer some advice?"

"Sure."

"Find yourself. Find what you love. I hear you love art."

"I do."

"So paint! And be true to yourself. That's always a good place to start."

Camila brushed the tears from her cheeks. "I'm going to miss my dad."

"I know. But know this. There are people in your life who care for you. I think you'll do well."

She looked at her watch. "I'm on cleaning duties! I can't be late. So long." She ran back inside, turning to wave at Reznick.

He waved back and walked with the priest to the boardwalk. "Keep a close eye on her, Father."

"I will, son. And trust me, so will Mary Perez."

Reznick thanked him again. Then he drove through the backstreets of Venice before he got onto the freeway, headed for LAX. The sky was cobalt blue. He turned on the radio. A Donald Fagen song was playing, wind in his hair.

He was starting his long journey. Back to the small town he called home.

Epilogue

Three months later, Reznick was sitting on his back porch in Rockland, Maine, beer in hand. He was wrapped up against the chill of November. He stared out over the calm, gray waters of Penobscot Bay.

When his cell phone rang, the caller ID showed a number he didn't recognize.

He wondered if it was Father O'Donnell in Venice Beach with an update on Camila's progress. The last he'd heard from him was a month earlier. Camila was clean and had moved in with her foster family in Topanga Canyon, far away from the craziness of the city. But when Reznick answered the call, it wasn't the priest.

A woman's voice. "I'm looking to speak to Jon Reznick?"

"Who's this?"

"Samantha Isaac. Your . . . LA attorney."

Reznick sat up in his seat. "Hey, Samantha, how the hell are you? I'm still waiting to be billed. Is that what this is about?"

"Hah! Don't worry about that. I believe that's been taken care of."

"Been taken care of? By whom?"

"The CIA was eager to pick up the tab."

"That's nice of them. Daniel Black involved?"

"Indeed."

"So, how are things in LA? Busy?"

"What can I say? I'm okay. Still clearing up the backlog of paperwork from your little visit a few months back. Quite an eventful couple weeks you spent in the city, Jon."

"I'm assuming the FBI, LAPD, and all the rest have no further questions for me?"

"Let's put it this way: you carried out the trash, free of charge."

Reznick swigged some more beer. "Glad to help. I have my moments."

Isaac laughed. "You certainly do. If you're ever out this way again, let me know. Drinks on me."

"Sounds like a plan. So I'm assuming you didn't call just for some small talk."

"You got it. Do me a favor . . . turn on your TV."

Reznick got to his feet. "Channel?"

"CNN."

Reznick went inside and turned on the TV. He channel-hopped until he got to CNN. Chopper footage showed police gathered beside a massive heart-shaped outdoor pool, palm trees in view.

The reporter's voice said, "Hollywood director Brett Miller was found floating in the pool late last night by his wife, who had returned home from a vacation. Mr. Miller's agent and his lawyer refused to confirm that he was being investigated by LAPD for five separate cases of statutory rape at the time of his death."

Reznick muted the volume on the TV, cell phone still pressed to his ear. "That's interesting."

"I believe you had a little run-in with him at a club in West Hollywood."

"He was playing lovey-dovey with an underage girl."

"Camila Ramos?"

"What do you know about this, Samantha?"

"I know that Brett Miller's predilections were an open secret in the industry in Hollywood. Major-league sleazeball. He was a super-wealthy and powerful pedophile. And he was protected by his money, allowing him to be insulated against retribution. Until he wasn't."

"And how did this all come out into the open?"

"A Haitian girl, Mirlande Jean-Baptiste. Miller had raped her. Just like he did with most of the girls he hung out with. Shortly before she died on a freeway, her mother got messages from Mirlande. They showed her daughter taking cocaine with Brett Miller. Having sex with Brett Miller. And from that, she gave an interview with *60 Minutes*. After it aired, Brett Miller's world slowly came crashing down. But the most damaging allegations emerged in the intel that you and Trevelle passed on to the FBI and the cops. The LAPD are investigating other directors and producers and actors across the city."

Reznick stared out over the bay. "I appreciate the heads-up. Tell me, what about the art dealer and his brother?"

"Robert Kassan was a regular at the sex parties at Brett Miller's house that catered to wealthy Hollywood clients. Kassan was also the money launderer for Hezbollah on the West Coast. The FBI are still investigating not only him and his brother, but how Lopez and the Mexican cartels were using the city as a hub for drug importation, child trafficking through tunnels, and myriad money-laundering schemes. The nexus of the Mexican cartels and Hezbollah operations is multifaceted. What you dealt with was only the tip of the iceberg."

Reznick sipped some beer, thinking of Angel Ramos and his terrible, monstrous murder. His Delta pal had deserved better. So much better.

"And just so you know, there's a wide-ranging inquiry into the homicide investigation of your friend's killing."

"Into the investigation itself? Negligence or culpability?"

"They don't know. A few officers from Homicide have taken early retirement. The Police Commissioner has also resigned to spend more time with his family. But get this. I'm also hearing that the Governor of California is under investigation. Bribes from his pals in Hollywood. But also, it turns out he has a thing for young girls."

"Why doesn't that surprise me?"

"Quite a fallout, Jon."

"Power, corruption, and lies."

"Like I said, we're only scratching the surface."

"Till next time," Reznick said.

"Take it easy, Jon."

Reznick ended the call. He gulped down the rest of his beer and set the bottle down on the table.

The sky was darkening over Penobscot Bay. The end of an overcast November day, far away from the Californian sunshine. He thought of all the forgotten people of Venice Beach—the poor, the neglected, the broken-down. But he also thought of Camila Ramos, now living a new life, high up in Topanga Canyon. She had a chance.

Angel's flesh and blood was alive.

Reznick closed his eyes and said a silent prayer.

Acknowledgements

I would like to thank my editor, Maisie Lawrence, and everyone at Amazon Publishing for their enthusiasm, hard work, and belief in the Jon Reznick thriller series. I would also like to thank my loyal readers. Thanks also to Faith Black Ross for her terrific work on this book, and Randall Klein, who looked over an early draft. Special thanks to my agent, Mitch Hoffman, of The Aaron M. Priest Literary Agency, New York.

Last but by no means least, my family and friends for their encouragement and support. None more so than my wife, Susan.

About the Author

Photo © Robbie Bald 2024

J. B. Turner is a former journalist and the author of the Jon Reznick series of political thrillers (*Hard Road, Hard Kill, Hard Wired, Hard Way, Hard Fall, Hard Hit, Hard Shot, Hard Target, Hard Vengeance, Hard Fire, Hard Exit, Hard Power,* and *Hard Duty*), the American Ghost series of black ops thrillers (*Rogue, Reckoning,* and *Requiem*), the Jack McNeal series (*No Way Back* and *Long Way Home*), and the Deborah Jones crime thrillers (*Miami Requiem* and *Dark Waters*). He has a keen interest in geopolitics. He lives in Scotland with his wife and two children.

Printed in Dunstable, United Kingdom

Follow the Author on Amazon

If you enjoyed this book, follow J. B. Turner on Amazon to be notified when the author releases a new book!
To do this, please follow these instructions:

Desktop:

1) Search for the author's name on Amazon or in the Amazon App.
2) Click on the author's name to arrive on their Amazon page.
3) Click the 'Follow' button.

Mobile and Tablet:

1) Search for the author's name on Amazon or in the Amazon App.
2) Click on one of the author's books.
3) Click on the author's name to arrive on their Amazon page.
4) Click the "Follow" button.

Kindle eReader and Kindle App:

If you enjoyed this book on a Kindle eReader or in the Kindle App, you will find the author "Follow" button after the last page.